Wild CHILD

A SOUL SISTER NOVEL

AUDREY CARLAN

Cover Design: Jena Brignola

Copy Editor: Jeanne De Vita

ISBN: 978-1-943340-15-6 (ebook)

ISBN: 978-1-943340-16-3 (print)

*To **Dorothy Bircher***
Thank you for sharing your pain,
your truth, and your friendship.
The sisterhood, and this book, are stronger for it.

A SOUL SISTER NOVEL

Chapter
ONE

TODAY HAS BEEN THE ABSOLUTE WORST DAY OF MY LIFE. Well, aside from the day I lost both my parents in a house fire when I was six. Not that I remember any of that night, nor much of my childhood before I arrived at my foster home twenty-one years ago.

This morning started with me spilling a cup of scalding hot coffee down the front of my only clean uniform, which meant I had to wear the grubby one I'd worn the night before and hadn't yet washed. Made me feel as though I smelled of greasy hamburgers and girl funk all day.

Then, my on-again, off-again boyfriend, if I could even really call him that, broke it off with me during my lunch break. I could hear the voice of a giggling woman in the background. His latest conquest or ten. I'd thought he might have been cheating on me, but for some reason I had hoped there was more to our relationship. Perhaps it was because I was tired of playing the field. And in all honesty, the sex was awesome. No complaints there. Now I wondered if it was *because* he was sleeping with every woman who hit on him at work that he was so good in the sack. Another downside was that I'd be seeing Trey at work tomorrow night. And of course, he'd be all smiles and how do you do's, playing me, while playing the field.

Grinding my teeth, I stared out through my windshield to the open, dark road and remembered what my jerkface boss at the diner I waitressed at said to me a half hour ago, prompting my bad day to become epically worse.

"You know, Simone, if you'd just be a good girl and give me what I want, I can easily ensure you a fifty-cent raise on your next check. And there will be more where that came from."

Of course, this was after he'd done a little grab ass, going under the stupid pale pink uniform skirt they made us wear. When I turned around and slapped him across his smarmy face, he claimed he was going to complain to the owner that *I was* the one harassing *him* sexually, when it was the complete opposite. That slimy freak hit on anything that moved, making not only the other waitresses uncomfortable, but even going so far as to bother the female customers. Ones who coincidentally never came back for a repeat performance.

After I slapped him, I took off my apron, tossed it in his shocked face, and screamed, "I quit!"

At least that'd felt good.

At the time.

Now I was down yet another crummy-paying job, but I needed the money. I couldn't pay for the business classes I was taking online at the community college if I didn't have money for the tuition. The money I made bartending was my primary source of income where every penny I made went to rent, bills, and gas. On Sundays I helped the local florist Mama Kerri was best friends with for some quick cash under the table, but it wasn't going to keep me doing anything but treading water. And living on the outskirts of Chicago in a safe neighborhood with great access to the city was not cheap. I'd get a roommate, but I already lived in a one-bedroom shoebox. If I did that, I'd be living on my own couch. The waitressing job I just quit brought in the money I needed for tuition and food. A lot of times I took home wrong orders or extras the cook set aside for me. I had three jobs and still could barely afford the crummy life I'd built for myself, but I wanted more. Hoped for more. Worked hard to achieve more.

I sighed heavily into the stale interior as I drove. More than anything, I wanted to live. To have a life where I could walk into a store one day and buy an outfit and not worry about what bill I wasn't going to pay in its place. Maybe go out to dinner once in a while. Stop mooching off my foster mom and my sisters by way of free food and clothes. To this day I still took my laundry over to Mama Kerri's, so I didn't have to use up my hard-earned tips on quarters at the laundromat.

"I am so lame," I grumbled. Not that anyone one could hear me. The radio in my car didn't work and I couldn't afford to fix it or get a fancy new CD player. One day, though, when I had my degree in business administration and could finally make something of myself, I'd get a shiny new car. One that didn't require ten *Hail Marys* and five *Our Fathers* in order to get it started every morning.

Seeing a gas station up ahead, I hit my blinker and drove my hand-me-down, four-door, fifteen-year-old Honda Civic up to a pump.

Digging through my purse I found a crumpled up twenty-dollar bill. "Woo hoo!" I did a little chair dance as I opened my wallet and grabbed the two fivers I'd received from a couple of nice people who had tipped me more than expected this evening. Thirty whole bucks on gas…AMEN!

Knowing I didn't have enough in my bank account to use my card, I dashed into the store, waited my turn in line, and spent my last thirty bucks on gas for my car.

"Thanks, brother." I waved and headed outside.

While my gas was pumping, I pulled out my phone and scanned the texts.

From: Sonia

I have a dinner in the city next month. Want to be my plus one?

I cringed as I read the message again, thinking of a way I could get out of it. I definitely didn't want to get all dolled-up prim and proper to go to another one of my sister's boring political dinners. Sonia was my only living blood relative and also happened to be a state Senator. Yep. The real deal. She managed hundreds of people and an entire state and has been doing so for the last four years. Youngest Senator there ever was. And here I couldn't even hold down a job at a crummy diner that paid minimum wage.

Skipping over her message I reviewed the next from my foster sister Addison, Addy for short.

From: Addison

Will be in town this weekend. Coming back from a photoshoot with Blessing. She's down to hook up too. Let's party!

Now that sounded like fun. Hitting the clubs with two of my foster sisters was exactly what I needed to lift my mood. With fast fingers I responded with a *Hell, yeah*, and moved on to the next message.

Trey. Ugh.

From: Trey

Hey babe. Sorry about earlier. Still friends?

I rolled my eyes and snarled under my breath, ignoring

his text too. God, I hated men like him. They broke your heart but wanted to stay friends? What was that? Then again, it's not as if I was crying in my ergonomic tennis shoes over our breakup either. The kind thing to do would have been to let him off the hook. After the day I'd had, I was not interested in doing the kind thing, or even the right thing. I was going to let him stew in his crap a little longer, because in truth, the punk ass deserved it.

Making that decision had me feeling a bit more upbeat about everything. Not much, but a little.

The pump clicked that it was done refueling. I replaced the pump, grabbed my receipt, closed the gas cap, and moseyed into my car. As I turned around and got into my seat, I saw the cashier waving both his arms in the air. Weird. I squinted and noted he was making a "come here" gesture.

Whatever it was, I did not have the time to deal with it. So instead I waved wildly and smiled, slammed my door, and motored off into the night toward home. I needed sleep, tequila, and the other half of a burrito I saved from my Chipotle run yesterday.

Mmm. I could already taste the meat, rice, and bean-filled goodness that would hit my belly soon. A little squirt of lime, maybe some sour cream…heaven. My stomach growled and I pressed harder on the gas.

I got about ten minutes away from home, and a good five miles from the gas station I'd just left when suddenly sirens started blaring. I glanced in my rearview mirror and saw red and blue lights flashing behind me. Unfortunately, the car was focused on me and not trying to go around.

Dammit to hell in a handbasket!

What next?

I inhaled full and deep as the tears started pricking the back of my eyes. I could not afford a speeding ticket.

Please, Lord, let him give me a verbal warning. Please, please, please. If you do, I'll go to that stupid dinner with Sonia and take one for the sisterhood.

Careful as could be, I hit my blinker and shifted over to the side of the road. The area was a bit creepy and located in the industrial part of town where not a lot of people spent time when it wasn't daylight hours.

Doing my best to keep calm, I employed the yoga breathing technique Mama Kerri taught me. Through the years our foster mom taught us weekly yoga, all eight of us "sisters" in a circle of unity as she called it, breathing and holding hands.

The tears still fell as I rolled down my window and checked my side mirror.

A tall, dark, male form was silhouetted by the single red and blue flashing light. The kind you see on an unmarked cop car. The man approached slowly. He had his gun out and down at his side. He was wearing dark slacks and a sportscoat but that was about all I could see. My entire focus was on the gun hanging at his side.

Were they supposed to have their guns out for a routine traffic stop? And why wasn't he in a cruiser? Why was he in a suit and not a uniform?

Oh my god! Did he think I was a criminal? I mean the car used to be in Sonia's name, but she gave it to me when she traded up. For a few seconds I filtered through tons of memories trying to figure out if her name was still on the car or my own. No, it was me. I paid the registration fee this year. Yeah. I nodded to myself as the officer got closer.

"Ma'am, hands to the steering wheel," a low and very deep voice demanded.

Shoot. I knew that. Everyone did nowadays.

I placed my shaking hands on the wheel and turned my head to the side and out the window a bit.

"I'm sorry, Officer. I mean…"

"Ma'am, please step out of the vehicle." His voice was direct and brooked no argument.

"Um, why? I didn't even know I was speeding. I swear. I have a lot on my mind and I just got fired from my job… well technically, I quit because my boss was harassing me and grabbed my butt and…"

"Ma'am. Now. Out of the vehicle," his request came again.

"But? Why? I-I…is this normal?" My voice cracked.

"I have reason to believe you stole this car and are carrying illegal paraphernalia in it. Please, do as I ask and get out of the vehicle. Keep your hands visible at all times. Do not reach for anything inside the car."

My heart pounded so hard I thought I might have a heart attack.

Drugs. Stolen car.

What the heck was happening?

"Officer…" I glanced down at the shiny gold badge clipped to his belt, but it didn't look like the normal badge a regular cop wore. The letters F-B-I glinted off the headlights from his car. "Really, this is a mistake. I am the rightful owner of this car and I don't have drugs, nor have I ever done them." I moved my right arm out toward the glove compartment. "I can show you my registration and…"

"Out. Of. The. Vehicle." He ground the command out.

"Okay, okay. Um, I have to unlatch my seat belt."

"Do it. Then hands up."

I did as he said, trying the latch twice before I could get it to release. As he required, I put my hands up into the air, reached for the latch, and pushed the door open. It squeaked so loud I shivered at the sound; all of the doors made that sound. It had been doing that for a full year and I didn't know how to make it stop. Trey, my useless no-longer boyfriend, didn't even try to fix it. No-good loser. Another in the con column that was Trey Barker.

My hands continued to shake, and tears fell down my cheeks as I stood with my hands up.

"Close the door," he demanded.

I did as he asked and squinted against the light.

"Now follow me. One foot in front of the other," he instructed as though he were speaking to a child.

"Are you arresting me?" A deluge of tears fell down my cheeks as my chest constricted and my stomach plummeted.

"Ma'am just follow me. Closer." He waved his non-gun-toting hand as he walked backward.

"I don't understand. This is so crazy. I didn't do anything wrong. I swear! It's my car and I don't have drugs. You can check it."

"And I will, when you're safely sitting in my car."

"Oh my God! You're arresting me!"

That's when I lost it.

I punched my hands into my hair, tugging on the long, beachy golden waves until they were hanging off my now heated neck.

"This is unbelievable! The absolute worst day of my entire life. And my parents died in a fire! At the same time!

And I had to go to foster care with my sister. And this day, oh my God. Sonia! My sister…no, Officer, you *cannot* arrest me. You do not understand what this will do to my sister. She's the…"

"Ma'am! Get over here now!" The officer grated through a super scary rumble pushing me into immediate action.

When I got closer, he latched onto my wrist and tugged me close to his body. My chest slammed against his and I placed my hands to his muscular biceps. I stared up into the darkest set of eyes I'd ever seen. Like a black cup of coffee, yet with little golden-brown flecks at the center. His skin was an olive tone, his jaw cut square, framed by cheekbones that were sharp slashes as though chiseled into fine marble. He had dark brown hair that was longer on top and shorter at the sides. If I had to guess, I'd put him in the dark Italian stallion category or Greek god.

He was beautiful.

One of his hands moved to my waist where he squeezed, and he dipped his head so close to my ear I could feel his warm breath against my cheek. "We received a report that someone crawled into the back of a blonde woman's red old-model four-door Honda Civic at a gas station. First two letters of the license plate are A2."

"W-what?"

"I need to check your car. Fast. If it's not you, another woman could get hurt."

"Oh my god! I did get gas." I held onto his biceps so hard I may have left nail imprints.

"It's okay, you're safe now," he murmured, and I closed my eyes, taking in his woodsy and fresh linens scent. It helped calm me instantly.

Until we both heard the familiar metal creaking sound against the quiet of the cool night.

I whirled around and saw a thin, tall man standing next to my car, a full ski mask covering most of his face aside from cutouts around the eyes and mouth.

Before I could do or say anything, I was grabbed around the waist and spun behind the cop as the guy in a mask lifted his arm, pointed a gun, and fired off two shots.

The officer took two to the chest as I screamed. He fell back against me as two more shots were fired. One must have whizzed past him because a blooming round of fire ripped through the side of my bicep on the arm that I'd placed around the officer to hold him up.

He fell backward and I went down with him.

I screeched in pain as I slammed into the asphalt, my hip smarting while taking the brunt of our combined weight. My hand scraped along the rough black surface, abrading the skin, but I didn't care about that. As soon as we fell to the ground, I looked up to see the criminal slam the driver's side door and take off in my car, tires squealing.

Focusing on the officer, I checked for a pulse and found a steady beat.

Okay, okay, okay. You can do this, Simone. I felt the officer's cheeks and patted them a few times. "Wake up, wake up. Please. He's gone! Wake up."

Nothing happened. I stood up and looked around. There was no one to speak to and I couldn't leave him lying in the road to get run over while I searched out help.

My phone was in my purse in the car that was now a getaway vehicle for a bad guy I did not want to think about.

I settled the officer on his side and rushed over to his

vehicle. I saw something that looked like a laptop and panel of electronic things that I had absolutely no idea how to work. Except one item looked like a walkie talkie on a cord with a button like regular cops had. I picked it up and pressed the button.

"Help me. Help me, please. My name is Simone Wright-Kerrighan. The officer that pulled me over has been shot. Send help, please!" I said on a rush and let go of the button.

Instantly a female voice came through the car's interior. "Ma'am, you've got dispatch. I'm sending a unit and an ambulance. Are you hurt?"

Which was when I realized my arm was blazing white hot fire, and blood was leaking down past my elbow. I lifted it to see how bad it was. There was a big, long gouge from the front to the back of my bicep like I'd been grazed or sliced, but it wasn't a hole. Still it seemed pretty deep and there was an awful amount of blood.

I hissed and pushed the button and spoke. "Um, I might have been shot too in the arm but I'm okay. He's breathing and I felt his pulse but he's unconscious. I don't know what to do!"

"You're doing just fine. A unit is two minutes from your location."

"Please hurry. The bad guy stole my car and got away." The tears fell again, and my nose ran like a faucet. I lifted the skirt of my stupid diner outfit that already had crimson staining it and wiped my nose.

"Just tell the officer that arrives what happened, and we'll take care of it." The woman's voice sent a layer of calm rushing through my system.

I dropped the walkie talkie thing when I saw the man's leg move through the car window.

"Don't move!" I hollered and jumped out of the car, rushing to his side. I bit back a curse as I fell to my knees on the raw asphalt and placed my hands to his cheeks. "You're okay. Help is on the way. I called them."

His eyes opened and closed several times as though he were waking from a long sleep.

"Where were you shot?" I looked at his chest but didn't see any blood escaping from him.

"Vest," he muttered through clenched teeth.

I frowned and then realized he was referring to one of those bulletproof vests. He must have been wearing it under his dress clothes.

"Yay!" I said stupidly and regretted it instantly.

His eyes squeezed together as though he were in great pain.

Off in the distance I could hear sirens approaching.

"They're almost here, just be still."

"Where is he?" He coughed and winced.

"The bad guy? He took off in my car. We're safe now." I held onto his cheek and prayed he'd open his eyes and keep them open.

My prayer was granted a moment later when he opened his beautiful brown eyes. "Name?"

"I don't know who he was! I swear!"

He closed his eyes for a moment and then gifted me a small, yet still pained, smile.

"Your name, gorgeous?"

I sucked in a harsh breath. *God, I'm so stupid.* "Simone. My name is Simone."

"Simone. Pretty. Agent Fontaine," he murmured.

"Um, thank you," I said, and the officer seemed to have

lost the battle with being able to keep his eyes open or to stay conscious for that matter as he passed out again.

The paramedics and cops descended *en masse* on us. I stayed close enough to see them cut through his dress shirt. Not one, not two, but *three* golden bullets wedged into the vest covering his broad chest.

They did a few medical things with a cuff, a pen light, a breathing mask, and then propped him up and put him on a stretcher.

"Can I go with him?" I asked needing to see him safe and sound after he'd thrown himself in front of a madman with a gun and saved my life.

"Honey, you need to be seen to as well. Yeah, you can come in the ambulance and I'll get you bandaged too." A short woman with a pair of glasses inspected my arm. "Gauze!" She held her hand out and her partner put a roll of white bandages into it. She promptly wrapped my bleeding arm. "Flesh wound. Just a graze. Still, you'll need stitches. Though looks like you were lucky."

No. I wasn't lucky. That's the last thing I'd ever been in my entire life.

"Is Agent Fontaine going to be okay?" I recalled the name he gave and realized he'd said Agent and not Officer.

"We'll know more when we get him to the hospital. Looks to be okay. The vest did the job, but we don't know what type of internal injuries might have occurred."

I bit down on my bottom lip and followed her into the ambulance.

"Miss, we need to get your statement," another burly officer holding out a notepad asked.

"Oh my god! Yes, you have to go after the guy that did

this. He stole my car. My name is Simone Wright-Kerrighan and I drive a red Honda Civic. I'm sure you'll find the details in the system." I finished off by giving him my driver's license number which I'd memorized.

"We'll meet you at the hospital, ma'am, to get the rest of the details on what happened here. Get fixed up first. The information about your car will be very helpful. Thank you."

I nodded and the cop shut me into the ambulance with my fallen savior.

Within moments we jetted off down the road. The paramedic had removed the agent's vest and was feeling around his taught, muscular abdomen and chest.

I made sure I was close enough that I could hold onto the man's hand as I closed my eyes and prayed that he'd be okay and that they'd find the man that did this.

When I was done, I opened my eyes to find him looking at me. His beautiful eyes focused directly on my face.

"I'm sorry," I whispered and pressed the back of his hand to my cheek needing to feel his life source directly. "Thank you for saving my life," I choked out, barely containing the emotions roaring through my system.

He didn't say anything, just squeezed my hand and closed his eyes, a soft smile on his beautiful lips.

Chapter
TWO

CLENCHING MY FINGERS INTO A TIGHT FIST, I BREATHED through another stitch being woven into my arm. I let out the breath when the physician's assistant stopped for a moment.

"You're doing really great," she said as she continued to close the wound. Thankfully she'd numbed the area around it first, but I could still feel the tightening, burning, sizzling sensation.

"Where's my sister!" I heard my sister's cool, don't-mess-with-me tone demand from a distance beyond the closed curtain where I was being treated in the Emergency Room.

"My daughter? Simone Kerrighan. Please…" I heard Mama Kerri's more seasoned and lilting, emotional voice come through.

"Over here, guys!" I hollered out.

The blue curtain was pulled away and there were my sister and my foster mother. Sonia put her hands over her mouth and tears filled her ocean blue eyes. With her white blonde hair, red painted lips and those eyes, she looked like an angel. A suit-wearing, super serious angel who was currently trying to hide her devastation.

"Oh, my goodness me, what happened to my girl?" Mama Kerri rounded the bed and cupped both of my cheeks.

"Mama, I'm okay, really. I uh…" I bit down on my bottom lip trying to determine what to tell them, not wanting to worry them unnecessarily.

"I want answers. Now." My sister had already turned toward the approaching doctor, arms crossed over her chest, her team of suits standing a reasonable distance behind her. The doc was short, Asian, and kept a flat thin line to his lips. He seemed unimpressed with my sister's demands and ignored her completely. I needed to take notes from the man.

"Ms. Wright-Kerrighan." He looked down at the electronic device he was holding, using my full name. "Gunshot wound to the arm, bruised hip, scratches and abrasions on the hands and knees." He flipped a page.

"Gunshot!" My sister gasped, her hand flying to her chest over her heart, interrupting the doc.

"I'm fine, SoSo, just a graze…" I attempted to soothe her concern.

"Just a graze! How? What in the world happened?" My normally insanely calm sister petered out, her bottom lip wobbling as a tear fell down the side of her cheek. She swiped it away as fast as it appeared lest someone see her crack.

Her crying made me tear up, and I was doing damn good considering.

The doctor assessed the work the PA was doing. "Looks great. Once you're stitched up, we'll set you up with some antibiotics to ward off an infection. The discharge nurse will go over the cleansing and bandaging procedure. You need to follow up with your doctor in a couple weeks though the stitches should dissolve over the next ten days or so. Leave them clean and dry for the next forty-eight hours but you can take a shower like normal after that timeframe. Any questions?"

"Yes. The agent that I came in with. Is he okay?"

"Can't say. You're not family, but a couple of officers would like to speak with you shortly. I told them to wait until you were stitched up."

"Thank you, Doctor. I appreciate it." I frowned and thought about Agent Fontaine as the doctor left us. The man had saved my life. I didn't even know his first name and he'd taken three bullets to the chest in order to keep me safe. He could have died. Thank God he was wearing that vest and the criminal took off. Not that I was thrilled he'd taken my car with him, but the alternative would have been worse.

"Sweetheart, what happened?" Mama Kerri squeezed my good hand as my sister came around to the other side of the bed and put her own on my shoulder, comforting me as much as herself. My sister had the ice princess thing down, but not when it came to me. I was her vulnerability in a big way. The weakest link in her armor. Which was also why I hated letting her down more than just about anything.

I swallowed and figured the best policy was always an honest one.

For the next half hour or so I explained what happened—from my douchebag boss, getting gas, the weird experience of the cashier trying to wave me back in that I ignored. Really wished I'd made a different choice at that moment. Then to the guy pulling me over with his gun visible, how I was scared that I was being arrested for no reason, then everything seemed to go dead silent in the room as I detailed what happened when the man crawled out of my car. It was like I was reliving it all over again.

The creak of metal from the door had me flinching.

Feeling the agent's breath so warm and comforting against my cheek sent a wave of warmth through my body.

His scent wafting around us like a blanket being place around me.

Seeing the light from the car glinting off the shiny black gun. I winced.

Those two eyes holes cut out of the fabric and the one for his mouth flashing like a predator standing over me. I shrank back into the hospital bed on instinct.

The boom of the gun as it went off. I jerked and cried out.

When I came to, blinking away the experience and the retelling of it, Mama Kerri was sitting on the bed and I was in her arms. The PA was done, and I was in the only maternal arms I'd ever remembered. She ran her hand along my hair and back, over and over, as I cried, my face pressed to her ample chest. The smell of fresh cut flowers filled my nose as it always did when Mama Kerri held me. I trembled as she spoke quietly.

"You're okay, my girl. Just fine. Right here with me and Sonia. We've got you, my lovely. I've always got you."

And she did.

From the moment Sonia and I had walked up to her door hand in hand, Mama Kerri took care of us. Like a beautiful earthy goddess. Long, curly strawberry blonde hair. Pale pink lips. Pearly white skin. Eyes that seemed to change from blue to hazel depending on the day or the emotion she felt. However, none of that beauty could beat the sound of her voice. It resonated at a timber and lilt that brought a sense of peace and serenity that couldn't be matched. Not ever.

"Mama," I sobbed and gripped onto her wherever I could, letting it all out. The fear. The hopelessness of the situation while it was happening and even the worry over my savior's prognosis.

"It's okay. Mama's here." She patted my back and whispered against my temple. "You're just fine. You. Are. Just. Fine." Her words broke as she held me tighter. "I'm so sorry you had to go through that. It sounds terrifying. Don't you worry though. I've got you. Sonia and I have you, dear."

I sniffled through my tears and took several breaths, allowing her to comfort me until I got myself back in check.

"Senator Wright, please excuse me. I apologize for interrupting, but we just got word the story has already leaked to the press. They saw you coming into the hospital and someone confirmed it was your sister that had been targeted."

Sonia sighed as I sucked in a huge breath trying not to cry more. "I'm sorry, SoSo. I didn't…"

"Wasn't your fault. This was a random act of violence and we need to be grateful that you weren't more seriously hurt."

"Actually, about that…" The cute man shuffled his feet and grimaced. "The news is reporting it was an attempt by the Backseat Strangler…"

"What!" Sonia screeched and her entire face went deathly pale.

"No…" I practically choked on the word.

The young assistant, I think his name was Logan, firmed his stance and lifted his chest as he glanced down at his phone. "He crawled into her car at a gas station. Hid in the back." He was reading something as though he'd been told my story directly. "The only other woman that got away stated he was tall, thin, white, and wore all black including a ski mask."

My hand shook as I lifted it to my mouth. Exact same thing happened tonight.

"He's killed eight other women in this manner. One of the women he attacked got away and has disappeared off the map, and now, uh, your sister." He licked his lips and seemed to gather himself, which if I'd been in a better mental headspace, I would have congratulated him for. Dealing with a pissed-off Sonia was no walk in the park on a good day and he was doing his best. "We're going to need to get on top of this…" He frowned.

"Right now I need to focus on my sister. You need to call Quinn…"

"And who's Quinn?" He wrote down the name on notepad and I sighed. He must be really new. Sonia tended to be a hard-ass and go through assistants like she went through the Sunday paper. Quinn was my sister's right-hand man, her BFF jack of all trades who also happened to be gay and dress fabulously. I was jealous of his abilities in all things. He even was capable of managing my sister, something no one had been able to do, not even Mama Kerri. However, I also knew he'd just gotten back from a much-needed two-week vacation. Hence the reason newbie Logan didn't know about him.

"Head of PR," she ground out. "He's just come back from the Bahamas. Explain what's happened, sparing no detail. I'll deal with the press after I've ensured my sister's safety and well-being." She waved her hand in the air, dismissing the poor guy. "Thank you." She added onto her instruction as if she'd realized how bitchy she sounded. "You may leave."

He nodded and scampered away like a long-lost puppy. Then two uniformed officers took his place.

"Ms. Wright?"

"Wright-Kerrighan." I held my foster mother's hand tighter. When each of the foster girls turned of age, every one of us changed our last names, hyphenating ours with hers. Kind of like a gift to her for all she'd done over the many years she raised us. I kept the Wright because it felt wrong getting rid of every trace of our biological parents. And since that's how Sonia kept her name, I followed along. Our other foster sisters did too. Sonia however used Wright-Kerrighan only in private. For professional reasons she chose to stick with Wright.

"Can we speak with you about what happened?" asked a man in a pair of navy slacks and an old beige sportscoat that had seen better days.

"Can they stay?" I nodded to my sister and mom.

"Oh, hello, Senator Wright. I'm sorry to be seeing you again under these circumstances." He had a shiny gold badge clipped to his worn-out belt.

"Captain Mandle, thank you for coming." Sonia offered a flat press of her lips as though she weren't actually happy to see him.

"Captain?" I frowned. How many crimes came with the Captain visiting one of the victims in the hospital the night of?

"This case is sensitive, the FBI is involved, and you're uh, well darlin', you're a living witness."

And that explained it. I was alive as opposed to being dead girl number nine. Awesome. This day just kept getting better and better.

"The Backseat Strangler." I swallowed the lump that had formed in my throat.

"'Fraid so. I'm going to need to ask you a lot of questions. Many you may not have the answers to, but just do your best, yeah?"

I nodded. "I will."

Peeking down the corridor, I noted a handful of officers standing around a single door at the end of the hall.

A nudge from behind had me shuffling into the open space before I'd gotten my wits together.

"Sonia, dammit! I was going for stealth mode!" I whisper-scolded under my breath.

"For what reason?" She hooked me at the elbow of my good arm, and we walked hip to hip toward the gaggle of men.

As soon as we approached, several of the uniformed officers turned around. One super tall white guy with longish layered dark blond hair that looked windswept held a hand up, palm facing out. He was dressed more professionally in a full pitch-black suit.

"This is a restricted section of the hospital. Authorized medical personal only," he started, but my sister stepped right up to battle.

"Hello, Agent." She glanced down his body.

He smirked. "Agent Russell."

"Agent Russell. I'm Senator Sonia Wright and my sister was attacked this evening. Your peer, Agent Fontaine, saved her life. We'd like to inquire how he's doing, and my sister would like to say a few words if he's up to the company."

My sister was a freakin' rockstar. I held her hand, interlacing our fingers, palm to palm sharing my thanks silently.

The man's face gentled. "You're Simone?"

"Yes. Is he okay?"

The blond man smiled, and it lit up his face, making his already handsome one rather stunning. Though the man who saved my life was far more attractive. I always swooned for tall, dark, and handsome though several of my sisters would have dug this guy.

"He's doing really well. A couple of fractured ribs and some serious soreness and bruising but the vest did its job. He'll be back to work in no time. Not that he'd ever rest. And how are you?"

I reached for my bandaged arm and held onto it. "Twenty-two stitches and bumps and bruises."

"The hand?" He glanced down at the hand that was wrapped and being held by my sister.

"Scratched up from hitting the asphalt. I'll be good as new in a few days. Um, do you think I could see him?"

He gave us a boy next door grin. "I think he'd like that very much. He's been asking about you. Come on." He led us through the group of men gathered around and opened the door.

I walked in and my knight in shining hospital gown turned his head and smiled huge.

My heart stopped.

All sound disappeared.

There was nothing but him and me in that moment.

No machines. No hospital. No people milling about.

Just us.

I rushed to his form and threw my arms around him the best I could. He held onto me and pressed his chin to my neck.

"Thank you. Thank you for saving my life. I can't ever repay that gift." I snuffled against his warm, *alive* form.

"Hey, hey, we're both okay. It all worked out." He cupped the back of my neck under my hair and kissed my temple. "It all worked out."

For a few long moments we held one another. Me standing over his bed leaning against him, him taking my weight and holding me close.

Eventually someone behind me cleared their throat.

I inhaled against his neck, the woodsy and fresh linen scent even stronger, but now mixed with something inherently rich and masculine. Pulling myself together, I leaned back and wiped the stray tears from my eyes.

"Oh, hello there. Whoa. Senator Wright?" Agent Fontaine said, clearly shocked to see my sister's presence.

My sister smiled softly, her entire face softening at the sight of my savior.

"Thank you, Agent Fontaine, for saving my sister's life. I am in your debt. If there is anything me or my office can do to assist the FBI or you with anything in the future, I am at your service."

"Wow. Uh, okay. Thank you for that." He shook his head as if trying to clear it before focusing on me.

I grabbed his hand and took the liberty of sitting on the side of his bed, not wanting to miss anything my living hero had to say. And honestly, the view was not bad. Even roughed up and on pain killers the man was possibly the most gorgeous man on the planet.

"Do you know when you'll be released?"

He smiled softly and I watched his perfectly shaped lips lift and fall back into place.

Dreamy.

The man was incredibly good looking, and if I didn't have so much adrenaline running through my system after all we'd been through, I would have been a puddle of goo at his feet.

"My name's Jonah by the way. Jonah Fontaine."

"Jonah." I tried his name on for size and found I liked it very much. A little thrill of hope rippled through my already over-sensitized system.

I trembled and he narrowed his eyes. "You need to get home. Except not your home. Since the perp absconded with your vehicle, I'm assuming your purse, phone, and address were in the car too?"

My sister put her arm out and squeezed my shoulder. I glanced over to her.

"You are not going home. You shouldn't be in that tiny box anyway. You're moving in with me," Sonia stated flatly, going right into Big Sister Says So mode. I hated that mode and found the off switch when I turned twenty-one, but she constantly tried to flip that sucker back on and make decisions about my life.

I shook my head. "No way. I'm going back to my house."

"The hell you are. I forbid it." My overprotective older sister positively vibrated as a red flush encompassed her cheeks and chest, showing her burgeoning anger.

"SoSo, I'm a grown woman. No, I will not go home tonight. I agree it's too dangerous."

Her shoulders fell two inches and a sigh of relief escaped her perfectly painted red lips.

I glanced back at Jonah. "Though I'm sure Agent Fontaine and his perfectly capable crew of hundreds can tell me when it's safe to return. I will need to go there tomorrow to pick up some things at least for the next week or so depending on what they say. I'll just stay with Mama Kerri in our old room until all this is worked out. No muss, no fuss."

"Damn, you're one helluva strong woman, Simone." Jonah ran his thumb over the top of my hand, and I felt the caress careen straight through to my heart.

"Thank you." I smiled. I'd never been called strong a day in my life. Resilient, yes. Strong, no. Most often people saw me as the people pleaser. The sister always willing to help out with anyone's desires or dreams but never having any of her own. I'd been pegged as reliable but not responsible. Late but always in attendance. Hardworking but never driven. I was good at a lot of things but master of none. Unfortunately, it was all true. Except hearing this man call me strong gave me a huge sense of pride when I very rarely felt that emotion.

"Simone, you can stay with me. The guest room can easily be transitioned into your room. You know I'd love to have you. And I'm rarely home anyway…"

I stood up and hugged my sister, wrapping my arms around her much taller and far more fit frame. Men considered me voluptuous and on the curvy side. My sister was elegance in motion. An athletic build she worked hard to keep. Said working out cleared her mind. I found my workouts by being on my feet slinging drinks and carrying dinner trays over my head, though I enjoyed eating and drinking far more than my sister. Hence the curves.

"You know I love you more than my own life…"

"And I you, that's why I think you should stay with me, in my guarded and secure apartment." She tried again.

"That's not a bad idea, Simone. There's a serial killer on the loose. And you don't get much more guarded than an elected official, unless of course you're the President or a celebrity," Jonah added.

I shook my head. "Sorry. I'd be more comfortable back at Kerrighan House. Plenty of room. Mom's there to feed and baby me. You know how it is. When something bad happens…"

"You just want to go home," Sonia said the phrase that meant so much to the both of us. We'd always been one another's safe place, but it was a bit different for me. I was only six when we arrived at Kerrighan House. She'd been twelve. It was the only home I really remembered or knew. To her, I was home. Not that she didn't love our foster mother to pieces.

"Besides, if I didn't go to her house, you know Mama'd end up at yours."

Sonia smiled wide breaking up the tension that had built in the room. "That is true. You're likely not going to get away from her for a while."

I shrugged. "Why would I want to?" My foster mother was the coolest mom ever. Everyone that met her agreed. She was one of those people you just adored being around.

Sonia nodded. "Okay then. I'm going to talk to the men

about perhaps seeing if we could secure a couple officers doing some rounds of the house during their patrols. It would make me feel safer knowing they have an eye on you and Mama Kerri."

"Sure," I relented. The woman would not settle if I didn't give her something.

Sonia nodded. "I'll leave you two to visit." She turned and left.

When I focused back on Jonah, he was opening and closing his eyes as though he were fighting a battle to stay awake.

"I'll take you to your house tomorrow afternoon. I don't want you, your sister, or mother going there alone."

"You really have done enough already…"

He pursed his lips and adjusted his position with a wince. "Promise me you'll give him your information and wait for our call?"

I patted his hand. "I promise. It's the least I can do. What's your favorite cookie?"

He frowned and shook his head. Sleep trying to take over. "Chocolate chip. Why?"

"Because I'm going to make you and the other officers that helped us some."

Jonah smiled. "Simone, you are something else."

"Like what?"

He closed his eyes. "I don't know, but it will be fun finding out."

And that was all he said before his head fell to the side and his chest moved up and down in a deep breathing pattern, telling me he'd fallen asleep.

I leaned over and went to kiss his forehead but in the

last moment, strayed down and placed my lips feather light against his, stealing a tiny kiss from the man that saved my life. A man I wanted to get to know better. In every way that counted.

"I'll look forward to that," I whispered and cupped his cheek, soaking in his dark, beautiful features one last time before I let him go and slipped out of his room.

I couldn't wait until tomorrow when I'd see him again.

Circumstances be damned.

Meeting this man, surviving what could have been a horrible tragedy, changed everything I knew in one evening.

It was time to live for me.

Work toward what I wanted, and grab hold with everything I had inside of me.

And the first thing I wanted...

To get to know my savior, FBI Agent Jonah Fontaine.

Chapter
THREE

S LEEP SLIPPED AWAY AS I FELT A WEIGHT ACROSS MY STOM-
ach and heat at both of my sides.

What in the world?

Blinking my scratchy eyes open, I came face to face
with culprit number one. Her bouncy brown curls were all
over the place in messy waves. Her perfectly shaped eyebrows, even in rest, gave her a sleeping beauty affect. Only
this sleeping beauty was little and a spunky Latina to her
core. My sister Liliana slept soundly, her face right against
my wounded shoulder but not hurting me in the least. Her
arm was slung over my waist holding on. Next to that arm
was yet another slender limb not of my own, this one ghost
white in color. Her perfectly painted nails were a startling
purple and the tattoo she had down the side of her hand of
a cross was prominent against her pale skin.

Her flaming auburn hair was a flat sheet of red against
the white linens. Charlotte. Better known as "Charlie," my
serial-dating bisexual foster sister let it all hang out, and often, depending on her mood.

I lay there for several minutes held between the arms
of two women I adored as if they were my very own blood
relations.

There were eight of us in total. Foster sisters. Well, me

and Sonia were related by blood. The other six came from all different walks of life. One thing remained the same. We'd grown up together in Aurora Kerrighan's house. Since we were little it had always been the nine of us.

Me. Sonia. Addison. Blessing. Liliana. Charlotte. Genesis. Tabitha. And last but not least, Mama Kerri. She'd taken each of us in and since I was around eight, the entire house had been filled with females. From then on, we were just sisters…a family by choice. We celebrated birthdays, holidays, graduations, jobs, and everything in between just like any other family.

Our lives weren't normal by any stretch of the imagination, but we made it work and it was filled to the brim with love and sisterhood.

I'd have it no other way.

I lifted my arms and put both of them around the two women. The jostling woke them and each one stirred. Liliana smiled huge, her dark gaze twinkling.

"*Dios mio*, you had us worried, *hermana*." She leaned forward and kissed my bandaged shoulder, and I could have imagined it, but I believed it did take away a little of the burn.

Sisterly magic. Worked like a charm.

Charlie on my right lifted my bandaged hand and brought it to her cheek, pressing lightly. "Mama Kerri said you'd been shot." Her voice cracked, and her eyes filled with tears.

"When did you guys get here?" My voice was hoarse, and I tried to clear it of all the cotton I felt coating my throat. Pain meds did a number on the body. Damn. Everywhere felt sluggish and lethargic, not to mention the aches and throbbing at my shoulder, hip, and hand.

"We rushed right over when Mama called," Liliana explained. "You were asleep when we got here. We didn't want to wake you up."

I tugged them close, closed my eyes, and breathed deep, allowing their presence to fill me up and give me the comfort I needed this morning.

"Are you really okay?" Charlie asked.

"How can I not be? I woke up warm and comfy to two of the best sisters in the entire world." I smiled and sighed.

"I see three little chicks cuddled up in bed," Mama's lilting voice came from the room's entrance.

The three of us glanced over where she leaned against the doorjamb, her purple fluffy robe in place, her long strawberry waves down around her shoulders. She had a pair of multicolored reading glasses on and a book tucked under her arm, a steaming yellow mug in her hand.

She was the sun. The moon. The bringer of everything good in life.

"Morning, Mama." I smiled.

"Girls, I see you couldn't stay away even though I told you not to rouse her. She needed her sleep after the night she had." She tsked but smiled through it.

"We didn't bug her, just cuddled up and crashed like old times," Charlie stated.

"Mmm, well come on my little chicks, let's get some tea and cookies into you. Nothing like a sweet in the morning to wash away a bad night, eh?"

I smiled and looked at Liliana and then Charlie. The three of us started giggling like the teenagers we once were. Every time we had a bad night, we'd wake to tea and cookies instead of eggs or oatmeal, which was normally on the menu. Mama Kerri had a firm belief that a sweet treat could solve any hurt, at least for a time.

Seemed to work as we grew up. Definitely wouldn't hurt now.

She clucked her tongue and disappeared.

The girls helped me get out of bed.

Charlie hissed as my panty-clad form was revealed. I should say, more that the bruise on my hip came into stark view. It was hideous. Black and purple and about the size of a salad plate.

Liliana and Charlie both studied it.

"Does it hurt really bad?" Liliana asked, her eyes filled with worry and concern.

I shook my head. "Not if I don't touch it." I grinned and she shook her head as though she were used to me blowing things off and making light of a bad situation. Part of my sparkling personality. Though I will admit yesterday took the cake for shitty days. I was more than ready to start today fresh and let go of all that came before.

"Come on, ladies. Remember, each new day is a gift."

According to Sonia anyway. She'd always tell me that, especially the first couple years we lived here after our parents died.

"Be grateful for each new day. It's truly a gift." She'd say that when I'd grumble about waking up, or having to go to school, or waking early on a weekend to go to my part-time job as a teenager.

I grabbed Sonia's old robe hanging off the back of the door, feeling instantly comforted by something that was worn by my big sis, who—knowing her—would be arriving any time now.

The three of us did our bathroom routine, the door completely open, one peeing, one brushing her teeth, and one washing her face before we'd switch. When you lived in a house with eight girls, you learned how to share space. That didn't change even though we were tipping the scales toward thirty.

One by one, we each took the staircase down to the kitchen where shocker of all shockers, my sister Sonia was already sitting at the table, phone plastered to her ear. The second she noticed us coming down the stairs, she barked into her phone, "Gotta go. Simone's awake. Yes, I'll tell her...mmm hmm. I'll tell Mama too. Got it." She set her phone down and set her gaze on me. "That was Genesis. She's freaked out to the max. Her and Rory will be here this evening. She didn't bring her over today so Mama could focus on you."

Genesis was the second oldest at a whopping thirty-one, a social worker in downtown Chicago, and a single mother of Rory, aptly named Aurora after Mama Kerri. We called her three-year-old daughter Rory for short.

"Aw, she didn't have to do that. I would have loved hanging out with my niece." I frowned and winced as I sat on the padded seat at the large picnic-style table in the rectangular kitchen.

Mama stood by the metal sink, plants dangling around the window, herbs sitting in neat little pots at perfect clipping distance, though it didn't hold a candle to the enormous garden in the backyard.

"That's what I told her. Don't keep my grandchild from me, but Gen never listens. Uses that degree in psychology and social behavior to determine that we shouldn't have more to deal with, when our Rory is not *something* we deal with but enjoy to the fullest. You can tell her I said so too." Her tone was indignant but not irritated as she poured milk in some teas, sugar in others, and both in mine because I loved most things in life. If it tasted good by itself, it likely tasted good with it all mixed in together too.

"Anyway, how's the arm?" Sonia asked her blue-eyed gaze running over my bandaged arm and hand as though she could see through the dressings and determine if they were healing right herself.

"Good, good. I mean…" I canted my head from left to right. "It burns a little and the stitches pull but overall it could have been a lot worse."

"Yeah, as in dead worse. Simone, Mama told us that the cops think it was the Backseat Strangler." Charlie slumped into the seat across from me.

Just as I was about to respond, a loud bang whistled through the air and two sets of high heels raced across the hardwood floors and into the kitchen.

The five of us stood silently, waiting for the train wreck to appear.

"We're here! We're here!" Addy cried as she practically tripped through the kitchen entryway, Blessing fast on her heels. Liliana reached out to help break her fall but at the last minute, Blessing caught hold of Addy's jeans and yanked her back toward her.

"Lord, girl, you almost killed the sprite!" Blessing admonished and I snorted out a laugh.

Liliana narrowed her gaze and practically stomped her foot. "I am not a sprite! I'm five foot three! Give me a break. Not all of us can be giants like you two!"

"What are you guys doing here? Last I heard you were coming this weekend and we were going to party! You were in France just yesterday?" My tone did not hide my shock at all.

"First flight out." Blessing let Addy go and sat next to me, pulling me into a deep hug. "Family first and my sister was shot and almost killed by a maniac. Don't think I wasn't gonna hightail my ass on outta Paris so I could see she's okay for myself. Shoot, girl, you be trippin'." She pressed her full pink lips together and gave me some attitude.

"Blessing," I choked out and looked at Addison. "Addy. You left a shoot…that had to be a lot of money and…"

Addy shook her head. "Nothing's more important than our sisters. Besides, we rushed through the shoot and Blessing pulled her fashion forward ideas straight out of thin air and the client was thrilled. It all worked out."

Addison was a high fashion plus-sized model. She had long dark hair with natural caramel and auburn highlights running through it, huge boobs, a size-fourteen body with a god-given hourglass frame, green eyes that shone like emeralds, and the perfect lush pout. Her body looked incredible in anything and knocked the socks off the more inclusive designers. She was also the number one "it girl" for lingerie.

Blessing was the exact opposite. An inch shorter than Addy at five foot ten, but her skin was dark and shiny as a river rock. She claimed it was all that coconut oil she swore by. She had a 'fro that was enviable and could be worked into a pineapple shape on top of her head, wild and out like a lion's mane, or soft and curly just hugging her stunning face and coal black eyes. She had these beautiful full pink lips almost as poufy as my own, but I took the cake in big plump lips. Though it was Blessing's smile that could heal the world. Big, bright, and genuine.

Addy came over and hugged me, dipping her head to my cheek and breathing me in. I could feel the wetness against my skin.

I cupped her nape and held her close. "Hey now, don't start crying or I'm gonna start crying and then we'll all get going and it will be a hormone fest."

She giggled against my cheek and then kissed me there before standing up, wiping her eyes, and moseyed over to our mama.

"Oh, my chicklets all in the same house. Now we just need Tabby and Genesis and life would be perfect." She put her arms out and Blessing and Addy each took their hugs.

"Has anyone heard from Tabby lately?" I asked as Mama handed me and Sonia our cups of tea.

She sighed and I swore I saw her shoulders slump. "Unfortunately, no. I've called and left messages."

"Me too," Charlie said.

"*Si,* me too," Liliana added.

"I've had my assistant attempt to call once a day in the hopes that at some point she'd pick up. Last I heard he got some male who told my assistant to screw off and stop calling. Though he didn't say screw." Sonia blew on her tea as she raised her brows for emphasis.

"I've sent weekly texts and have heard nothing in two months. Has anyone gone over there?" Blessing asked.

Charlie nodded. "Yeah, Gen goes over at least once a week and tries to catch her since her apartment is close to her work, but no dice."

"I've attempted to catch her at the bars she's frequented in the past and nothing. Ever since that blowout with the dude who stole from Mama Kerri, she's been incommunicado. My guess, she's feeling really embarrassed and not taking it well. I'll try her house again too." I sipped my tea and sighed.

"Tabby's loser boyfriends are the least of our concerns. She should be here. I left a message last night telling her that Simone was shot at and almost became a victim of the Backseat Strangler and heard *nothing*. No text. No call. Zip. What the heck is that about?" Charlie asked on a snarl, her bright red ponytail swinging with her anger.

Sonia ran a hand down my back. "She's right. Family sticks together and she's avoiding all of us, especially when we need her most. We need to find her, sit her down, and give her a little intervention of sorts. Help her work through whatever's going on in her life. Cut out the riff raff, scrape off the losers, and help her get back on her feet. I'm really worried about her."

"She's always been a little different," Mama commented as she placed a tea towel over her shoulder. "Tabby never has been able to handle her demons the way you girls have. It's always been a struggle, but she's our family and we'll be here for her, no matter what the cost. That's how I raised my girls and I expect you to go to your sister with open arms." A blonde eyebrow rose in question as she looked at each one of us.

A chorus of, "Yes, Mama," rang through the open kitchen.

"So, what did the cops say? Do they really for sure think it was the Backseat Strangler?" Addy asked.

I nodded and then shrugged. "I'm supposed to touch base with Agent Fontaine this afternoon. He should know more. He's the agent who saved my life. Thank God he was wearing a vest…" My eyes glazed over as I remembered the four shots ringing out into the dark night.

I jerked a few times as the memory of each shot going off jolted through my system.

Sonia scooched over to me and wrapped her arms around me from behind. I leaned against her warmth, shaken by the memory.

"It's okay. You're safe," she whispered.

I shivered for a moment and then bit down on my bottom lip, trying desperately to ward off the tears that wanted to come.

"I'm stronger than this…" I whispered, and she nodded against my shoulder.

"Yep. One of the strongest people I know," she agreed.

Each one of my sisters came over to me, Blessing and Addy at my sides, Charlie and Liliana down on their hunches. Sonia at my back. Every one of their hands on my body felt like a bolt of energy powering through my form and charging me up with their love and support.

"I love you guys. So much. I don't know what I'd do without you." I swallowed down the emotion and sniffled a little.

"Good thing you're never gonna have to find out," Charlie rubbed a hand down my thigh. "Right, ladies?"

"Sho'nuff!"

"Sisters forever!"

"*Hermanas!*"

"Family," Sonia said against my ear before placing a kiss there. "Love you."

"Man, I'm the luckiest woman in the world." I had most of my family around me, safe and sound, except for Genesis who I'd see tonight along with Rory after Genesis got off work. And hopefully Tabby soon, if that damn woman would get her head outta her booty long enough to talk to one of us.

"Okay, well, I'm gonna need to shower and do some serious baking in order to get through today. The agents are coming later and I'm heading over to my place to get a week or two's worth of clothes. Mama, it's cool if I stay here?"

"Chicklet, don't be silly or absurd. This is your home. You always have a place to stay. All of you girls do, and any family you make in the future. Now, who wants cookies or cake? I have an excellent German chocolate I baked yesterday and some snickerdoodles too."

I grinned and waggled my eyebrows at Charlie. "The snickerdoodles are mine!" I jumped up at the same time she did.

"No way! You're hurt. I can totally outrun you! Nothing's keeping me from first dibs on those cookies!" She dashed toward the cookie jar like a burst of red lightning streaking by.

"Dammit! No fair!"

"Mouth," Mama warned. One thing our foster mother did not tolerate was profanity. She believed from the moment you could cogitate that you had the ability to choose your words, and a person should do so wisely, as to not offend others. She felt you could always use your vocabulary to get the point across without being profane.

Drove some of the girls nuts. Me, I liked that she had little quirks. Made her more human and less goddess. She was

40

already worshiped by every single one of us for being our ultimate savior. Her quirks made her relatable and loveable. Then again, I loved everything about all of them. They were my family. All I had in the world.

"Ah-ha!" Charlie held up the first snickerdoodle as though it were a bar of gold she'd found in her search for mighty treasure.

"Whatever!" I groused good naturedly.

"There's plenty to go around for all my girls. It's most certainly not my first day being your mother, is it?" She nailed the two of us with her blue-green eyes and a twitch of her lips giving away her amusement.

"No, Mama," I pouted.

"No. But I scored the best one," Charlie attested, taking a big bite then moaning.

I glared at her. "You'd eat the best one after your sister was shot and almost strangled! How rude!"

"Jesus!" Blessing griped. "Those two."

"Blessing, that better be a prayer!" Mama warned.

Her eyes got big and she made the sign for zipping up her mouth and tossing the imaginary key over her shoulder.

"Fine. You can have half of the world's greatest cookie," Charlie bartered.

I smiled wide and held out my hand. "Thank you, Charlieeeee."

She rolled her eyes and slapped half a cookie in my hand as if it were the last one, but it definitely was not. Still, the fact that she'd give it to me and share was what mattered. It had been a lifelong game between us. And yet, we always shared. Except when it came to men. That was one thing none of us would ever do. That wasn't even girl code. That was sister smackdown. If ever one of us went for the same guy, never, not ever, would any one of us date a man that had first been on a date with one of our sisters. No way. No how. That ship would sail before it ever even tried to dock.

The sisterhood was far more important than any man.

Perhaps that was why we were all single...hmmm. Something to ponder at a later date, for sure.

Speaking of dates, Mama's cellphone that she had charging in the kitchen went off.

I chewed the cookie faster and looked down at the phone hoping it was Agent Fontaine. I'd given them my mother's cellphone as mine was in my purse in my car which was in the hands of a killer. I shivered at the thought.

When I saw an unknown caller, my cheeks heated and my heart started to pound. I stupidly fluffed my hair and cleared my throat.

"Oh no. She did not just fix her hair for a phone call. And who, pray tell, is callin' my sista'?" Blessing hugged me from behind and looked at Mama's phone. "Unknown. Oooh, I do love me a mystery."

I shoved her back with my bum, and she cackled and stepped back.

"Hello, this is Simone."

"Hey, Simone? This is Jonah, uh, Agent Fontaine."

"Yeah." I smiled wide. I couldn't help it. Just hearing his voice had butterflies fluttering in my stomach. "Hi. How are you this morning?"

"Discharged. And you?" His voice was deeper than I remembered or maybe it was just my imagination running away with me.

"Fine. Sore. But my uh, most of my sisters are here and

we're at our mother's having tea and cookies, so…yeah. I'm good."

He chuckled and I sighed.

I glanced behind me and every single one of the women in the room, besides Mama, was staring right at me, not even pretending they weren't listening in.

I crinkled my nose, bugged out my eyes, and waved at them.

"Look, I'm going to go home, shower and change, meet up with my team, and secure an update from my boss the Deputy Assistant Director. Then I'll head over to where you are and pick you up to take you to your place."

"Honestly, you've done so much. You really don't have to do that…"

Why the heck was I trying to get out of seeing him when not seeing him was the absolute last thing I wanted?

"Simone, I told you I'm gonna keep you safe and I'm committed to that. You're in danger. No matter how strong you are or how many family members you have around you. The situation is still dire. A very bad man has your contact information, ID, cellphone, and car. That's too close of a connection than I'd like anyone to have on a single woman who's as sweet as you."

"You think I'm sweet?"

Oh my God! He thinks I'm sweet!

He laughed heartier this time and I felt a flush of embarrassment work its way across my cheeks and down my neck and chest.

"Simone, you got out of your car in a tiny pink uniform that made you look like cotton candy. You're kind. Strong. And you were more worried about getting your sister into

43

trouble because of the possibility that you'd get a ticket or be arrested than you were about yourself. You took care of me. Got us help. Yeah, I think you're sweet."

"Um…thank you."

"No problem. So, text this phone the address to where you're at…"

"I can have someone bring me, if it's out of your way," I offered not wanting him to take me up on it.

"See? Sweet. And no, I'd rather escort you. We want anyone who may be casing the place to know you're in FBI custody. Meaning unavailable to hunt and hurt."

I covered my mouth with my hand as I gasped.

"Don't worry. I've got you covered. I promised to keep you safe. I did that last night, right?"

"Yeah." I let out the single word as though it were a whisper.

"And I'm a man of my word. When you're with me, you'll always be safe, Simone."

I swallowed down the sudden emotion making my throat dry. "I'll text you the address."

"Fuckin' sweet. Christ," he blurted.

"I'm sorry?"

"Nothing. See you this afternoon, yeah?"

"Okay, Jonah. Thanks again."

"You got it. Until then," he said and hung up. No good-bye or farewell. Just, until then.

I pressed the button and turned around to a bunch of smiling faces.

"Don't even start…" I warned.

"Oh no, we are sooooo getting into this. Jonah? You're calling the agent by name?" Blessing noted right off the bat.

"Of course, I am, because it is his name," I fired off and set the phone down.

"And you're flushed, as though you're happy to talk to him. Reeeeaaaallly happy," Charlie added. "I know that look, girl. I feel that way every time I visit one of Addy's photo shoots and see all those naked or half-dressed women. Who am I kidding? Even the men."

"You hit on everything that moves," I countered.

"True, but that doesn't change the fact that you are into this guy! The FBI guy who saved you," she teased.

"I think it's romantic. Like a fairytale." Liliana put her hands in a prayer pose at her chin, her eyes filled with rainbows and unicorns.

"Mama! Get them to lay off," I requested.

"And ruin all the fun? I want to hear about this Jonah fella. I left the hospital before you two. Sonia said you'd chatted with the FBI agent who saved your life, but she didn't say you took a liking to him. Do tell?" She leaned over the counter on her elbows and put her cheek into her hand.

"You guys are impossible!" I harrumphed.

"No, we're your sisters, and you're hot for a guy and we want to know more! Like, what happened with that good-for-nothing boyfriend of yours, Trey?"

"Oh blech." I made a gagging sound. "He broke up with me yesterday. Let me start at the beginning of my day so you're all caught up…"

"And then you'll tell us about Agent Jonah Fontaine?" Liliana demanded in her singsong, life-is-amazing tone.

I took a deep, fortifying breath. "And then I'll tell you about one heck of a hot FBI agent."

Chapter
FOUR

W HEN I OPENED THE DOOR, I WAS NOT ONLY GREETED by Jonah, but also the blond agent from the hospital.

"Hi, Simone, this is my partner, Agent Ryan Russell."

I smiled. "Nice seeing you again. We met briefly last night." I glanced at Jonah and his dreamy dark gaze was planted directly on my face, as though he were cataloguing my every reaction. My stupid traitorous cheeks heated.

The agent held out his hand and I shook it, trying to focus on what I was doing, not on my savior.

Right behind me, Mama put her hand to my shoulder and peeked around the door. "Well, hello, gentlemen. Come in. May I offer you some coffee or tea perhaps?" She held the door open fully.

"Uh yeah, goodness. I should have offered. Would you both like to come in?" I gestured with a thumb behind me.

Agent Russell grinned and Jonah bit down on his lush bottom lip. Oh, what I wouldn't have given to be the one to taste that bit of flesh.

"Gratitude, ma'am. Unfortunately we need to get Simone to her home. Agent Russell is working right now." He gestured to his partner who was in a dark suit, much like the one he'd worn last night, while Jonah looked scrumptious in a form-fitting kelly green, long-sleeve thermal. His dark jeans had definitely seen better days if the fray around the pockets and the fading down the thighs were anything to go by.

Agent Russell put his hand over his heart. "Wonderful offer. How's about a rain check?" His light-eyed gaze traveled from me to Jonah and then back to my mother. "I have a good feeling we'll be seeing more of each other," he stated in a very forthcoming manner.

I'm certain my eyes widened, and my heated cheeks went from hot to absolutely flaming.

"Um, let me just grab my sweater." I turned around, dashed to the coat rack, and pulled off a slouchy, long gray cardigan I'd left here the last time I stayed over. It was soft, comfy, and had a hood. Felt like I was wearing a blanket all day. I loved it.

The men led me to a black SUV, and I got into the back. I folded and unfolded my hands repeatedly as I checked my surroundings.

"Technically this is not the first time I've been in a situation with the police," I shared unnecessarily and then immediately tried to fix it. "I mean, not for anything *serious*. Actually, it wasn't even my fault. It was my foster sister Tabby's idea." Neither man said anything and the quiet in the space felt stifling, so I continued. "We were playing a prank on one of our teachers and things got out of hand..." I clenched my teeth together and mentally smacked myself silly, for stupidly sharing an embarrassing story. I did that all the time. Shared too much. Talked too much. Gave too much advice.

"How so?" Jonah asked, saving me from feeling the burn of humiliation.

"We, uh, stuck a hose in the front door of the house and toilet-papered his trees and bushes. He'd given Genesis, one of my other sisters, a bad science grade because she refused to participate in the dissection of a pig. She's a real human and animal lover, and anyway, she's the one who's a social worker downtown. It was going to go on her permanent record and she really needed perfect grades to get a good scholarship, so our plan was to get back at him. Mama Kerri had already worked out an arrangement with the teacher, though we didn't know that at the time. Swear!" I crossed my heart with one finger.

Agent Russell chuckled. "Brother, you got yourself a *live* one," he murmured, and I wasn't sure if him saying that was a compliment or not. I couldn't tell from his tone either.

Shoot. I was making myself look like a complete dork. "Never mind. I always do this. Talk too much. Ignore me." I waved my hand and stared out the window.

Jonah turned around, the window between us open so I could see his handsome face unimpeded by the heavy plastic partition. "No way. Don't stop now. The story was just getting good." He grinned. "What happened after the toilet papering and the water hose?"

I swallowed and sucked in my bottom lip. His gaze stayed on my mouth and I watched in extreme fascination as he licked his lips. My body started to heat and the space between my thighs throbbed. It felt like long minutes passed between us as we stared at one another instead of only maybe twenty seconds.

"Um, well, I didn't know that Tabby had turned the hose on, so by the time he woke up the next day, his house had flooded. Did some pretty serious damage to his floors."

"No shit!" he exclaimed.

"'Fraid so. The cops were called. Apparently, he had a video doorbell and caught Tabby's face as she held the water hose and me as I papered a bush. Officers came to school and took us right out of our classes. I was so scared…"

"What happened next?"

"Mama Kerri talked to him. Explained our backgrounds, how we were both foster children trying to find our way, yada. He dropped the charges, but we had to pay for the damage and apologize in person. We spent the entire summer raking lawns, cleaning houses, babysitting…whatever it took to pay back the damage. All of our sisters helped though. It was pretty amazing. Everyone spent the summer paying off what Tabby and I'd done to get back at a teacher who was being unfair with Genesis. All for one, and one for all." I shrugged.

"Wow, that's something else…" Jonah's voice was low and held a note of praise.

"The toilet papering?"

He shook his head. "Nah, the fact that your foster sisters and your foster mom all stepped up to help get you out of a bind. It's like me and Ryan here." He playfully punched his partner's shoulder. "We're brothers by choice. You are sisters by circumstance, but your love is a choice. Powerful stuff."

I smiled wide with a sense of pride that he understood the connection I had with those women. "I think so too. Thank you."

We stared at one another again, lost in the moment until Agent Russell announced, "We're here."

I dropped my head down to look at my lap and tried

my darndest to hold back the outrageous smile stretching across my face.

Before long, the back door to the SUV opened and we all filed out.

The second we reached my complex, I knew something was wrong. The slider of my upstairs window was open, the billowy white curtain flapping in the wind.

"That shouldn't be open." I gripped onto Jonah's forearm and stopped in my tracks, afraid to move even a single muscle.

He lifted his chin toward my apartment, which was on the second floor. "That your place?"

I nodded.

"Okay, stay here, out in the open. We're going to go in first. "

I stood by a big tree, hiding most of my body, and watched while the two men climbed the concrete stairway up to my apartment, guns out and ready.

When they got to my door, they didn't even need a key. Officer Russell just pushed the door with his hand and went in with his gun up. Jonah right behind him.

Please don't let anyone be there. Please don't let anyone be there. Pleasedon'tletanyonebethere.

I prayed over and over, my heart pounding so loud I could hear it acutely. All the rest of the sounds outside disappeared. No more cars. No more neighbors. No birds singing. Nothing. Just the sound of my own breath moving in and out of my body. My heart beating as loud as a base drum in a full marching band.

Until Jonah appeared at the front door, his face flat, his jaw tight.

Without thinking, I just ran. Flew up the stairs so fast I took them two at a time and slammed into his form when I hit the top, wrapping my arms around him. He went back a step and grunted, but held strong, bringing me close, his hand at my nape and one at my waist. I shook against him and waited until my nerves relaxed.

"It's okay. You're okay." He rubbed the back of my neck.

When I could feel my heart rate going back to normal and my body no longer shaking, I pulled away. Nervously, I pushed back a long lock of hair, placing it behind my ear as I looked at the ground. "I'm sorry, I just…freaked out for a minute there."

He grabbed my hand and squeezed. "Pretty normal response. Though I will tell you right now, it's not pretty in there. You can't go in."

"What?" I hollered, pushed the door so hard it slammed back against the opposite wall, and slid by him before he could stop me.

And that was when I smelled it.

Blood.

I glanced around as Jonah tried to yank me back.

My home had been completely ransacked. The couch cushions shredded as though Freddy Krueger and Edward Scissorhands had been staying at my place and things got a little crazy. The TV was shattered, something having been thrown into it. Seemed as though it might have been one of my potted plants as the plant's remains were in a pile of dirt mixed with leaves, glass, and other detritus from the carnage that was my living room.

The coffee table was lying on its side, a table lamp broken on the floor. The desk drawers were out, papers strewn about everywhere. I stepped farther in but when I headed toward my bedroom, the tangy, coppery smell that permeated the air got thicker, and my mouth started to water with a sour taste, my stomach clenching tightly.

Agent Russell appeared at the doorway of my bedroom and held his hands up, palms facing out like he did last night at the hospital, trying to block my way with his large body.

I faked to the left and then dashed to the right only a couple feet inside my private quarters. I was not prepared for what I saw.

On my bed was a woman, bloodshot eyes open unseeingly. Her neck was purple and twisted at a weird angle. Her brown hair was ratty and tangled all over the place, mixed with blood. Red, bloody stripes were down her back as though someone had tried to write something. My giant butcher knife appeared to have been left on the bed, blood curdling down its silver edge and wooden handle.

I covered my mouth as I noticed the woman was completely naked and worse, I knew who she was.

I backed up blindly on my tiptoes. "Oh my god, no!" I sucked in a huge breath but all I smelled was death.

My stomach churned, the cookies and tea I ate this morning swirling violently in my gut. On a full toe spin the likes you'd see from a ballerina on the stage, I pushed past both agents and flung myself bodily into the bathroom, falling to my knees and retching into the toilet. Everything came up until there was nothing more than bile, but I kept heaving.

The dead woman's bloodshot eyes filled my vision every time I closed my lids, bringing up another round of heaving.

All of a sudden, I noticed a wet, cool cloth on the back

of my neck, then at my forehead, someone holding my long hair away from the mess.

Then *he* was there.

Everywhere.

All around me.

Hovering around my form.

"I'm sorry you had to see that." His words were soft and soothing.

I heaved some more, and he stayed with me, holding me, doing what he could to comfort me from behind.

"I've called it in to the team. The police captain is also on his way too," Agent Russell said from somewhere farther away, maybe in the hall, but I didn't turn my head to look.

I grabbed the washcloth Jonah held at my forehead and wiped my mouth with it, then flushed the toilet, my stomach clenching fading away slowly but surely as I breathed in and out in measured breaths.

Jonah helped me to stand and I went to the sink, rinsing my mouth out before loading up my toothbrush with a huge application of toothpaste, shoving it in my mouth, and getting down to business. I couldn't stop tasting blood. It was insane, and didn't make any sense, but that was all I could taste on my tongue.

Jonah calmly rubbed my back as I finished up, rinsed my face and washed my hands before leaning both hands to the basin and holding myself up.

Agent Russell led me out into the living space, and I sat down at my small kitchenette trying to make sense of what I'd just seen.

"I, uh, know her."

"Who?" he asked.

"The woman," I said while tracing the patterns and knots in the wooden kitchen table with my fingertip. Over and over. Each swirl. One after another.

"Who is she?" He crouched at my side and put his hand to my knee. I flinched, curving in on myself. He removed his hand as if he'd been burned. "I'm sorry."

I shook my head but didn't say anything for a little bit.

Then my savior was back. His hand at my shoulder, his warmth seeping straight through to my marrow. I sighed and tipped my head up toward him, wanting to be closer, not farther away.

"I knew her." My voice cracked. "It's the manager. Of the complex. Katrina. I don't remember her last name, but I pay her every month, and see her at the pool in the summer. She plants flowers in the spring, and we always seem to use the small gym at the complex around the same time at least once a week. She's really nice. Super pretty. And everyone, *everyone* likes her! Why is she dead in my bed?" The emotions roared through me so fast my body quaked and convulsed as I wrapped myself in my sweater, pulling my knees up into the chair and rocking back and forth.

"Who would do this to such a nice person? She never hurt anyone! And if you were late on your rent a day or two, she didn't even charge the late fee! She was so nice. Everyone loved her!" I continued to rock my body as Jonah pushed a chair next to me and wrapped his arms around my form.

"I'm sorry about your friend. We won't know what happened until the team has investigated, but it's not a co-incidence that she was killed here on the same night the Backseat Strangler took off in your car with your purse and contact information."

"Oh my god! My mom! My sisters!" I screeched and stood so fast the chair slammed back behind me. I moved to go, not knowing what I was going to do, or where I was going to go. I hadn't even driven here. I shoved my hands into my hair at the roots and looked around at the destruction. "My entire life is so messed up and someone I know is dead! I don't know what to do!" I hiccoughed into a sob, the tears tracking down my face.

Jonah pulled me into his arms again and held me tight. "You're going to breathe. Then we'll go over everything you know about last night and what you know of the victim. Agent Russell and I have been tracking the Backseat Strangler all over the state. We're going to find him. And then the FBI and the criminal justice system are going to throw everything we have at him. Which means he's going to pay with life in prison."

I shook my head, thoughts of what happened last night mixing with everything I'd just seen. "No, he's going to get away with it. Just like with all those other women. He's going to get away with it!" I screeched and cried at the same time.

Jonah cupped my cheeks and held my head still, his dark gaze tethering me to the here and now. "I swear to you, Simone, we will get this man. He will pay for what he's done to those women, to you, and to your friend. I won't stop looking for him until he's found."

"He's going to find me and do t-th-that to m-me." My teeth started to chatter.

His face turned to stone and he gritted through a snarl. "No man will ever fucking touch you. Not even one finger to your beautiful hair." He wiped my tears with his thumbs. "That's a promise you can bet I'll be keeping, sweet girl."

I stared into his eyes and watched the brown and gold flecks swirl. This was a good man. An honest man. A hero. Someone I knew with my whole heart I could trust.

It took all my will power, but I whispered, "I believe you."

And I did. As long as my savior was near, I knew I'd be safe.

But what would happen when I was alone?

I'd been sitting at my kitchen table with a dead woman in my bedroom for well over an hour. I'd given Captain Mandle and the guys everything I knew about Katrina and the last time I was home. Yesterday, before the diner shift. Then I'd been pulled over by Agent Fontaine and the shootout occurred where we were both injured, and the perpetrator took off in my car. He already knew everything that had happened at that scene, but together, Jonah and I pieced together the accounts of what we experienced as it occurred, detailing anything that we may have remembered since last night.

The police captain stepped outside to discuss the information with others while Jonah secured approval to remove some of my clothing and Agent Russell checked in with their Director. Everything was placed outside of the apartment ready to be taken with me.

I didn't dare go back into the bedroom, but every so often I'd hear a buzzing sound like something was charging up and then a clicking from what I assumed was one of those big cameras with the giant flashes you saw on television.

I was never coming back to this apartment. Not ever. I'd get some friends or someone to come in and salvage what they could. Or maybe I'd start new. I didn't care. There was no way I'd be able to unsee Katrina's dead and bloodied body lying in my bed.

As I sipped on my lukewarm coffee the Captain entered the front door, maneuvered my way, and stood a few feet from me. He put his hands in his pockets and rocked back and forth from heel to toe as though he was working through something in his head.

Eventually he spoke. Direct and to the point. "Victim is Katrina Dushay, manager of the Valley Oak Apartments. Worked here for six years. After talking to the boyfriend, we believe Katrina left her apartment last night at midnight because she'd received noise complaints from a couple neighbors. We've interviewed them and all they could tell us is that they heard glass breaking and loud thumps coming from your apartment as though someone was trashing the place. At approximately twelve-thirty the neighbors said the noises stopped. That's the last anyone heard or saw anything. The boyfriend fell asleep and didn't even know she was missing when we showed up. He's contacting her parents."

Katrina was killed in my apartment between midnight and twelve-thirty. Thirty minutes and then a vibrant and beautiful young woman was taken out of this world. And no one was the wiser.

"How could something like this happen? There was so much blood..." My hands shook so I put down the mug. "She had to have screamed."

"Look, Ms. Wright-Kerrighan, I can't get into

particulars, but I will say the killer left a message." Captain Mandle frowned deeply and rubbed at the back of his hairy neck.

"A message?" I reached out and Jonah took my hand under the table.

Just having his presence there to lock onto kept me from passing out cold.

"Hide and seek," the Captain said.

I frowned. "I don't understand."

He closed his eyes. "I really didn't want to share this, but he carved the words into her back using a knife he found in your kitchen. Killed her on your bed. We believe he's escalated from his activities as the Backseat Strangler. She was definitely strangled, but the added violence wasn't there before in any of the other cases. He wrote those words for a reason and I think they're a message for us, or perhaps for you. We need to proceed with extreme caution. This man has your phone, ID, your car, and knows where you live." He lifted his hands around the room. "I need you to look around the room and see if there is anything you can tell may be missing."

I blinked as though he'd asked me to search a beach for a long-lost diamond. This was needle in a haystack territory, not to mention my nerves were so far gone I wasn't in the realm of reality let alone capable of truly seeing anything through the mess.

"I, I, d-don't know. There's so much…"

Jonah squeezed my hand. "We'll do it together. Just try, yeah?"

I nodded and he helped me to stand. My arm was throbbing, and I needed a pain pill, but I had to get this over with and get back to the safety and comfort of my mother's home. Bury my head straight under a stack of blankets and make all of this disappear.

Jonah held my hand and led me over to the center of the living room. "Start with the couch, tables, anything on them that's not on the ground now."

I scanned the space seeing my candle holder, coasters, magazines all spread out on the floor. I shook my head.

"Bookcase." He brought me to the bookcase. All the books were on the floor. I used my foot to move them around. It was nothing but books and CDs.

"It looks like it could all be there, but I'm not sure. It held mostly books and CDs I'd collected over time."

He nodded. "Okay, good. Now the entertainment center."

I noticed the broken TV, the mangled plant and dirt, some other knickknacks, and just as I was about to move on to the next space, I crouched down and pushed the items around. Then became frantic in my pursuit as I shoved things in different directions.

It wasn't here. I surveyed the rest of the room, my gaze jumping from point to point. "It's not here."

"What isn't?"

"A picture. A framed picture of me, Sonia, my six foster sisters, and our foster mom. We had one taken in front of the house a few years ago. It was a gift for Mother's Day, but Liliana made one for all of us. It's gone."

"Dammit," Jonah growled and prowled over to Agent Russell and Captain Mandle. They said some hushed words and the Captain nodded before Jonah stormed back over to me.

"Come on, we're going back to your mother's. Now. We need to contact all of your sisters. Do you know their phone numbers by heart?"

I nodded, then left his side and raced over to the kitchen drawer where my old cell phone and charger was. I'd just gotten a new one after saving for months.

"We'll get that hooked up on the way. Contact your mother. Make sure all of your sisters meet us at her house at five."

"They're already supposed to come over for dinner. Why do you want to see them?"

"If our killer took a book, a piece of jewelry, or something of not much use, I wouldn't be so worried. He took a photo of you and your family."

"Does that mean he's going after my family?"

He inhaled so hard his nostrils flared. "I don't know, but I'm not willing to take any chances."

Chapter
FIVE

THE SECOND MAMA KERRI OPENED THE DOOR TO GREET US I jetted toward her, smacking right dab in the center of her chest. The tears flowed as my mother's arms came around me securely.

"Dear girl, what has frightened you?" Her hands held me close, but I didn't respond, just cowered into her chest like the small girl I was when I showed up holding hands with my big sister after our parents died all those years ago.

"Ma'am, I'm going to bring in her bags and then we need to have a chat," Jonah said from behind us.

Mama patted my back and head. "Yes, of course. Come on in." She tucked me to her side like one of her baby chicks. I soaked up her essence, allowing all the nastiness that came before this moment to dissipate.

I couldn't help trembling as she rubbed my good arm up and down and led me into the living room. She sat me down, grabbed one of her homemade throw blankets, and wrapped me up in it. She bent down, tugged off my shoes, and grabbed the pair of her slippers sitting next to her chair and put them on my feet.

"There now, you rest, and I'll make some chamomile tea. You hungry?"

I shook my head and cuddled further into the blanket,

leaning my head down on the arm of the couch and watching while Jonah brought in one suitcase and bag after another.

Mama noticed the number of bags he'd brought in. "I see you're staying home for a while then? Tell me what happened?"

I firmed up my lips and breathed through my nose, closing my eyes and trying not to remember Katrina's vacant look so I wouldn't break down in tears again.

Eventually I didn't have to because Jonah took over telling Mama the entire story. Besides covering her mouth and putting her hand to her heart, she received the information far better than I would have expected. Then again, Mama Kerri had been through a lot in her sixty years on this earth. From her husband dying when she was in her late twenties, to when she opened up Kerrighan House and started to fill the home she'd planned on having babies with her husband with lost and orphaned young girls instead. She'd seen it all.

Back then, it was much harder for a single woman to adopt children, but not as difficult to foster. And since we were all orphaned, we stayed until we aged out, and even past that. Some of us attended college while still living here.

At some point I must have dozed off because when I opened my eyes back up the living room was filled to the brim with my sisters.

Little Rory was full out lying in front of me, cuddled up to my chest. I must have sensed her because I had the blanket curled around her and her sweet smell in my nose. She was giggling at something and then turned around. Her golden amber gaze met mine.

"Hi, Auntie." She patted my face with her chubby little three-year-old hand. "You 'wake?"

I brought her hand to my mouth and kissed her palm then blew a raspberry into it. She laughed heartily and it filled me with such extreme love I couldn't help but snuggle her, kiss her neck and face, and hug her precious form dearly.

She shrieked and giggled as I teased and played with my niece. Her curly black hair was a wild halo around her chestnut-colored skin. Her mom, Genesis, was half African-American and half Korean. Her daughter's father was African-American and Caucasian. Together, the two of them made the most gorgeous child on the planet. Her brown skin was effervescent and was paired with stark, black hair and those amber eyes. She could have graced the cover of any magazine and sold a bazillion copies.

I lifted the toddler bundle of love and set her on my lap facing the room. Sitting in various positions, on the chairs, the floor, and standing close were every single one of my sisters. Except freakin' Tabby.

"No Tabby?" I asked the room.

Each sister looked away, gave a pissed-off face, or just sighed.

"I stopped by her apartment when I left work," Genesis said. "Her place was quiet. I'm thinking next time I need to touch base with the manager and see if we can't get in. I'm starting to worry about her safety. That rat-infested place is scary and I'm certain there are drug dealers sitting on the stoop. It was so bad, I went there before I picked up Rory because I don't want her there."

"I'll go, I have a key," Mama said as she came in with a tray filled with meats, cheeses, jams, and crackers.

"Not alone you won't." Charlie threw her two cents in. "Drug dealers, nut-uh. Not happenin', Mama." My sister shrugged and then put her hand out to Blessing who gave her a fist bump that exploded after they touched.

I grinned at the two.

"Now that you're all here, Agent Fontaine has some news he needs to share. However…" Mama held out her loving, eager arms to her grandbaby, wiggling the fingers and all. "This conversation is not for little ears! You want to help Grammy frost some cupcakes, my lovely?"

Rory bounced up and into her grandmother's arms. "I wike pink cupcakes!" she exclaimed.

"Oh, I know, my girl. I've got pink with sprinkles ready!"

Rory raised her little arms into the air and cheered. "Yay!"

Genesis patted her daughter's back as they walked by and Charlie kissed the girl's cheek as they passed the threshold of the room where she was leaning against the jamb.

"Ladies, this is not good news so I'm going to get straight to the point. You are aware of what happened to Simone and me last night?"

Each of them gave their own nod or soft reply. He took the time to look each one of them directly in the eye. I appreciated that about him instantly. Wanting to ensure he had everyone's attention, no one left out.

"Today my partner and I took Simone to her place to gather some of her things. Since the perpetrator took off with her car, ID, house keys, etc., it wasn't safe for her to go alone and I'm very glad that we did. When we got there, we found a body…"

"A body!" Blessing blurted out. "Excuse me, sir. I do *not*

think I heard you correctly." She placed a hand to her hip, the other held in a cup shape behind her ear. There was nothing but sass in every ounce of her form. "Say that one more time?"

He licked his lips and sighed. "When we arrived, the location had been trashed."

"Oh my god!" Genesis covered her mouth.

"No shit!" Charlie blinked staring at Jonah with her mouth hanging open.

"*Dios mio.* No!" Liliana added.

"That's it. You're outta there. *Permanently.*" My sister Sonia stood up, phone in her hand, buttons already being pressed.

Jonah stood up and put his hands out in front of him and waved the air in a calm down gesture as though the air itself were pressurized.

Me, I just brought my legs up and curled my form around my knees and waited for this to blow up.

"Let's just settle down so I can explain everything without having to repeat myself." Jonah's FBI authoritative voice came out and was stern, demanding, and held no room for defiance.

A little thrill of excitement shimmered down my chest to settle low in my belly, warming me from the inside out.

"The body had been strangled, defaced, and left for Simone to find on her bed."

Another round of gasps from the peanut gallery and some curses. Fear filled the room. I could practically feel the desperation and anxiety pumping off my sisters in a collective rush, battering my soul like a choppy ocean wave against the shore.

"Who was killed?" Sonia crossed her arms over her chest, her phone tapping against her bicep.

"The building manager, Katrina," I answered, her face ghosting past my vision. I held back the tears but only just. The roller coaster that had been my life the last two days was not one I'd like to ever ride again. Now I just wanted it all to stop. Bring me back to the safety of my bartending job, my schooling, and time spent with my sisters. Except I wasn't stupid. With a killer on the loose, my entire life was going to change in every way imaginable.

"The FBI is handling the case in tandem with local law enforcement. We will keep you apprised as information becomes available. However, the manner in which this woman died was violent and intentional. He chose her by convenience but not what he did or where he did it. Your sister is not safe. Frankly, I'm not comfortable saying any of you are safe. I'd like to suggest you pair up for a while. Prevent yourself from ever being alone while we hunt this man and bring him to justice."

"Why do you think we're at risk?" Genesis, the ever-smart, methodical, and logical one asked. She also had the most to lose, since her three-year-old was her entire world.

"We know the perp has your sister's phone, though she has informed me that it was password protected and has a GPS. We've got a tech guy monitoring it to see if it goes on. Right now, it's off. Simone also tells me she didn't have an address book at home nor specifics about where any of you lived. However, he did take a family portrait of the nine of you standing out in front of this house. It's easy enough to recognize Sonia and figure out that she is the Senator. That puts her in a very high-profile public position. If someone searched for her, they could unearth her past here and at Kerrighan house. Eventually it's all a matter of records. We don't know what he's capable of. Which is also why I've decided that Simone will come and stay with me at my home until this is all settled."

His words went in through my ears, percolated around my brain and then still didn't come up with one plus one equaling two.

"Wait, what?" I stuttered not sure I heard him correctly.

"It's the safest plan. I share a house with Agent Russell. Two FBI agents in one place. Pretty damn safe."

"I'll say!" Addy finally piped up for the first time tonight, her long brown hair falling all over her shoulders in pretty, full waves that many women would beg, barter, and steal for. She looked Jonah up and down, her eyes sparkling with mirth. "I most certainly *would not* be passing up the chance to stay in his bed, Goldilocks." She came over and plopped down on the side of the couch, her arm going around my back and hugging me to her ample bosom.

I nudged her back. "Horn dog," I teased lightening the tension in the room a little.

"Um, have you seen him?" She continued to prod me.

Jonah covered up a laugh by pretending to cough, though when his gaze met mine, it was filled to the brim with an unspoken heat.

"No one is denying Agent Fontaine's obvious..." Sonia looked him up and down as though she were assessing not only his looks but his brawn, and his command of the situation. "Attributes, and/or skills as a protector, but I have a team of people to keep her safe and alive in a high rise, with a doorman, and Fort Knox-style security. Why the hell wouldn't it be most prudent for her to stay with me?"

"You're the first person I'd go after if I was in the killer's shoes and looking for her sister."

I gasped and intense fear sliced through my gut. I bent over my knees and tried to breathe deep. Addy rubbed my back.

"Shhh, shhh, she's fine. No one would dare mess with Sonia. Her team would eat them up. Plus, she can be really scary," Addy whispered and ran her hand through my hair and down my back until I sat back up. I'd lost my fight with the tears, and no longer cared if I looked weak and weepy. A serious load of crap had landed in my life and it felt like everything was falling apart at the seams.

Blessing put both of her hands to her hips, firmed her jaw, and with a grit to her voice said, "I could talk to my dad. No one would touch her."

"No!" I screeched knowing what that meant.

"Absolutely not!" Sonia shifted around and put her hand up in a stop gesture.

"Jesus, Mary, and Joseph," Liliana blurted, her hand immediately moving in the sign of the cross on her forehead, shoulders, and chest.

Blessing's biological father was a member of a street gang in the heart of Chicago. A bad one. He was in the kind of gang where the members wore red and black, had tons of prison tattoos, carried around guns like some people carried newspapers, and probably killed for funsies. It had been rule number one since Blessing came to stay at Kerrighan house. Her father Tyrell Jones was never allowed to visit the premises. Tyrell had been found an unfit parent when Blessing's mother was murdered. He didn't fight for custody, but he did contact Mama Kerri after Blessing came to stay and worked out an arrangement to see his daughter every couple months or so. To this day, I didn't know how connected my sister was to her dad. It had always been a taboo topic of conversation, though the overall consensus had always been no contact with any of us.

"Someone has to do something! This is family. I'm not going to come home to Mama's one day and find her dead in her bed because of some lunatic. Been through that once. Don't plan on going there again." Blessing scowled, her naturally dark skin turning a deep garnet at her cheeks and down her neck with her anger.

Jonah held his hands out. "Which is why I am suggesting that she stay with me. I'm off work for at least a week and can protect her. She'll never be alone."

"What about when I have to go to work?" I perked up at his "never be alone" commentary.

"Simone, you're gonna need to take a leave of absence," he started but I stood up, the blanket falling to the couch as I started to pace.

"There is no way I can take time away. I'll lose my job and I already lost one of them last night that I still need to replace!" I finagled my fingers through my ratty hair and gripped the roots. "I can't provide for myself if I don't have a job."

"And you won't be able to provide for yourself if you are dead either!" Sonia pointed at me, her pretty eyes going dark as night.

I shook my head. "This is insane. I have to work. I have to. There's no other option. I'm already out of a home.

They could burn the place down with all my stuff in it for all I care. I'm never going back there."

Addy came up to me and hugged me, following her natural inclination to comfort first and think about the situation later. "We'll figure something out."

"Yeah, like her sister will take her in and provide for her until all of this mess gets cleaned up…" Sonia ordered.

"No. I'm not living off my big sister!"

"Why the hell not?"

"Because I make my own way! I pay for my life. Me!" I tapped at my chest. "You do not get to decide my life for me. You've been trying to do so since we came to live here. You have to let me go!"

"It's because you're too damn wild, Simone! Always leaping before you look! Running before you walk."

"You mean *living*? That's what people who live their lives fully do. Take advantage of every day they are given because as we both know, they are precious. Remember. You always say each day is a gift. I believe that with my whole heart! You on the other hand stay with your feet firmly planted on the ground. Making decisions for everyone in your life. Heck, you even make decisions for the entire state of Illinois and yet it's still not enough for you. You want to control me too!"

"I want you safe!" Sonia cried out, tears falling down her porcelain cheeks, the dam that held the waterworks back exploding along with her temper. "I want you alive!" Her voice rose. "Is it so wrong to want my only blood relative on this earth to be where I can touch and talk to her?" She sniffed and wiped at her nose. "You are reckless, Simone. Always have been. Every day of your life I worry about you."

"Maybe because my big sister has always held on too tight! I love you, Sonia. More than anything. But you can't keep me locked in a gilded cage like some exotic bird. You can't clip my wings and expect me to stay around. I'll always find a way to fly."

Sonia sucked in a sob and tilted her head down as her shoulders shook with her grief.

I went over to her and wrapped my arms around her form. "I'll be okay. Jonah is going to help me out. Keep me safe. Together we're all going to figure this out. We have to." I glanced up and into Jonah's dark gaze. There was sadness but also a strength and calm resolve. His hands were fisted at his sides and it seemed like it was taking everything in him not to approach me and my sister. For what, I didn't know. All I knew was that gaze pierced straight through my soul and made a promise. A promise to keep me safe, and I believed him.

After Mama Kerri made us all a lasagna dinner complete with salad and garlic bread, my sisters helped me go through all of my bags and narrow things down to a couple suitcases with enough clothes and toiletries for a couple weeks. I could always go back to Mama Kerri's to get more of my things. It turned out that Mama wanted to stay with Genesis so she could watch her grandbaby like she usually did three days a week. Blessing and Addy paired up because they were used to traveling together for photo shoots and fashion meetings. Charlie and Liliana agreed to both go stay with Sonia and all of us would continue to try and get a lock on Tabby.

That brought me to now, where I followed Jonah's broad

form into a small brick house in one of the Chicago area suburbs, just outside of the city but closer to my bartending job at Tracks where I worked most weeknights.

"And this will be your new abode." He gestured to the small but cozy living space. Right in front of the entry was a living room with a small L-shaped navy-blue microfiber couch. A square chrome and glass coffee table sat smack dab in the center of the L. Across from the couch was a matching recliner shoved into a corner next to a bookcase that didn't hold a single book. Nope. It was filled with DVDs or video game cases and CDs. A huge TV filled the entire wall opposite the couch.

I couldn't clearly define how big the thing was. I wasn't a super tall girl at five foot six, but if you stretched my arms out in a T, that's how wide that TV was. Mine at home seemed a quarter of the size. Not that it mattered since it was destroyed and was on the ever-growing list of the parts of my life I now had to rebuild.

"Wow. That's a...big TV." I smiled.

He grinned. "Gotta be able to watch the game."

"And pretend you're actually there?"

"Definitely!"

"Hey, bro! How goes it?" Ryan exited a part of the kitchen I couldn't yet see with two beer bottles in hand. "How you doin', beautiful?"

My cheeks heated and I glanced down at my mom's slippers I hadn't bothered to take off. They were comfy and made me feel more at peace. "Good, thank you."

When I glanced up, Jonah was glaring at Ryan and purposely bumped one of his shoulders into his friend, then winced as though he'd hurt himself in the process.

"Jonah! Honey, be careful!" I admonished and then realized what I'd said. "I mean, I say that to everyone. I mean, I call everyone honey, and sweetie and cutie and…"

"Simone. It's cute. I liked it. Chill." Jonah smiled softly and winked.

Winked.

Yep, Agent Jonah Fontaine was definitely dreamy.

"You want a beer, *Simone*?" Ryan enunciated my name perfectly which I'm pretty sure was for Jonah's benefit and not my own. I rather liked being called beautiful by a hunky FBI guy. Though I'd have preferred it come from Jonah instead of his roommate and partner.

"Nah, prefer the hard stuff. I'm more of a shots and cocktails type of girl."

"My kinda woman." Ryan suavely maneuvered around my form heading toward the kitchen. "Gotta get you a real drink. What's your poison?" he asked amicably.

Next to him, Jonah was leaning against the kitchen counter, his arm crossed over his midsection as though he were holding onto his sore ribs. "I think I can handle getting Simone a drink."

"Wouldn't want you to pull or strain something while you're healing. Besides, what are best friends for?" Ryan teased while opening the cabinet across from where Jonah stood. "We've got whiskey, vodka, and tequila."

"What do you have to cut it with?"

"Got a couple a Cokes in the fridge but me and the sourpuss over here don't usually drink anything but water, coffee, milk, beer, and liquor straight."

"No problem. I'll take the tequila as is."

"You got it." He pulled down a clear bottle of Patron

Silver along with a tumbler, not a shot glass. Guess we were going whole hog tonight.

He filled the glass about one and a half fingers and passed it my way.

I took the entire thing in one go. "Another," I requested.

Jonah's eyes widened.

"You lucky son of a bitch." Ryan glared at Jonah and shook his head on a chuckle.

"How you figure?" I asked wondering what the male posturing was about. It was not as if Jonah and I were together or anything. Sure, there was some attraction, but he hadn't said or done anything overt to express his intentions. Other than moving me into his home after a hell-acious night and day. Hmm, maybe I needed to think on that a bit harder.

"If I hadn't had my little sister's dance recital to attend last night, I'd have been with Jonah in the car. Usually we pair up, but I couldn't bail on family and we hadn't gotten a lead on our guy in a solid week. Could have been me you'd met last night if I'd have gotten the call out." He grinned salaciously and filled my cup again. This time he gave me a full two fingers, so I sipped it.

Jonah stepped right in front of his friend chest to chest and looked him dead in the face. They were about the same height. Both a couple inches over six feet if I had to guess. "Brother, don't."

Ryan held his hands up. "Just pointing out the obvious. No need to get your panties in a wad." He grinned then looked over at me.

"I'm not sure I understand what's happening here?" I entered into the fray.

"And she's sweet too?" Ryan's eyebrows rose up toward his hairline.

"Something you're never gonna find out. Now how's about you head out. You're dressed for trolling; you better get on that before all the good ones are taken." Jonah addressed Ryan's dark gray slacks and burgundy button-up shirt. The sleeves were casually rolled up his forearms and I had to admit, he looked damn good. Would definitely score with the ladies if he were as smooth and forthcoming with them as he'd been with me so far.

I sucked in both my lips and turned my head to survey the living room, trying to give them a speck of privacy.

"And if I want to stay? Get to know our new houseguest a little better?" He continued to taunt Jonah and my cheeks and neck flamed so hot I shrugged off my big sweater and hung it over one of the barstool seatbacks.

Jonah's mouth tightened into a grimace. "Russell, don't fuck with me." Jonah said those words through a clenched jaw and in a timber so low, I could sense there was a double meaning.

"Bro, it's cool. I'm sorry. I was just messing with you. Teasing. Jesus. Lighten up." He looked up at me. "Simone, you've got your work cut out for you." He tugged Jonah around and put his arm over both of Jonah's shoulders. "My boy here is intense. But he's the best guy in the entire world. If he lets you in. Be cool, yeah?"

"Cool?" I questioned and he nodded. "Uh, sure. I can be cool." I sipped at my tequila allowing it to burn its way down my throat and into my gut where it warmed my entire body.

"Get outta here." Jonah shoved Ryan off and finally gifted us both a genuine smile.

"If I hook up, I won't bring her here. Don't wait up?" He dumped his empty bottle in the recycle bin in the corner of the kitchen near the small four-seater table.

"Be safe!" I called out last minute, not knowing what else to say.

"Safety first." He grinned and saluted us both as he grabbed his coat and keys that were hanging over the couch.

Jonah sighed and rubbed at his eyes before grabbing my hand. There was a spark of something the second his palm touched mine. A sizzle of recognition, of familiarity. Of peace and security.

"Come on, I'll show you where you're going to sleep."

I held onto his hand and followed him down the hallway. Without wanting to think about it fully, I was pretty sure I'd follow Agent Jonah Fontaine anywhere he wanted me to go.

Just as long as he held my hand.

Chapter
SIX

L AST NIGHT, JONAH GAVE UP HIS MASSIVE KING-SIZED, SUPER comfy bed for me. I opened my eyes and glanced at the clock. Ten-thirty. A little earlier than normal, but I crashed pretty hard the second I cuddled up in his fluffy comforter. The thing was amazing. One of those down-type blankets but didn't have those pokey feathers most of them have.

Looking around the room, I took in the masculine vibe. He had nothing on the walls except for a cityscape of the Chicago skyline over his bed. The furniture was a dark thick wood and squared off at every edge. The comforter was a pristine white which I found incredibly soothing. He swore he'd just changed the sheets two nights before, and I could still smell the strong fabric softener scent as well as the woodsy notes I'd come to associate with Jonah. Now I knew why that woodsy scent came with the fresh linens. It was his fabric softener. Still, on him it was delicious, and I wanted to burrow straight into it and never come out to the light of day.

Except, I was not the type of person to waste a perfectly good day when there was adventure and fun to be had, life to be lived.

Popping out of bed, I used the facilities, pulled my hair

up into a messy bun, and brushed my teeth. My face was clear of makeup and the ribbed navy tank I wore really brought out the gray-blue of my eyes. I had on a pair of drawstring tan lounge pants that fell all the way to my toes.

I shrugged. Welp, if Jonah didn't like the way I looked first thing in the morning, who cared? I lied to myself in order to let it all go and just move on with my plan.

Making sure to be quiet, I tiptoed into the living room and found Jonah lying with his feet stretched out across the length of the couch, wearing jeans, a T-shirt, and bare feet. He had his eyes on a game on the television with the volume turned all the way off. His dark hair had a sheen to it that suggested he'd already showered.

"You already showered?"

He turned his head and his dark gaze took in my ratty appearance from top to toe.

"Yeah. Do you always sleep this late?"

I opened my eyes wide and looked out the window seeing the sky was nice and blue and the sun was out.

"Uh, this is early for me. I work nights in a bar. I usually get off around two, help clean up until three, and then come home to eat something and then crash until around noon."

"Noon? Wow. How many jobs do you have?"

"Three. Well, I had three. As I told you last night, I quit the diner I worked at three of the nights I don't work at Tracks downtown. There I usually work Tuesday or Wednesday through Friday or Saturday depending on the shift."

"And the third job?"

I smiled and made my way around the back of the couch and sat down on the comfy chair across from him.

"I help out one or two days a week at Perfect Petal in Oak Park arranging flowers, cleaning up, doing the odd things that might be needed. The shop owner is Mama Kerri's best friend and she pays me in cash under the table. I use that as my gas money for the week."

"And you said something about a credential?"

"Usually after I wake up, I spend an hour or two on my studies online. I'm almost done. One more class and I'll have my associate's degree in business administration."

"You work three jobs, and go to school part time?"

I tucked my feet up and to the side of me. "Yep. How about you?"

"Usually I try to work four on, four off, twelve-hour shifts unless we have a serious threat like this one then it's all hands on deck with unpredictable hours until the killer is found and put in jail. Would you like some coffee?"

"Do you have tea?"

He smiled and shook his head. "We'll get you some."

"Coffee is fine too, thank you. Do you like being an FBI agent? Not that I know exactly what that all entails."

He disappeared into the part of the kitchen you couldn't see from where I sat, and I heard him pull down a cup and pour the coffee.

"Cream and sugar?"

"I'll try it how you make it. I like to be surprised." I stared out the window noticing the kids playing a game of stick hockey in the street. He lived in a nice area, not fancy but well-loved. The sidewalks could have used some help as some of the trees' gnarled roots had broken through the concrete, creating breaks in the path. Still, having large shade trees was always preferred in Chicago. In the summer, the heat could be sweltering, the humidity life changing, and not in a good way. I'd bet those trees kept his car from becoming a hotbox of lava.

"Shoot, my car," I murmured as Jonah handed me a steaming mug.

"We've got an APB out for your car and the local boys in blue patrolling. Hope to get some hits soon. This is the first time he's hit this close to our offices."

I frowned. "Yeah." I sipped the coffee and found he'd made it with cream and sugar, and it was divine. Exactly how I liked it. "This is perfect."

"Yeah?"

"Perfect. Exactly the way I like it."

"Me too."

I smiled and held the mug in front of my face, allowing it to hide my overwhelming excitement in the fact that we liked our coffee the same way. It was such a cheesy thing to be happy about, but I couldn't help it.

"So, I've got an idea! Let's go out today and have some fun!" I stood up and shimmied a little where I stood.

"Fun? Simone, you've been through absolute hell the past two days and I'm supposed to be taking it easy for the rest of the week and keeping you safe. I'm surprised you don't want to hide out and just chill."

"One thing you're going to learn about me, I'm not a Netflix and chill type of woman. Not when there's life to be living, places to see, and people to enjoy spending time with."

"Did you want to connect with one of your sisters or friends?" He rubbed his hands down his long muscular thighs.

I frowned. "I'll check in with them, but they all have work and their own lives to focus on. Regardless of what crazy things are happening in mine, they need to carry on just as much as I do. We can't let this psycho control every step of how we live. Otherwise he wins. Besides, I want to hang out with you. Get to know my savior better."

"Ah, your *savior*, right." His jaw hardened and he glanced away.

I tipped my head and focused on his body language. "Did I say something wrong?"

He sighed and shook his head. "Not at all. It just all makes sense."

"What does?"

"You're attracted to me because I saved your life."

I jerked my head back in complete shock. "Say what?"

He stood up and swished his hand through the air like it was no big deal. "It's totally normal. Common actually. Hero worship. It happens more often than you might think."

I made a face like he'd just stepped in something rank. "I'm not sure where you're getting this from. Attracted to you because you saved my life? Um, no. I'm *thankful* to you because you saved my life. So grateful. Which I still need to repay by doing something nice for you. But I'm attracted to you because you're smokin' hot. Now, you think on that while I go get showered and changed. We'll be heading out and I have a great idea where to go."

"Simone…"

"Nope! You stepped in it, dude, not me. I'm choosing not to take offense…yet. And while I'm showering, all naked and wet in your shower, how's about you think about why you're attracted to me? And I can sure as hell bet it isn't because you saved my life, or you loved seeing me in a pink, greasy day-old diner outfit." And as I walked out of the room, I waved my ass to the best of my ability, showing off whatever I could.

Hero worship.

For the love of all things Holy. I couldn't wait to tell my sisters about that. Charlie would lose her mind. Blessing would laugh her butt off and Addy would tell me to use that to my advantage. Still the way he responded, cutting himself off from me when I called him my savior was not a pleasant reaction and said more about him than it ever could about me. Definitely a story there.

And just like a dog with a bone, if I wanted something, I'd work to get it. So far, Jonah was a male of true worth. I just had to find out what had gone wrong in his past that made him skittish when it came to women. Or more specifically, a woman he'd saved.

Still, there was a beautiful day to be had, and some bad crap from the last two days to get off my chest and fill with nothing but the good things life had to offer.

I'd take Jonah kicking and screaming with me if I had to.

Poor, sexy, smokin' hot FBI man had no idea what he'd gotten himself into moving me in.

"Navy Pier. That's where you've directed me?" Jonah's voice did not hold a lot of excitement, but I knew I'd bring him around. Otherwise, I wouldn't, and he'd be a bump on a log and yet, I'd still have a blast. His response would also determine if he was the man for me or not.

Simple.

"Yes, sir! First stop. Breakfast!"

He parked the car, got out, walked around, and opened my door for me before I even had my bag situated with all the stuff I wanted back in it, as I'd put my makeup on in the car while he drove. Something he found absolutely fascinating if how many times he kept glancing my way was any measure.

"Some of us early birds already had breakfast." He grinned.

"Suit yourself, but I'm getting a churro and we're taking it on the big ferris wheel. It's going to be awesome!" I jumped out of the car and strapped my purse over and across my body, the slouchy part hanging right in front of me. A girl could never be too careful with her purse or her pocketbook in Chi-Town.

Once he locked the car, he held out his hand.

Gentleman opening my door. Check.

Holding my hand. Double check.

I grabbed his and couldn't help but beam while looking at his gorgeous face, his pretty eyes hidden behind a pair of dark Ray-Bans.

He stared at me for a long time, his face dipping a tad closer almost as if he were going to kiss me.

I waited what felt like an eternity when he inhaled slowly and said, "I could do a churro and the ferris wheel."

Inside my heart was pounding, my body tingling and butterflies filling my belly. I squeezed his hand and said, "Triple check."

He smiled. "What's that supposed to mean?"

I smirked. "Maybe one day you'll find out. Now come

on, you've got a woman to feed and you do not want me to get hangry. That is not a pretty look on me."

He chuffed. "I find that hard to believe."

"You find what hard to believe?"

"That any look wouldn't be pretty on you."

I swung his arm and nudged him forward. "Such a charmer."

He didn't say anything, but his cheeks seemed to get a tiny teensy bit red.

"And a little bashful too."

"No way. You've got the wrong idea." He led me to the ticket counter. "Do you just want to ride the ferris wheel?"

"That's like asking someone if you just want a slice of pizza. No, I want as much as can fit in my belly!" I edged in front of him. "We'll take the Play the Park pass for two please!" I tugged out an old wallet that had nothing in it but some cash since my wallet and bank cards had been taken by…the Strangler. Before I knew it, a masculine, well-muscled forearm was wrapped around my stomach and I was physically lifted up and over to the side with a grunt.

"Hey! I was paying for you. It's the least I could do! I still owe you. And I heard that grunt Mr. I-Bruised-My-Ribs-Bad-Just-A-Day-Ago." I huffed and pushed my wild hair out of my face.

"Two, please." Jonah ignored me and handed the teller his bank card.

I glared and tapped my foot as he turned around holding our wrist bands. "Now come on, don't be salty. If you're out with me, you are not paying. Ever."

"Because this is a date," I hedged.

"Well yeah, I mean no." He frowned and looked away. "Just give me your wrist."

I smiled wide and held out my good arm where he wrapped a hot pink paper bracelet on me and handed me his to do the same.

Instead of grabbing my hand he hooked his arm around my shoulder, careful not to jostle the bandaged one. "Over there. I see the churro booth."

"Are you going to let me buy you a churro?"

He shook his head. "You just can't help yourself, can you?"

"Nope!" I skipped out of his hold and over to the churro man and passed him a twenty-dollar bill from what would have been part of my rent money. Shockingly, the perpetrator hadn't gone through my kitchen last night which was where I kept a big yellow envelope that I put all my weekly tips into that I then deposited into the bank at the beginning of each new week.

As the churro man handed me two warm cinnamon-tastic, ropelike pastries, I felt Jonah come up behind me. He placed both of his large hands to my hips and pressed his nose into the back of my neck. "You're going to try my patience at every turn, aren't you, sweet girl?"

His warm breath at my neck sent a shiver down my spine and heat to settle low in my belly.

I glanced over my shoulder and gave my most sultry smile. "You better believe it."

He chuckled and took the churro I handed him, taking a giant bite before closing his eyes and humming while he chewed. "Holy hell, this is amazing. I haven't had one of these in ages." I watched fascinated by his tanned throat working as he swallowed, his Adam's apple bobbing with the effort. He hadn't shaved this morning, so his face held a good day or two's worth of scruff that I wanted to touch... with my tongue.

Instead, I bit off a good chunk of the warm pastry, closed my eyes, and moaned around the perfect texture, the crystalized sugar mixing with the heated dough and cinnamon.

When I opened my eyes, he had pushed his sunglasses up and into his hair, his dark orbs blazing with desire.

I licked my lips.

"Fuck it!" He growled, pulling me against his form with one arm wrapped around my waist, locking his hand at my other side, while the opposite hand still had a hold on the churro, but that didn't stop him.

His head tipped down, mine went up, and our lips molded to one another's.

He tasted of sugar and spice and wet, hot, man. I dropped my churro, lifted both of my hands, and drove my fingers into his thick, soft hair. I opened my mouth farther, got up on my toes, and kissed him deep, gliding my tongue along his until we were glued together, both fighting for dominance of the kiss. For a few seconds I'd win, then he'd turn his head, growl, and take the kiss where he wanted it to go.

It was the best kiss of my life.

And it went on.

And on.

Until neither one of us could breathe and he pulled away while biting down on my bottom lip, letting it go at the last possible second with a little snap.

I gasped at the pinch of erotic sensation and sucked it

back into my mouth, tasting his rich flavor on the swollen flesh. I was dizzy. Filled to bursting with excitement and the desire to do it all over again.

"You are a fantastic kisser." He pressed his forehead to mine, and I smiled and closed my eyes, allowing the fresh air to enter my lungs and bring me back down to Earth.

"You are not so bad yourself."

"Not so bad?" He leaned back and smiled.

I cheesed out. I couldn't help it. The man made me positively giddy. I jumped a little in my shoes and planted my hands to his hips. "Okay, maybe a little better than not so bad…"

"Mmm hmm?"

"Maybe even possibly the best kiss of my life," I admitted honestly.

"Now *that* I believe since it was sure as fuck the best kiss of my life too. Now let me get you another churro."

As we turned around the churro man had two new steaming hot churros wrapped and ready to go. The ones we'd dropped were gone and likely tossed in the trash by the same fella.

"What can I say? I'm in love with love," the man said handing us the treats. "On the house."

"Thanks, man." Jonah clapped the guy on the shoulder, hooked his free arm around my waist, and brought me close to his side as he dipped his head toward my ear. "I believe we have a date with a ferris wheel?"

"Heck, yes!" I held my churro out and up toward the giant circle against the sunny horizon. "Lead on!"

Jonah chuckled but snuggled near my side and kissed my temple. "You're a nut."

"Oh, honey, you have no idea what I'm capable of. Hope you're the kind of guy who likes a good adventure."

"Babe, I'm an FBI agent. Every day of my life is an adventure."

I stopped in my tracks, churro almost touching my lips. "That. Is. True!" And it was. Law enforcement officers had no idea what they were going to encounter in the field day in and day out. Anything could have happened. "Huh, I never thought about it that way. This is great."

He chuckled again. "Do tell?"

"Well, I'm not into boring men. And it just dawned on me with your answer that FBI agents are probably the farthest thing from boring there is! Every day is a new possible challenge and risk. You're lucky."

"I enjoy my job, definitely. Not sure I'd say I'm lucky seeing as I was shot the other night and the woman I was trying to protect was grazed and is still in mortal danger. There's also the little fact that there's a serial killer out on the loose."

Properly chastised, I answered, "Well, besides all of that."

Jonah smiled. "You really do take everything with a grain of salt. Nothing bothers you."

"Well I did spend a couple of days crying my eyes out like a little girl so I wouldn't exactly say *nothing* bothers me, but I'm not going to hole up in your house and hide, not living my life to the fullest because of some wack-a-doo. Every day is a gift. We can't sit around and let it pass us by."

"Wack-a-doo?"

"It's an expression."

"Not anymore it isn't." He laughed.

"Yes, it is!"

"Maybe fifty or sixty years ago, babe. Trust me."

I rolled my eyes and ignored him by eating my churro. The second one was almost as good as the first, but I wouldn't compare them because the first one led to our first kiss and I couldn't wait to lay my lips on his again.

Jonah led me to the line for the ferris wheel.

"Would you kiss me again at the top of the ferris wheel?" I asked as we showed the operator our wrist bands for access.

Jonah's lips pursed together. "Maybe."

"Maybe?" I harrumphed.

We settled into our seat and the ride started its stop and go procedure letting people on and off for the next few minutes before it really started to move.

"Are you always this forward with men you're attracted to?" He cupped my cheek and held my chin with his thumb and forefinger.

I licked my lips and watched his eyes dilate at the sight.

"Yeah, if I want something, I ask for it. You don't get anything in life without asking for it, working hard, and sacrifice. The worst that could happen is you say no." I shrugged one shoulder.

He leaned close enough that I could feel his breath on my face. "And what would you do if I said no?"

"I'd be sad, but I'd try to respect your answer."

"And if I said yes?" He grinned.

"Then I'd kiss the heck out of you right now." My voice was breathy and needy.

"Ah, but you asked me to kiss *you*, did you not?"

"Are you going to kiss me?" I whispered.

He smiled. "Yeah, Simone. I'm going to kiss you. I'm going to kiss you until you forget where you are. I'm going to kiss you until you forget all that has happened these last couple days. And I'm going to kiss you so that the only thing you can remember going forward is the taste of me on your tongue and in your mouth. Then I'm going to do it all over again."

A river of arousal rushed through my system making my sex throb to the tempo of my heartbeat. I'd never been this turned on or desperate for a man's kiss.

He had me obsessed with need.

And then his lips touched mine and I was lost. Gone to the rich texture of his tongue sliding across mine. His lips pressing, easing his way until our teeth touched and the slick heat of his tongue danced and twirled. In and out we chased one another, smooth silky lips learning, taking, connecting. Teasing, tasting, nipping, and sighing as the world around us spun in an endless loop we had no part of.

When we broke away, the operator had the door open and was urging us out.

I blinked and looked at him and then Jonah. "But we haven't gone yet?"

Jonah laughed so hard I could feel it against my belly which was also when I realized that I was on his lap, facing him, a knee to each side of the seat, his hair twined in my fingers.

"Nice, bro, but you gotta get." The operator hooked a thumb over his shoulder.

"But I didn't get to see anything!!!" I grouched.

"Look, man, there's a twenty in it for you if you let us go around again, yeah?"

"Done." The guy shut the door on the little glass cage thingy.

Jonah's hands squeezed my hips. "You didn't even know we had ridden the entire ride," he teased. "I'd have to say *that* was the best kiss of your life."

I swiveled off his lap and to the side, pressing my fingers over my lips trying to calm my raging heart, mind, and libido. "You'd be correct."

"I like that about you." He put his hand into mine and then set them both on the top of his thigh.

"Like what?"

"Your honesty. You say exactly what you're thinking. Which often is funny as hell, but most of the time is cute, sweet, and truthful. I like knowing where I'm at with the people I share time with."

"Have women in your past not done that with you?" I finally got the opening to bring up the weird vibe I'd felt this morning.

"Let's just say I've had my share of seriously dishonest people that went on to break more than one heart. I'm not into games. Lies. Or half-truths. I don't share. I won't ever covet another man's woman and I'm not the easiest man to get to know. It's not easy for me to let people in."

I brought his hand up to my cheek and nuzzled it. "Challenge accepted."

"Simone…" he warned on a sigh.

"No, really. I'm no different. Well, I'm totally the opposite." I grinned. "I lay it all on the table. Wear my heart on my sleeve. Have been screwed over by every man I've loaned my heart to but, I still see the good in people. Still believe that one day I'm going to find my perfect match, my other half. The man that suits only me."

"It's a pretty dream," he sighed.

"Dreams come true every day. All you have to do is work hard and put the good out into the Universe. Eventually karma will come through."

"I want to believe the way you do. Life would be so much easier."

I leaned forward, pressed my lips to his with my eyes still open, and watched him while I kissed him softly. "Stick with me and I'll make you a believer."

The ride came back around to a stop. Jonah got up, pulled his wallet out of his pants, passed the guy a twenty, and then helped me out of the box.

"If anyone could make me a believer, Simone, you just may be the one to do it."

I smiled wild and dragged him away from the ride. "Up next, the carousel."

"Whatever you want, sweet girl. Whatever you want."

"I'll have to remember that."

Chapter
SEVEN

SKIP-JUMPED, SWINGING HIS HAND WHILE HEADING TO HIS CAR. "That was a blast!" I raved as he opened my door and waited until I folded myself in and shut the door safely behind me. I watched as he scanned the surroundings, ever watchful. That trait could have been engrained in him as a gentleman or a product of his training in the FBI. Either way, I found it sexy as hell.

Technically I found everything about Jonah Fontaine sexy as hell. From his muscular lean frame, to his long-tapered fingers, to the dark olive hue of his skin tone. And he kissed like he was made for it. I wanted more. So much more and I hoped even with his bruised ribs I could encourage a bit longer make out session. Heck, I'd take it all the way to experience this man fully.

Usually I had a rule about sleeping with a man I was interested in. Typically I'd wait at least a few dates, to make sure they were worthy of a roll in the hay. With Jonah, I'd toss the dice and go for it. Even though Trey was good in bed, we hadn't actually hooked up in a few weeks and I was a sexual person by nature. Sex felt amazing. Relieved stress. And it was the best, purest way to connect with a man. At least in my opinion. I could tell by the way a man kissed if he was going to be good in bed, and after Jonah's kisses, I knew he'd be stellar. I couldn't wait.

"Why the smile?" He smirked as he started the car.

"I had a really good time. Thank you for taking me," I answered.

He smiled. "Honestly, it's the most fun I've had in a while. This case has put a lot on our team and if I hadn't happened to be close when the call came through, I shudder to think about what might have happened."

I let my shoulders drop and ran my hands down my jean-clad thighs. The last thing I wanted to think about in the world was what could have happened if he hadn't been there. "I'm not the type of person who thinks about what could have happened, Jonah. You were there. You saved my life. The alternative is horrifying so it's best not to think about it." I reached for his hand which was resting on his thigh and covered it with my own. "Let's just move on. Instead, how about we decide what to eat. My treat!"

He brought my hand up to his mouth and did something no man had ever done before. He kissed the back of my hand and smiled. I felt his lips shift against my hand, and I shivered in response.

"Sweetheart, it's never going to be your treat. We've already had this discussion. But I do actually have plans for dinner. You can come with or…" His lips tightened and he brought my hand back down to his thigh. "I can drop you with Agent Russell."

I laughed out loud. I laughed so hard and for so long my eyes watered.

"What's so funny?" His pretty, dark eyebrows were furrowed, his facial expression set at concerned.

"You. You're what's funny. You don't trust me with your partner."

"He's the *only one* I trust you with, actually. He'd die to keep you safe," he affirmed.

I shook my head. "That's not what I meant. You're worried he'll hit on me."

"Not worried, no. It's a guarantee he'll hit on you. Repeatedly, the bastard." His words were stiff, and he adjusted in his seat as if he were suddenly uncomfortable.

I covered my mouth trying not to chuckle. "Do you think I'd be interested in him? After an incredible day with you? Complete with churro-and-ferris-wheel-kisses aplenty."

His jaw tightened and I focused on the little muscle in his cheek that seemed to tick there. "We don't know one another that well," he admitted. "I can't be sure exactly how you'd respond."

"Still. That would be a super bitchy move to fall over myself for one guy and then turn around and do the same with his partner?" I scrunched up my nose. "What kind of woman would do that? My sisters and I have a super fat unbreakable pact that we all made. We'd never, ever go for the same guy. Second, the biggest deal breaker of all, you are never, ever allowed to date one of your sisters' exes. Think of how awkward that would be. To have to see your ex at a family function." I made a gagging sound. "No way, Jose. Not happening. And it never has. You just don't go there."

"Yeah, right. You just don't go there," he murmured sadly. "Unfortunately, Simone, not all people think like you."

"And you don't trust your partner not to screw you over like that?"

He shook his head. "No, I do. Mostly. Let's just say, I've been fucked over royally by people who meant everything to me."

I figured it was time to lighten the heavy in the car. "Well, that sucks. I'm sorry you've been hurt. So, in answer to your original question, if I'm not going to be in the way, I'd be happy to tag along with you." My belly took that moment to growl. "As long as we're going to eat." I smiled wide and covered my belly with my hand.

He chuckled and hit the blinker taking us off the freeway and closer to Oak Park where I grew up in Kerrighan House.

I watched the landscape as he drove into a pretty, older neighborhood, very much like my mother's. Though Kerrighan house was huge, these were moderate sized with nicely kept yards and long driveways. Each house had a deep span of grass from the curb to the house. The house we stopped in front of was one story with half of it covered in white horizontal paneling and the bottom half faced with old brick. There were two big pots out front bursting with foliage and purple flowers poking out the center.

Through the big rectangular picture window at the front of the house, I could see a soft yellow glow inside. The front door was painted a deep navy and had a brass knocker in the center. I waited until Jonah folded out of the driver's side and came around to open the door and help me out of the car.

"Such a gentleman," I purred and winked.

"Yeah well, my ma's probably watching through the window, and she'd have a hernia if I didn't help a woman out of the car."

I opened my eyes wide. "Your mother?"

He grinned and just as I was about to question him further, the front door opened and a petite woman with long black hair liberally mixed with silver, wearing a red ruffled apron, stood watching as he grabbed my hand.

Her dark gaze, exactly the same as her son's, clocked the hand holding and she smiled wide. "Jonah, you brought a woman home for dinner. This is a great surprise, son."

I nudged his shoulder and grinned.

"Ma, this is my friend, Simone. Simone, this is my mother, Loretta."

"Your friend?" She squinted and assessed her son with a shrewd eye.

"Yeah, Ma, my friend." Jonah ran the fingers not holding my hand through his hair making it messy sexy.

"What kind of friend?" She held her hand out toward me.

Before Jonah could answer, I did for him. "The kind who spent the entire day on a date with him, kissed him twice, and who he brought home to his mama," I offered candidly.

"Fucking hell," he growled, and I laughed.

Loretta smiled and held my hand and patted the top with her other one. "Aw, that kind of friend. I see. This makes me very happy. My boy needs a woman to look after. He's happier when he has someone to take care of, and someone taking care of him in return."

"Oh really?" I laughed. "Tell me more, Loretta. I'm all ears." I smirked at Jonah.

"Come, come. I've got pasta and meatballs on the stove." His mother waved.

My mouth watered at the visual. I gripped Jonah's hand and followed his mother inside. "Come on, honey, let's have dinner with your family," I teased.

He tugged my hand so hard, I landed right against his

side where he dipped his head straight to my ear. "You're not at all bothered that I brought you home to meet my mother on the first date?"

"No. Why would I be? Moms always like me. What can I say? It's a gift." I shrugged.

His dark gaze traced my face and he lifted his hand and cupped my nape. Then he brought his lips to mine where he kissed me softly. "You're not like any woman I've ever known."

I smiled. "Thanks, baby. That's sweet. The kiss is even sweeter, but my stomach is about to eat itself if I don't get something inside of it and your mom is Italian. I'm counting on this being some really awesome spaghetti and meatballs, so can we get to the part where you get over how weirdly cool I am and feed me?"

He smashed our lips together in reply, touched his tongue with mine, and I instantly forgot how hungry I was, suddenly all about being hungry for more of Jonah.

"Kids!" I vaguely heard his mother call out from somewhere in the house. "Good Lord above," his mother gasped from over my shoulder.

"Sorry, Ma. Try and make a little more noise when you approach next time," he joked.

I started laughing and turned toward his mother, likely beet red. I hooked a thumb at Jonah. "I'm sorry I couldn't help myself, but he started it. And have you seen him? You made the most beautiful man on earth, Loretta. I plain turn stupid when he puts his lips on mine."

This had his mother beaming with what I assumed was pride. "No sorry needed. His father is the same."

"Where is Dad?"

"Garage, tooling away on that old car."

He smiled. "My father's hobby is fixing up classic American vehicles."

"Cool," I said in awe. "Can we check it out?" Cars were great at getting you from point A to B. Though all the new shiny bling and curves kind of took the fun out of the deep rumbling engine and smooth edges of sculpted metal from eras past. If I had my pick, meaning the money to buy whatever I wanted, I'd totally buy a muscle car. I wanted to feel the rumble of a car underneath me as I drove. Be one with it. My old hand-me-down sedan definitely did not have that feel. Alas, another in the long list of things I loved but wasn't sure I'd ever have, not to mention the car I did have had been stolen by my would-be captor.

"He'd love nothing more than to show you his baby…"

He was cut off when I heard a man's voice from deeper in the house holler. "Loretta, woman, your man is wasting away in here!" A booming laugh could be heard from the other room. "What's the hold up?" His dad then appeared in the living room from where I guessed was the kitchen.

It was like looking at Jonah thirty years from now. The same dark brown hair and facial features. Wisps of gray at his temple and curls around the sides of his ears. Still a full head of hair, thankfully. He stood tall, an inch or two over six feet. Similar build, though it was obvious that his dad partook of his mother's cooking and didn't hide it if the small rounded stomach was anything to go by. His eyes were a clear blue though.

"Son," his dad called out. "Why didn't you tell me Jonah was here already?" He stomped into the room and took Jonah into his arms and clapped him hard and loud on the back. Jonah sucked in a hiss. His father jerked back. "You hurt?"

"Yeah, Dad, bruised some ribs is all. You know how it is?"

"Oh, has your dad been shot before too?" I turned my gaze to him. "Are you in law enforcement?"

His dad's face took in mine and then turned hard. I glanced at his mother and she paled. Shit.

"I'm fine. I was wearing the vest," Jonah rushed to say.

His mother's eyes filled with tears. "My son was shot. Why didn't you call us? When did this happen? Oh, my Lord. Are you okay?"

I bit down on my bottom lip and crossed my arms over one another before I mouthed, "Sorry," to Jonah. Always sticking my foot in it. Dammit, I need to keep my mouth shut.

"I'm well. I was working a case. It's how I met Simone. How's about we talk about it over dinner? What I can tell you anyway."

That had me giving him big eyes and he shook his head. He knew what his family could handle hearing about his job. I was pretty sure the idea that he'd been shot by the Backseat Strangler wasn't exactly going to make for polite dinner conversation, but what did I know. I was the outsider in the mix.

"Yes, come. Dinner's ready." His mother urged us with a wave. "Simone, would you like something to drink? Wine? Water. Pop?"

"A glass of wine would be heavenly. Thank you, Loretta. Is there anything I can do to help?"

She shook her head gracefully and I followed behind her into the kitchen. It was an average U-shaped kitchen with a six-seater dining table in the bit of open space. Cabinets oc-cupied two of the walls with a door by the fridge that likely led to the garage.

Jonah led me to a seat next to him and we sat while his mother put a big bowl of cooked spaghetti, another big pot of sauce with a ladle, a platter of fresh garlic bread, and a bowl of salad all in the center.

"We eat family style. Feel free to serve yourself. Guests first," Loretta said then poured two glasses of wine.

She moved to give her son one of them, but he shook his head. "No booze while I've got Simone on my watch."

"On your watch?" His dad interlaced his fingers and set his chin on them staring at his son. "Explain. Now."

For the next fifteen or so minutes Jonah updated them on some of what happened. Leaving out the part where he got shot three times, me once, and the loss of Katrina to the psycho. He did tell them who he was protecting me from and that he was off work for the next week to heal. His parents seemed thrilled that he would be on babysitting duty and not out there chasing after the serial killer.

"And when did the two of you decide to be a couple in all of this?" his mother blatantly asked.

Jonah choked on a piece of his bread and I chuckled while smacking his back.

"Ma, we are um…"

"Seeing each other?" I offered.

He let out a relieved breath. "Seeing each other. Yeah, that."

"What's the difference?" She frowned.

"A lot, Ma, but that's between me and Simone. Let's just say it's new and leave it at that, yeah?"

"Don't get that tone with your mother, son. Mind your manners," his dad chastised.

And I lost it. Snort-laughed and put my head down so I was looking at my lap as I tried desperately to control my laugher.

A warm arm sliced across my back and Jonah pressed his chin to my shoulder, and whispered, "Keep it up, baby. You're gonna get it."

I swallowed and cleared my throat, then reached for the glass of wine and taking a hefty sip, allowing it to warm my body from the inside out. Jonah watched me like a hawk. So much so that I turned my head and taunted, "Oh yeah, you gonna give it to me?"

He smirked. "Only if you're good."

Damn.

Check. Mate. He won.

Just as I was reaching for another hunk of supremely amazing garlic bread to sop up the rest of the sauce on my plate, lest it go to waste, someone rang the doorbell.

His father growled low in his throat clearly annoyed by being disturbed during dinner. I got that. It was annoying. Like when you'd just sat down to eat and the phone rang and it was a freakin' telemarketer and not someone you could easily just tell, "Hey, I'll call you right back when I'm done with dinner," and they let you. No, you were stuck on the phone with someone who wanted to sell you a new warranty on your stove that you didn't even know had a warranty in the first place.

Jonah stood and set his napkin on the table. "I'll get it."

"So, Simone, what do you do?" his mother asked.

"That's a rather loaded question. It would be easier to

ask what I don't do." I smiled. "Most of the time I bartend at Tracks downtown. I also work in my mom's best friend's flower shop a couple days a week, and I just recently as of two days quit my waitressing job."

"That's a lot of jobs. A hard worker. I like it," his father complimented.

"Thanks. It's not hard work except for the fact that it's tiring and physical a lot of the time, but I'm almost done with school. I have one more class in order to get my associate degree in business. Then I hope that will help me get into an office management type position where I can make higher pay, secure healthcare benefits, and one day toss my old hand-me-down junker my sister gave me. Well, if I ever get it back."

His dad, who I later found out was named Marco, pointed at me. "You work for what you get. This is admirable. It will mean more. When you get that degree, you come see me at our offices. We're not a huge construction business, but me and my other son Luca run the jobs. We have about thirty men under us. Our office manager is leaving us in six months to have a baby. She wants to be an at-home mother raising her children. We'll have an opening…"

"You just met me and you're offering me the possibility of a job?" I pressed my hands to the table so they wouldn't see them shaking with excitement.

"I like people who are hard working and driven. Willing to work three jobs in order to make something of themselves. That's all I need to know about you. The rest being you came here with my son who wouldn't bring a woman to his mother's home if she didn't mean something to him. And he's a good judge of character, being a junior profiler in the FBI hunting down madmen. Doesn't hurt you're beautiful. Part of the job is dealing with people so that helps. You're social and outgoing. We'll have you meet Luca, do a walk around, learn about the job, get details from Lisa who's leaving us, and see if you'd make a good fit."

"Wow, this is so unexpected, and I...well, I don't know what to say." I covered my pounding heart with my hand.

"Say you'll come check out the offices. Meet my men. Meet my other son."

"Definitely. I'd love it. Um, we might have to wait a little bit but let me go ask Jonah." I hopped up and out of my chair excitedly sprinting into the living room.

"Jonah, you're never gonna guess what your dad just offered me!" I called out to his back. He flicked his gaze my way and held up a hand to ward me off.

He'd have to do a lot more than hold up a hand if he was going to get me to listen. I had news and he needed to be the first to hear it.

"You didn't hear me!"

"Simone. Not now," he grated through his teeth and then faced the doorway again. His entire body was stiff and wired to the point I thought he might jump at whoever was opposite him.

"Jonah, come on, this is ridiculous. Take the check!" I heard a high-pitched woman's irritated voice screech.

"I don't want your money, Helen. I don't want anything from you, or from my brother."

"Don't be that way. It's not his fault and you know it. Frankly, the fact that you are playing blameless in this is rich. Just like you to play the victim," she sneered.

"It's not me who fucked Luca. That was you." He

pointed and scowled as I pressed up close to his back, my hands curled around his biceps.

I didn't speak but I could tell in the line of his body that he was angry and concealing that anger by being as passive as possible. He was hurting and whoever this woman was, she was the source.

I curled around his side, ducked my head under where he was holding the door jamb, and pressed my cheek to his pec. "Hey." I waved to the tall brunette whose hair was cut at a severe line at her pointed chin. She was super thin, with an angular, pretty face. A little like Sandra Bullock from her *Speed* movie days. "I'm Simone."

"Helen. Here." She handed me an envelope, one I just accepted automatically, hoping it would make her leave.

"I can't believe you came here. How could you?" Jonah groused.

"It's Thursday, same night of the week you have dinner with your folks when you are in town. I took a shot."

"I wish you hadn't. Please leave and don't ever come around again. It's over in a way it's never not going to be over."

"Cash that check. Half of the money is yours. And, have a nice life, Jonah. I know I will without you," she huffed snidely.

"Fuck you." He spat the words as though he couldn't get them off his tongue fast enough.

She made a pinched ugly face. "Nice. Real nice. Good luck with that one, Simone. You're gonna need it."

"Aw, thanks. I'm pretty happy with what I've got. You know, you should look into some Botox for those frown lines around your mouth." I canted my head to the side and pursed my lips. "Nah, never mind. You'll still be ugly. Don't bother." I let out a long breath. "Well this was fun, but I need to tell my man some really great news and you're kinda putting a damper on my joy. Hope to see you never." I curled my hands around Jonah's hips and pushed until he let go of the doorjamb and backed into the house. I gave a jaunty wave before slamming the door.

"Guess what!" I pressed my hands together still holding the envelope. "Your dad offered me a job!"

Jonah looked at the door, then at my face, down to the envelope, and back up to me. "What?"

"Your dad said he needs a new office manager. I told your parents about being one class away from my associate's degree and he practically offered me the job at his company!" I bounced up and down on my feet. "Honey, this is huge for me. Ginormous. Gargantuan."

He shook his head as if to clear it. "Big news. Got it." He pointed to the door. "Do you uh, have questions about what just happened with my ex-wife?"

The word wife had me clamping my mouth shut for a moment before I blurted, "That was your wife?"

"Ex-wife."

"Huh. And she cheated on you with some dude named Luca." I frowned for a moment as I put it all together. "Oh, hell no!" I covered my mouth in shock. Then my entire body got hot. Sweltering hot. Burning with rage. I clenched my hands together, my wounded one smarting a bit as it was just scabbing over, so it didn't need more than a couple bandages to cover it. I narrowed my eyes and reached for the door. I pulled it back so hard it jarred my shoulder which I barely felt.

Jonah looped me around the waist and pressed me back against his form, grunting in the process. "Where are you going?"

I shook out of his hold. "I'm going to start one helluva cat fight with that skank! She fucked your brother! She deserves to have her ass beat!" I roared and pushed myself further out the door.

Jonah hooked me more firmly around the waist and hauled me up and off my feet like he'd done at Navy Pier today bringing me right back inside. "Easy, tiger."

I smacked at his arm. "Let me go. She's gonna get away," I argued. "That woman is the worst of the worst. Not only did she cheat, she broke every girl code known to mankind, not to mention her vows to her husband! Eww. She's the scum on the bottom of your shoe. Now let me go rub her face in it!" I fought until Jonah whirled me around once more, locked his arm around my waist, and smashed his lips to mine.

Before I knew what was happening, I was opening my mouth and his tongue was delving inside. My anger quickly turned to lust and I gave what I got and then some. Turning my head from side to side, tunneling my fingers through his silky hair. One of his hands was cupped at the back of my head trying to keep control of the kiss, the other shifted from my waist to my ass.

Total ass man.

He gave a squeeze and I mewled into his mouth. Before it got too hot and heavy Jonah eased back, nipping at my top lip playfully and then sucking on my bottom one.

"You good?"

"Mmm." I was in a Jonah kiss-daze, swimming in his dark eyes while my heartbeat settled to a more normal beat.

He chuckled. "You were pretty mad, baby. Seems my girl has a temper hiding under all that sweet."

I pinched my lips together. "I don't like your ex-wife."

He huffed. "I'm getting that. Though I'll say, that's just fine since I don't like her either."

"You kids done?" Jonah's father asked. "Get the wicked witch of the Midwest to stop coming around? Swear I saw her car drive by each week for the past month."

"Yeah, Dad, we got rid of Helen."

"What's this?" I picked up the envelope that I dropped in my mini-freak-out and handed it to him.

"My half of the house. She sold it and our divorce decree stated I got half. This is it."

"Why wouldn't you want your own money?" I balked.

He shrugged. "Guess I just didn't want to deal with her. It's hard enough dealing with my brother."

"Now, son…" Marco tried to enter the conversation but Jonah shook his head.

"Dad, don't." His words were firm and succinct.

His father shockingly pressed his lips together for a moment. "Your ma's got dessert going. Wants to wow Simone with her chocolate cheesecake. You okay to stay for dessert and a cuppa?"

Jonah sighed. "Yeah, Dad, cheesecake would be great. Thanks. We'll be right in."

His dad left the room and Jonah looked at me. I lifted my hands to his face and cupped his cheeks. "I'm serious about beating her up. We can call it temporary insanity from the other night. They would totally let it slide."

That had my guy smiling. "You are too much. What am I going to do with you, huh?"

"Um, feed me cheesecake?"

"Uh huh." He hooked me around the shoulders.

"Kiss me?"

He laid a hot one on my neck and I sighed.

"Fall madly in love with me so that you never want to kiss or look at another woman ever again?" I batted my eyelashes and grinned wide.

He laughed. "Maybe." He said the one word the same way he did when I asked him to kiss me on the ferris wheel, and that ride went smashingly so I figured I had a good start toward more.

"Maybe's good."

Chapter
EIGHT

ONAH OPENED THE DOOR TO HIS HOME AND LED ME INSIDE. His mood had been sullen ever since bitch-face Helen had come knocking.

I followed him and set my purse on the kitchen bar. Jonah didn't speak, just went straight to a cabinet and pulled down a bottle of whiskey. "Drink with me on the patio?"

"Sure." I leaned over the bar and watched him take out two tumblers and fill both of them with two fingers of Jameson over ice.

Without a word, he passed me the drink, grabbed my hand, and brought me out the back door to a raised wooden deck. The yard was small but immaculately landscaped.

I sat down in a comfy-looking loveseat that had a dark red cushion. He sat his ass next to me and we both put our feet up onto the matching small ottoman.

"Amazing yard. Did you plant all of these?"

He sipped his drink and stared out at the variety of small bushes, trees, and flowers dotting the yard. "Nah. The house is Ryan's. I moved in a little over a year ago when Helen and I separated. Just haven't had the time to find my own place and since Ryan and I work together on the same team, it didn't really matter. I pay half the bills which he uses as his play money. Not that he has much time to play but the man is social. Every minute we're not working, he's finding time to be out and about. Says he needs to soak up humanity and all the good there is in it otherwise he'd be swallowed by the horror we deal in day to day chasing serial killers and profiling criminals."

"Sounds like a really hard job. You gone a lot?"

His body went stiff next to me. I reached for his hand and laced our fingers. We both held our drinks in the opposite one.

"Yeah, it's part of the job."

"Do you get to see anything?"

"In what way?"

I shrugged a shoulder. "Well, you know, if I had a job where I traveled, I'd be visiting all kinds of attractions, old relics, festivals, that kind of thing."

He smiled softly and stared into my eyes. "I'm sure you would. We don't usually have much time for that. When my team in the FBI is called in, it's usually a bad situation. Multiple deaths, often across state lines. We get in, profile the criminal and work with local authorities. Once our job is done, we jet back home."

"Like *Criminal Minds*?"

"Kind of, but that's more glorified. Ryan and I are criminal profilers, but we have a bit broader scope. There are a lot of FBI offices. Ours is downtown Chicago but we could be called in for anything. Depends on the job. Sometimes we don't travel for months because we can do a lot of things virtually. Meaning review case files across the nation and give feedback, act as consultant on criminal cases, and more I can't really get into."

"Meh, it's okay. I don't need to know everything. How long have you been working with Ryan?"

"Since the beginning. We were best friends in college, both transferred to Quantico, and have been paired up ever since. It's been mostly luck that we've gotten to stay in the same branches."

"What type of woman is he usually into?" I ask thinking about my sisters. He was super hot and I could see any one of them being into him.

Jonah dipped his head toward mine and cocked an eyebrow. "Why?"

"Because I'm a woman with seven sisters. A good man who's hardworking and hot is hard to find."

He chuckled. "He's always dated a wide variety of women."

"Does he date out of his race?"

For a minute he seemed to think about it. "Yeah." He nodded. "Actually, I've seen more women of color leaving his bedroom in the morning than I have white women."

I grinned wide. "That's awesome. My sister Blessing is Black, but her preference is white dudes. She's dated a few brothers in the past, but for some reason they've never had staying power. She's also a fashion designer who travels all the time too so a man who traveled and was okay with his woman traveling too wouldn't be a problem to her."

Jonah ran his nose down my neck and I trembled, squeezing his hand. "And what about you? Do you have a problem with a man who travels for work?"

I licked my lips and I could have sworn his eyes dilated. "No. People have to do what they love. I'm always busy and if my man was gone, I'd take that time to do hobby-related things, spending time with my sisters and mom. I'm not exactly the type of girl who ties a man down. Nor do I sit still for long. I respect people for what they need to be who they are. And I expect that in return. Would you have a problem with the fact that I planned a vacation with my sisters, and you happened to be home that weekend?"

He shook his head. "Never."

"And what about when you want to have children?"

That had him letting go of my hand and rubbing at his forehead. "I want children in the future. Helen wanted them right away after getting married. I wasn't prepared to give them to her when we were twenty-five and just married. I was in the beginning of my career at the FBI and needed to put the time in to solidify my position. Something I've since done."

"How long were you married?"

He groaned and cracked his neck. "Seven years. I'm thirty-three now."

I curled my hand around his thigh appreciating the muscles flexing under my palm. "I can understand that. I'm twenty-seven. You're the same age as my sister Sonia. And she doesn't have kids or a husband yet. It's okay to want to be settled in your life and career before bringing children into it."

Jonah let out a long, weighted breath, then sipped more of his drink.

"What happened with Helen?"

He let his head fall back and sucked in a breath.

"Never mind. You don't have to tell me. It's none of my business. I'm being nosy."

He turned his head and looked at me intensely, then kissed me, hard. He used his hand to hold my head in place. He didn't take the kiss farther, or deeper, just a hard press of his lips as though he were trying to say something without using his words.

I sighed dreamily when he pulled back. "It absolutely is your business. If we're starting something here, which it feels a hell of a lot like we are, you deserve to know what you're getting yourself into."

"Okay." I pulled up my legs and turned sideways so I could sit cross-legged and focus on him and him alone. "Lay it on me, I can take it." I sucked back a huge swallow of whiskey and let it out. "Ahhhhhh. Ready."

Jonah shook his head and laughed. "You amuse me. A breath of fresh air from what I've experienced in the past with women."

I held up a finger. "First and foremost, you need to stop comparing me to other women. You already said it yourself. I'm not like other women. Part of that is because I'm me. The other is probably because I was raised in a house with eight other women including my foster mom. I have a super over-bearing blood-related sister in Sonia, and I don't remember much about my real parents, but I lived at Kerrighan House since I was six. All of those personalities in the same place, you learn to adapt and form your own path. Mine seems to be tolerance. I can handle just about anything people throw my way, unless it's about my family. Then I turn into a raving lunatic. Oh, and when I'm confronted with a bitch-face ex that cheated on my new hot guy in the worst way possible."

He snickered and tried to cover his response by sipping more whiskey. "Noted."

"Since we got that out of the way, what happened with Helen?" I pressed my free hand back to his thigh to keep our connection close.

"You really aren't bothered by the fact that I was mar-ried before?" His tone was one of awe.

"Nope. It's in your past not your present. Can't dwell on it now."

He nodded but took his time before speaking. When he did it was a low, tired sound that made me wish we were lying in his big bed in the dark while he told me. Though sitting outside, drinking in the beautiful backyard and quiet of night wasn't too shabby.

"Helen and I fell madly in love in college. I met her and Ryan around the same time. When I transferred to DC, she followed me and finished up her schooling there. We were married three years later after I'd completed my training and became a special agent. Ryan and I were both eager to get back to Chicago, as was Helen, so when positions opened up in Chicago, we applied and were lucky to both be accepted."

"That is really cool that you get to work with your best friend."

"It is. Ryan's a great guy. Always been there for me. Especially after Helen cheated. Offering me a place to live with no end on that condition. If he doesn't bring a woman into his life, I think he'd happily share a place with me forever."

I grinned and ran my finger in squiggly designs down and around his thigh. "How did the Helen thing go down?"

His nostrils flared and his body went rigid once again. I unfolded my legs and got close, pressing my chin to his pec. He curved his free arm around my back and held me to his side.

"I'd been on an extra long case. Gone three weeks. It was brutal. The time away, the endless nights, sleeping on cots half the time in an FBI branch conference room. Remember the headlines about the couple who kidnapped two little kids, a brother and sister, and then killed them by pushing them over high cliffs in national parks?"

I lifted my head. "You worked that? My goodness, that's horrible. Wasn't it six pairs of children?"

"Yeah, though ten ended up dying. Two of the children, one boy and one girl from different families, survived the fall. They were able to tell us a little bit about the couple. After we were able to piece together a few sightings of the couple with the children, we were able to nail them down. They already had two more kidnapped kids in their RV when we found them."

"Jesus, that had to be awful."

"It was. It lasted what felt like forever. I didn't get to call home often, but Helen knew the score. This was nothing new. The night we found the kids, I was desperate to get home. Hold onto my wife even though we'd been fighting nonstop for the six months prior to that. My heart was shredded, my mind filled with images of dead children and mourning families, and I wanted nothing more than to fill my mental tank with the goodness of home. So, I took the red-eye home. Didn't call. She had no idea."

"Honey…" I squeezed my arm around his middle and pressed my face into his chest, already expecting what was to come.

"I walked into the house and noticed the clothes all over the living room floor first. My wife's. And a man's. Like a dead man walking, I went straight to my bedroom. I'll never forget the sound of hearing my wife in the throes of pleasure, screaming the name Luca as she orgasmed. I knew that sound. Had been hearing it for eight years when I made love to her."

My eyes filled with tears, but I didn't interrupt. I couldn't. Something inside me knew he'd never told this story in detail to another soul. As much as I hated everything he was saying and what it cost him to say it, I knew I needed to listen. To be there for him in this moment so he could fully move on to the beauty that the two of us could have without this past transgression in the way of his happiness.

"I pushed open the door, watched as if I were outside of my body as she rode my brother. He then turned her over and fucked her sloppily and very hard. And I watched the entire thing as she came again screaming out like she only ever did with me when she was drunk and randy as fuck. Which is another thing. The room was pungent with the smell of liquor and sex. They'd been at it a while. It was my job to know these things. Take in a scene. Scents. Sounds. The little things you are trained to notice at a crime scene. Which is probably why I stood there until they finished. Then when my brother got off and fell on top of my wife, sated, I pounded on the door."

"Jesus," I whispered, still holding him tight around the waist, the tears tracking down my cheeks and wetting his shirt.

"The two of them were so far gone, their eyes glazed with booze and euphoria it's like they didn't even know what they were looking at. Until my brother's eyes widened, he stared at me, then at Helen with horror in his face. And he said one word, as though it was torn from his throat. Brother."

I closed my eyes imagining everything he said and feeling the intense waves of hurt flooding my entire being.

"I left without a word and crashed at a hotel. Drank

117

myself into oblivion until the next day when I called Ryan. He picked me up and I moved into his spare bedroom."

I pressed off his chest and looked into his eyes, while he reached for my glass and set both of them, now empty, on the side table. Then he cupped my cheeks and wiped away my tears with his thumbs.

"You crying for me, sweet girl?"

My lips trembled as more tears fell. "Yeah, because it was an incredibly sad story. I'm sorry you lived that, especially after all you dealt with on the case prior to it. To come home to that…" I shook my head and sniffed. "It's inconceivable."

He pressed his forehead to mine. "At the time, yeah, it was. Which is why I'm so fucked up about women. Especially women I've saved, since my ex-wife was one of them."

I lifted my eyebrows in question.

He sighed deeply. "There was a party near campus. Ryan and I were there picking up girls, shooting drinks back. You know how it is."

I nodded with a grin, wiping at my eyes.

"Some jock was out of his mind, having a bad trip on acid. He was dating Helen. She was fighting with him, telling him to stop freaking out and to calm down. The guy pulled a gun out of the back of his jeans and started shooting wildly screaming about people not being people but aliens from another planet. Then he pointed the gun at her head point blank and told her that her face was melting off before his eyes. Which I knew meant he'd lost it completely and was about to kill this woman in front of my eyes. Ryan and I ran up from the side and I tackled him and scrambled for the weapon. He got off a couple more shots but none of them hit anyone by the time that Ryan and I wrestled it away. The cops came and he was taken in and charged."

"Holy shit. You've been through a lot."

"Says the woman who lost her parents at a young age and was raised in foster care."

"Sure, but I was loved and never part of anything like that, well, until the bad guy hid in the back of my car." I frowned. "You have a knack for hooking up with damsels in distress, huh?"

He chuckled. "No. Just Helen and now you." He ran his hand up and down my back then yawned.

"We could go to bed…" I bit down on my bottom lip and looked into his dark eyes as I reached my fingertips out and ran them across his sexy pout. "I'm certain we could find some other really wonderful things in order to make us both smile."

He tunneled his hand through my long hair to curl around my nape. "I want to drown myself in you, Simone, let it all go, and live in the moment."

"That sounds awesome." I ran my finger down his chest until he gripped my wrist with his other hand.

"We gotta do this right. You need a little more time to process all that's happened in the past three days. It wouldn't be right for me to take advantage…"

"You wouldn't be taking advantage. I want you."

He smiled, dipped his head, and took my mouth in a brief, sweet kiss. "I know. And I want you. More than I've wanted another woman. I haven't been with anyone since Helen and after just seeing her, reliving my story, I…"

I pressed my mouth to his, wrapped my arms around his neck, and tangled my tongue with his. We kissed for a long time, slowly and luxuriously. I plucked at his top lip and then bottom lip the same way he was so fond of nipping at mine. I rested my forehead against his as we both panted, taking in air.

"It's okay. I get it. We have all the time in the world," I reminded him. "I'm not going away. Well, eventually you and Ryan and the team will catch the bad guy and I'll be in my own place. Though it won't be that apartment, I can tell you that much right now."

"Simone," he cut me off.

"What?"

"Shut up and kiss me," he teased and took my mouth in another blistering kiss.

"Howdy, kids," Ryan's voice came from the doorway behind us.

We both turned our heads and saw the man grinning, arms crossed, the fingers of one of his hands curled around the neck of a beer bottle.

"Your timing is impeccable...as always," Jonah grumbled.

"Just wanted you to know that you're needed for the meet up tomorrow morning at eight."

He frowned. "Can you go hang out with your sister Sonia tomorrow?"

I scrunched up my nose. "My sister's workplace is really boring. Can you drop me off instead at Perfect Petal? I'm supposed to be arranging flowers and helping out. I can tell Auntie Delores that I can't leave the shop or be alone for any reason. She'll be cool with it. Her and my mom have been best friends since the dawn of time so I'm certain she's already up to date on what's going on."

"We can put a patrol outside the area too," Ryan offered.

I clapped my hands together lightly. "Yay!"

Jonah sighed and got up from our clinch. "You need to get some sleep."

"I would sleep better if I had a big hunky FBI agent cuddled up next to me." I laid out the bait.

"And that's my cue," Ryan chuckled and walked away leaving us to ourselves.

"I don't think that's a good idea…"

"No, it's a great one!" I snuggled up against his warm, tall body.

One of his hands automatically soothed down my back and went straight for my ass, pressing me up against a very sizeable erection.

I moaned.

"Believe me when I say I want to. Lord knows I want to, but it's not smart. You need time. I need a little of my own, after all I shared tonight. The first time we share a bed, Simone, I do not want the ghost of my ex in it."

That had me pouting because he was right.

"Fine, be logical, but I'm stealing one of your T-shirts, and you're tucking me in." I grinned.

"Yes, to the T-shirt. Fuck no to the tucking in. If I see you laid out in my bed, I won't have the fortitude to do the right thing."

"And what about tomorrow? Will tomorrow be enough processing time to get over the doom and gloom and bitch-face?" I tucked myself against his body and ran my hands down his frame to cup his hard ass making my intentions one hundred percent clear.

His lips twitched. "Maybe."

I smiled wide. "I love your maybe's."

"Mmm." He kissed me for a long time until it started to get heated. Then he pulled away, physically turned me toward the house and smacked my ass. Hard. "Get to gettin', woman, before I lose all control and do the exact opposite of what I promised I'd do."

"Hey, you're not going to get any help in that department. I want the naked time with my new hot FBI guy."

"Simone," he grumbled.

"All right, all right. I'm moving. Spoilsport."

He chuckled as we went back into the house. He brought me into his room where he pulled open his drawers and pulled out a T-shirt that said Quantico on it. I promptly pulled off my shirt so I stood in only my bra and jeans and smirked. He turned around gritting his teeth, pulling out a pair of plaid pajama bottoms and white T-shirt.

Win for me.

When he was done, I was already in only his shirt and slipped back the covers.

"You sure you don't want to join me? There's plenty of room in this monster-sized bed."

He stood stock still and breathed through his nose, one of his hands in a fist, the other clenched around his change of clothes.

"Suit yourself." I shrugged and made a big deal about bending over to fluff the pillows so he'd get a nice shot of my hipster panties that were cut high at the ass to show a little cheek.

I didn't win him joining me in the bed like I hoped, but he did tuck me in and lay a hot kiss that had me squirming and reaching for him before he pulled away, kissed my forehead, and said, "Sweet Dreams."

I fell asleep thinking about Jonah wearing only his PJ bottoms and how I planned to enjoy removing them from his gorgeous body in the near future. Stupid Helen screwed up huge, but I'd be there for my sullen FBI guy, and it would be me he'd rush home to in order to bury his burden in something sweet one day.

The connection I felt to Jonah Fontaine was thrilling and exciting. I wanted to know everything there was to know about him. I wanted to share all my highs and lows, and the craziness that was my family by choice. I wanted to sit and eat Italian meals with his parents and maybe even one day work at the family business. This was just the start of us but what he gave me tonight about the worst experience of his life, proved that we were heading somewhere important. I felt deep in my bones that we were meant to meet that night. He was chosen to be my savior and I wondered if there was more to it.

Fate.

Destiny.

Soulmates.

I didn't know for sure, but I knew there was a lot I'd do and risk, in order to one day be the woman that was having sweet dreams sleeping side by side with Jonah.

Chapter
NINE

THE NEXT MORNING, I WOKE TO THE SOUND OF INCESSANT buzzing. Without opening my eyes, I reached my arm out and patted around on the end table until I found the culprit. Blindly, I fumbled through unplugging the offender and brought it to my chest as I slipped back into dreamland. It worked for all of a minute before the damn phone buzzed against my sternum and I groaned, opened my scratchy eyes, and looked blearily at the thing.

My fucking sisters.

All of them texting me as if it were their job. Apparently, you don't forget to check in with them for a full day when a madman is after you.

I sighed, pushed up to leaning against the headboard, and started to go through the list. Sonia of course was first. As I scanned the list of unread messages I saw that she had her BFF and right hand man Quinn on the task too as there were several from him as well. I opened Sonia's first.

Where are you?

Why haven't you checked in?

This is so like you.

You're scaring me, Simone.

Please call me.

Simone? I'm activating the tree.

Oh shit. The tree. Fuck my life. That's why my phone was blowing up. Next in the string of a bazillion texts was Quinn.

Your sister is in a snit. You better call her.

Your sister is unbearable not knowing where you are.

Dammit Simone, I can't deal with her tears.

You are so off my chocolate almond butter clusters list for Xmas for this.

Call your fucking sister woman.

Then Blessing's texts.

I know you're blowing off your sisters because of hunky Agent Fontaine but seriously, you need to check in with your sisters. Sonia has lost her shit. I blame you. Love your face bitch.

Next was Addison.

I hope the reason you haven't checked in is because you're too busy drowning your sorrow in Jonah. Can you send out a quick "I'm alive" text. Sonia's driving us bonkers. Love you.

Then Liliana and her sweet self.

You've got us worried. Please call or text. Te quiero mucho.

I got a bunch of the same from Genesis and Charlie. No Tabby of course, because she was MIA, which was really starting to piss me off. I wondered if I could talk to Jonah about my concerns and we could do a drive by or something.

There was only a single voicemail. I clicked on it and pressed the phone to my ear.

"Hello, my darling girl, I'm sure you're just fine spending the day with Agents Fontaine and Russell, but can you please call your Mama and check in. I'm very concerned that I haven't heard from you all day. I know you're processing all that happened, but you have us all worried. I love you, sweetheart, and I very much look forward to hearing from you soon."

Oh shit. My eyes teared up as I pressed the button to call Mama Kerri.

"I'm so glad you called." Her tone was filled with relief and instantly I felt like a heel.

"Mama, I'm sorry I didn't call. Time got away from me and…"

"I understand. You've had a lot happening. Your sister Sonia however is not taking your independence well, as ever." She laughed and it sounded like a pretty melody, floating along my frayed nerves and soothing them.

"I'll text everyone next. I can't deal with her brand of crazy this morning. It's too early."

"For you I'm sure it is. What're your plans for the day?" Her warm voice sounded in my ears and it soothed my shaky nerves.

"I want to go to Auntie Delores's and work. I need to make some money. Especially now that I won't ever be going back to my apartment. I'll have to start all over, but I do have some great news!"

"Oh? Do tell." I heard the sound of her moving around her kitchen, then pouring what I assumed was tea from the kettle into her cup.

"Well, yesterday Jonah and I spent the day at Navy Pier. Just letting go, you know?"

"I do. And can understand the need to do something upbeat and positive, especially during a time like this."

I nodded in agreement even though she couldn't see me. "Then after, he took me to his parents' house for dinner."

"Really?" Her words rose in surprise. "That's very forward of him."

"Right! And a big fat whopping step toward *more*, in my opinion."

"It is, baby. Sounds like you had a good time meeting his folks?"

"They're awesome. His mom is little and Italian and makes the best spaghetti and meatballs and his dad fixes up classic cars. He's working on a 1969 Charger right now that would knock your socks off, Mama. It's bad ass."

"Don't say ass, darling. It's not becoming."

"Sorry. Anyway, that's still not the best part."

She chuckled. "Well get to it, my lovely. I'm not getting any younger."

That had me laughing and getting out of bed to hit the restroom.

While I peed, I told Mama about the job opportunity.

"Chicklet, that is good news. Will you have time to finish the course before the woman leaves?"

I finished my business and then held the phone to my ear so I could wash my hands.

"Honestly, yeah. My last course is online and at my own pace. Of course, my laptop was in my bedroom at the apartment." I shivered where I stood. "I'm gonna have to get a new one now."

"Honey, that's not true. Yours can be picked up by one of us if you don't want to go back there. It's horrible what happened to Katrina but that wasn't your fault. She was in the wrong place at the wrong time. Remember, we don't question why we were spared. We send up our thanks to the Universe and God and we go forward with grace and gratitude."

"I know, Mama. It just hurts that a good woman was killed for no other reason than to taunt me and the authorities."

"You didn't court a madman's attention. You were also in the wrong place at the wrong time when he got into your car. Then Jonah was in the right place at the right time in order to protect you. It's unfortunate and heartbreaking the same did not happen for your friend, dear, but again, you share no burden for a sick man's transgressions. Do you understand what I'm telling you, sweet pea?"

"Yeah. It still hurts."

"I know, baby, and it will for a while. These things are hard to shake because they are devastating to all involved. Just know that you will move on with grace and gratitude like I've taught all my girls. Now I want you to breathe with me. Let's set ourselves up for the day."

I grinned and closed my eyes.

"In for four full breaths and hold at the top…" She breathed in and I followed along. Her voice was tight when she said, "Now let it all go for four counts…three, two, one. And again."

We did five full rounds of breathing and my entire body felt electric and alive, the fear and frustration that was clawing at my insides dissipated and finally disappeared on the last breath.

"I love you, Mama."

"And I love you, my darling. Please contact your sisters. I'll bring Rory to the shop today and visit. That will help keep your state of mind in a good place. Children make everything in the world seem better and less about you, and more about them."

Seeing my gorgeous niece would definitely fix the little 'tude I'd woken up with. "Would love that, Mama. See you later. And thanks."

"Anytime. That's what I'm here for. My girls."

I smiled and hung up the phone, bouncing through the room and into the hallway. Jonah was just coming out of the hall bathroom, one of his hands scratching at his bare chest.

My mouth watered and I stared openly at his gorgeous body. Broad shoulders that tapered into a V-shape at his rib-cage. Boxed abdominals, six of them. Who had a real six pack these days? I mean, come on. It was insane. He had a smattering of dark hair across his pecs and down his abs heading to his crotch. His pants hung loosely off his hip bones so I could clearly see those crazy sexy indents that made smart girls stupid. Me included. My nipples hardened at the sight and my body warmed.

His hair was spiked up and all over the place as though he'd tossed and turned from side to side and had been run-ning his fingers through it. His gaze slid to my bare legs and up my body. I was still wearing just his shirt and at seeing him I squeezed my legs together and bit my lip.

Something in him and me both snapped but he was faster. He stormed to me, cupped the back of my head as I lifted up on my toes, wrapped my arms around him, and took his brutal kiss. He grunted, turned me to the side, and caged me against the wall. His mouth drank deep from mine. One of his hands slid down my body, under his shirt, and straight into my panties to cup my bare ass. He ground his stiff length against my center and I mewled in delight. His mouth left mine but wasn't gone for long when he ran his tongue along the length of my neck. I tipped my head to the side so he'd have better access and hiked a leg so I could get more action rubbing against my happy place.

We were going for it. Lost to the passion between us. He yanked my shirt off and tossed it somewhere, I don't know where. Then he curled a hand around my breast, lifted it up to his mouth, and sucked. Hard. I moaned deep and clenched around him. Arousal spearing through my body at an alarming rate. I wanted him. Inside me. Now.

"Baby...please," I begged.

At this he took my mouth, palmed my ass, and lifted me until my legs were off the floor and wrapped around his waist. I could tell by the grunt of pain it cost him but he wasn't letting it get him down or stop this train from barreling to its most awesome destination.

Lost to each other, we didn't notice Ryan storming around the corner until he blurted, "Oh, shit. Fucking hell."

Immediately Jonah turned me around so all Ryan would see was his bare back. I smiled like a loon and waved at him.

"Dude, I'm sorry. You have no idea how sorry I am, but we have to go. Simone's car was found. And shit, brother. There's another woman's body in it."

I frowned and let my head fall to Jonah's shoulder. He walked me into his room and kicked the door shut. I unhooked my legs and he let me slide down him until my feet touched the floor.

"To be continued," I whispered and looked into his stony face, hopeful yet sad about why we were interrupted.

"Yeah." His voice was thick as molasses but not nearly as sweet.

I cupped his cheeks. "I'm sorry, baby."

He swallowed and I watched his Adam's apple bob

enticingly, wanting so badly to kiss it and other things, but knowing he had to go.

"Gonna hit the shower in the hall. You shower here. Be quick, yeah?"

"Fast as lightning. Promise."

He dipped forward and took my mouth in a slow kiss that had a tiny touch of tongues. "We'll have our time."

"Yeah." I let my head fall forward. "Go shower. I'll be quick."

"Thanks, baby."

I nodded and let him peck me on the lips once more before he grabbed some clothes from his dresser. I rummaged through my suitcases for something easy to work at the shop in. When you worked in flowers and thorns, you made sure to cover the skin that might get punctured. I grabbed an old pair of jeans and a tank and my gold oval locket that had a picture of my biological parents in it. Mama Kerri gave me and Sonia each a locket on the one-year anniversary of living with her. Said she wanted our parents to always be with us, and while they weren't, she would be. Apparently she'd found pictures of them online because we had absolutely nothing left from the house fire.

I took the fastest shower, leaving my hair wet and tossing my small makeup bag into my big fringed purse once I hit the kitchen.

"You gonna dry your hair?" Jonah asked while finishing up making coffee. He wore black slacks and a white button-up shirt. A deep navy-blue tie with black and white geometric patterns was hanging undone around his neck. His shirt was open at the collar showing a tasty morsel of skin that I wanted to explore. His hair was wet and combed back.

I shook my head. "Nah, it will air dry quick."

He nodded and handed me a bagel with cream cheese wrapped in a napkin and a to-go coffee cup.

"Let's hit it. Ryan already headed out. I'm taking you to the flower shop but won't leave until a patrol unit shows."

"You really don't have to do that. There are tons of people in the shop working. I'll be safe."

He shook his head. "Can't be too careful. This guy is unpredictable and he's escalating. Which is usually when they make mistakes. He's got a hard-on for you and I don't want you unattended."

I scrunched up my nose and made a face at his "hard on" comment. "You just ruined the awesome of the hard on I did have on me earlier. One I really wanted." I pouted. "Now you're gonna have to work me up all over again."

He chuckled and shook his head. "Come on, sweet girl. Let's get you to work."

When we arrived at Perfect Petal a patrol officer was already waiting. Jonah saw me inside, looked around shrewdly, and nodded before briefly pecking me on the lips and giving me a strong edict to stay inside at all times. No doing delivery runs or going out to get lunch. I confirmed we'd order lunch in and I'd be too busy working and playing with my niece later on to worry about getting out and about.

Once I updated my Auntie Delores about the coming and goings and texted all of my crazy sisters, I set about getting to work. I was a machine. Needing the mindless work to allow my brain to think about all that had happened.

A few short days ago I was shot, saved by a hot FBI guy, and fell into a deep crush on said hot guy. Then my apartment was ransacked by the same crazy man who would have killed me had Jonah not saved me. I'd lost a friend, not a best friend, not even a super close one, more of a good acquaintance, but I liked Katrina. She was cool and so nice. She didn't deserve to be caught up in this. Then again none of the women he hurt, including myself, deserved anything this psychopath was doling out.

Then I had the most amazing day with Jonah, met his parents, and met his nasty ex-wife, which turned out to be a blessing in disguise because it gave my guy the opportunity to open up about her. Finding out how she'd ruined their marriage was a blow. It would have been for anyone. Learning that your wife betrayed you with your brother would be hard enough, but seeing it in living color had to be like watching a tornado shred through your childhood home. And I could tell from how repeating the story gutted him that the wound was still sore. Though I truly believed him sharing it with me, offloading that hurt onto someone else's shoulders, helped take some of the weight off him.

And now there was another body.

In my freakin' car.

I shook my head and clipped some big fat pink Gerbera daisies and plunked them into the waiting vase. The person who ordered them had chosen a sunshine yellow glass vase that would look amazing with a mix of bright pinks, whites, yellows, neon green, and some pops of purple. It was a birthday order and I loved doing the happy designs. Made me smile with all the joyful colors.

Just as I wrapped a bright green satin bow around the

yellow vase, finishing off the order, a pitter patter of tiny, fast feet came running into the big, open design space in the back.

"Auntie!" Rory screeched as she entered the back room.

I crouched down and opened my arms. She slammed right into me and I lifted her up and spun around in a circle making her squeal with glee. I kissed her all over her pretty face and neck until she started kicking her little feet. Those suckers were like mini punches. She'd make a good soccer player one day.

I tucked her to my hip and focused on her see-through, amber-colored eyes. Genesis wasn't one to boast or brag, especially since she worked her butt off in school and college to become a social worker but her child was the most beautiful I'd ever seen. Her African-American, Korean, and Caucasian genetics made my niece stunning. Genesis was constantly getting stopped by people in stores to admire Rory. And on top of it all, the little girl was the most social creature ever. Loved everyone and everything.

"How's my big girl doing? You ready to help Auntie make flowers?"

"Yes!" She clapped her hands.

"Where's my little doll-face?" Mama Kerri's voice echoed through the room as she entered. She placed her hands on her hips. "I see you found Auntie Simone." She came over to us both and kissed me on the temple than grabbed Rory's chubby little hand and kissed the inside of her palm until she laughed. "You got her? I'm going to help Delores with some customers up front. They've got the two front desk clerks out doing deliveries."

"Of course." I bounced my girl. "We've got this."

"Yay!" Rory clapped again, her joy clear on her face. I used a towel to shove aside any dangerous clippings that she might get into then set her on the table. She got up onto her knees and reached for a white daisy. "Pwetty."

"It is, baby. It's a daisy."

She repeated the word. I grabbed the next vase, this one a short, squat, fat, dark green glass. I took the daisy and clipped half of the stem off. "Now put it in the vase like I taught you."

Rory placed it in the center. For a while I clipped flowers and greens and handed them to her to place into the vase. Every time she put one in, she'd look at it and repeat, "Pwetty." To her it was a game and I was on board for it. Hearing her joy and laughter and seeing her cute toddler smiles was filling up my cup to full. Soaking my soul in pure innocence. Exactly what I needed.

Mama Kerri entered and leaned against the worktable, watching Rory place the flowers. They were haphazardly put in, but I could move them around just so and it would be perfect.

"She balance you out?" she asked knowingly.

"Filled me right up to full with love and light." I smiled wide.

"Excellent."

"You didn't have to come today, you know." I clipped another flower and handed it to Rory.

"I do know. I also know that one of my youngest girls is going through something tough to manage. Which means it's time for her mama and sisters to rally around her and show her the way of sisterhood and family, in order to keep her head above water."

I hooked my mother around the shoulders and pressed my face against her neck, feeling her pulse thump against my face. Her flowery scent mixed with all the others in the room, but I could still feel her energy wrapping around me in a blanket of comfort.

"Thanks for coming by today," I whispered against her neck.

"It's my pleasure to check in on my girls. No thanks needed. I'm glad you got some time with your niece. Sometimes seeing life lived through the eyes of a child can heal many hurts. I wish more people could find that peace."

"Yeah, me too. Now check out what Rory did, Grandma!" I pointed to the wonky flower display. Rory put her arms out exactly like I did, copying me, her little tongue poking out of the side of her mouth.

"See Gam-Ma, pwetty!" Rory exclaimed happily.

Mama made a big deal oohing and aww-ing over the bouquet.

Which is also when I heard a booming voice rumble, "Where is Simone?" from somewhere in the front of the shop. I knew it was Jonah even though I'd never heard that frightening tone from him.

Mama and I looked at one another worriedly and beat feet to the front.

The second his haunted gaze hit mine, I ran to him. He wrapped me in his arms and pressed his face to my neck. His entire body trembled, gooseflesh appearing on his forearms. I could see Ryan standing outside pacing back and forth, his cellphone plastered to his ear, an angry expression marring his gorgeous features.

I reached for Jonah's hand and turned, then dragged him

to the back room so we could have some privacy. When we got to the back, he immediately came into my arms once more. I held him close while he burrowed into me. Jonah was becoming more affectionate with each day we spent together, but didn't seem to be a toucher naturally. I, however, was. Since we met, I'd been finding ways to be close.

This was different.

Wrong, different.

Unbearable pain oozed from every single one of his pores as he shook.

I reached for his face and he lifted his head.

There was only one word I could come up with for the scorn and desperation coating the features of Jonah's handsome face.

Ravaged.

Something broke my man today. No, *shattered* him.

Staring into his broken, beautiful face, I had trouble getting the words out, fear replacing all the light and happiness I'd soaked up from Rory. "What happened?"

For a long time he just stared at me as though he were cataloguing the details of my face. Then his eyes filled with tears and they fell in tandem.

"He got to her." The words came out sounding as though his throat had been scraped by sandpaper.

"Who, baby? You're scaring me," I choked out, tears filling my own eyes at seeing the raw, gut-wrenching pain spilling from his own.

"Helen." The name was said in a gritty tone filled to the brim with tortured emotion.

"Helen, your ex? Who got her, honey?" I kept my hands to his cheeks and his gaze on mine.

"The Strangler." He closed his eyes and more tears spilled down his cheeks, wetting my palms.

I gasped as what he said dawned on me.

His next statement confirmed it.

"He killed my ex-wife and left her dead, desecrated, naked body for me to find in your car."

Instantly I reached out and wrapped my arms around him holding him so close you couldn't have slipped even a piece of paper between us. I tightened my grip wanting him to feel me and my strength straight through to his bones.

"Hold on to me, baby. Just hold on to me. And breathe. Hold on and breathe."

Chapter
TEN

"I WON'T LET HIM HAVE YOU."

This was the first thing he'd said since I led him out and into Ryan's SUV, got him home, and wrapped around me, fully clothed and in his bed, covers and all. Though I did remove our shoes. Ryan had come in twice. Once to bring Jonah a full glass of whiskey, setting it on the nightstand. He hadn't touched it. He popped in again to see if I wanted him to order food. I told him pizza because everyone loves pizza. It was one of those foods that's practically impossible to hate, unless you were one of those people that freaked out if there was pineapple on your pizza. I've found that particular ingredient has caused some serious wars between friends, and on social media. Me, I didn't care one way or the other. My mom liked broccoli on pizza. That item I could argue was far stranger than pineapple, but what did I know. I liked most things, even broccoli and, yes, pineapple, on my pizza.

I ran my fingers through his hair over and over in the same pattern, hoping to soothe and comfort him.

"He's not going to get to me," I murmured at the crown of his head.

Jonah was tucked to my side, my right hand in his hair, the other across his chest. He was tracing the lines of my fingers one at a time then up my forearm and back down again.

"I'm off the case." He let out a long breath, his body shuddering with the exhalation.

"Probably for the best. You need to grieve."

"This is personal now. And it gets worse. What he etched across her chest." He shook his head and sat up abruptly, reached for the whiskey, and downed at least half in one drink. He wiped the wet from his mouth with the back of his hand.

"Tell me," I urged.

He shook his head. "It's bad, baby. You don't need that in your head."

I reached for his hand and squeezed. "You don't either, but my guy is beyond hurting. I need to know everything in order to help you get through it. We need to get past this together."

He gritted his teeth and scowled so fiercely I almost didn't recognize him. "He's either following us and saw the fight we had outside my parents' house last night, or he looked me up and found out about my ex-wife and our divorce through the county recorder's office. Hell, an online search these days can bring up half the details of someone's life." He sucked back more whiskey.

"Okay, so what else is there that you aren't telling me? Did he, um, did he violate her?" My words were spoken so low I could barely process them myself.

"Not as far as we can tell even though her body was naked. We'll have to see what the autopsy reveals. It was obvious she was strangled." His head fell forward, his chin to his chest, shoulders drooping. He looked exhausted, as though the last ten years of his life had been lived in a single day.

"What was the message?"

His voice shook when he said, *"You're Welcome."*

I gasped and covered my shock with my hand over my mouth. "No. Jonah do not take this on. You did not ask for this. Just like I did not ask for Katrina to be killed in my apartment or any of those other women."

"It was a gift." He said it as though the words seared his very soul. "To *me*. Killing my bitch of an ex-wife and displaying her in my new girlfriend's car like a fucking trophy."

I was so *never* touching that car again.

I placed both of my hands on his shoulders. "Look at me, Jonah."

He ignored me.

"Look at me, honey. Please."

Either the please or the honey got him to look up.

"You had nothing to do with his decision to kill Helen. Did you want her dead?"

His entire face turned an angry red. "Fuck no! I wanted her to hurt like I did when she obliterated our marriage by sleeping with my fucking brother, but I didn't want her dead." He stood up, swung his arm back, and threw the whiskey glass against the brick wall opposite his bed. It smashed on impact, glass shards going all over the wood floor, golden-colored liquid dripping down the wall.

"Fuck!" He roared, his hands going into his hair and tugging on the roots. "He killed Helen! He wrapped his hands around her neck and snuffed the life right out of her. The first woman I ever loved. A woman I planned on raising children with, growing old with. And now he wants to do the same to you. He will not stop until he's got you. And he'll start by picking off other people we love. No one is safe. Not my parents, your sisters or your mom. No one."

I knee-walked across the bed until I could reach him. Then I tugged his shoulders until he slumped back in a sitting position, his elbows to his knees, his head in his hands.

I plastered myself against his back, wrapping my arms around him the best I could. When I got my hands in front of him, he grabbed them and kissed them repeatedly before pressing them to his heart.

"What do you need me to do?"

"I don't know. Just don't leave me. You're not to be out of my sight until this man goes down. Understand?"

I nodded against his neck. "What do we need to do to keep our families safe?"

"Get them the hell out of town. Maybe out of the country."

"Sonia won't go. She can't and I'm sure the media storm is going to hit big time when they find out that the Senator's ties to this serial killer just got more complex."

He sighed as the door to his room opened and Ryan held it open.

"Senator Wright is here with her entourage in the living room. The media are crawling all over the front of the house and I need to get on this. Brother, I want to be here for you, but you need me working this, for *you*." He glanced at the floor and noticed the mess. "I'll pour you another glass before I go." He moved to leave.

"Ryan?" Jonah called out, his voice hoarse.

"Yeah?"

"Find this motherfucker."

Ryan's face twisted into one of extreme confidence and true grit. He lifted his chin. "I'll do my best."

"I know you will. And thank you." He reached his hand out.

Ryan took hold, yanked Jonah up, and clapped him on the back in a brotherly man hug. "Take care of our boy, eh?" he said to me.

"Absolutely."

Jonah reached for me and I stood up and he held my hand as I walked to the other side of the bed where the glass hadn't spread and put on my mother's slippers. "I'll clean this up after we deal with Sonia and her team."

He held my hand and led me into the living room where we only found her and Quinn. Her team must have been outside.

My sister stood, her entire face pale, her red lips and sky-blue eyes looking so bright against her skin. "Jonah, I'm...I...I'm sorry for your loss."

He nodded. "Thank you."

I moved over to my sister and she immediately pulled me into an embrace. Her hold was tight, and I could feel her shaking as she tried to get her emotions under control. She cupped one of my cheeks. "You okay, Sis?"

"Yeah."

"I was so worried about you and then the media started reporting on the latest victim and tied it to Jonah and your car and I..." She didn't finish just pulled me into her arms again.

"I'm okay, Sonia. It will be okay. Ryan is going to kick some ass and take some names and find this guy. I have to believe that." She nodded against my shoulder but didn't let me go.

Sonia pulled her face back and we stood nose to nose. "You're everything to me, Simone. You know that, right? I cannot lose you. I simply can't."

That time I cupped both of her cheeks. "Look into my face. I'm right here. Alive. Perfectly fine. I mean, I'm not fine-fine, but I'm alive. And I have faith that the FBI will get their man. They have to."

"SoSo, the press outside want a comment." Quinn shuffled toward our huddle. He was impeccably dressed in a black bespoke suit, a gray dress shirt, and a shimmery green tie. His dark red hair was slicked up and coiffed perfectly to the side and out of his face. Quinn McCafferty was one hundred percent Irish from the tip of his toes to the top of his red hair and emerald green eyes.

"They can want all they want. My sister's boyfriend's ex-wife was just brutally murdered and placed naked in my sister's car. The same car he planned to strangle and kill my sister in, Quinn. The press can take a flying leap off a building for all I care right now."

"Okay, so…" He typed into a handheld mini-iPad or some type of electronic device. "Senator Wright is not currently giving any comments on the horrible events that happened today or led up to today's attack on Agent Fontaine's ex-wife or her sister Simone. She requests the media give her and her extended family the time to process and grieve. Got it." Quinn spoke succinctly and left the room and out the front door.

I could hear the roar of the media from all the way in here.

"He's worth his weight in gold, SoSo."

She gave me a small smile. "I know. I was lost without him while he was on vacation with his husband the last couple weeks."

Quinn was married to Niko Chinn-McCafferty who is a

mixed martial arts fighter and instructor. When I first met Niko, I swooned big time. Well, for all of ten minutes until I found out he was gay and dating Quinn. Then he just became Quinn's hot MMA man.

"I can imagine." I grinned knowing that Sonia did not do well without Quinn. He balanced her out in the workplace the way I hoped a husband would in her personal life.

While we were speaking, I could see Jonah head through the hallway and then come back a few minutes later with a dustpan filled with glass.

"Babe, I was going to do that."

"My outburst. My mess to clean up. Sonia, would you like a drink?"

Her eyebrows rose and she gestured to the new glass that Ryan had poured before he left. It was sitting on the edge of the bar next to a pizza box none of us had touched. "That whiskey?"

"Yeah."

"I'll take it neat."

He grinned. "Woman after my own heart," he teased.

"Hey!" I fired back. "I resent that." I pursed my lips and put my hands to my hips. "I'll take a glass too, please, and thank you very much!"

Instead of making two new glasses, Jonah grabbed the one on the counter and brought it straight to me. "First, I take care of my sweet girl. Then I'll pour her sister a drink, yeah?"

I pouted. "Thank you. Except I should be making you a drink not the other way around."

"How you figure?" He kissed me quick and all too brief, then left to go back and make himself and Sonia a drink.

"Because I should be taking care of you in your time of need. And besides, I'm a bartender. I'm an expert at slinging drinks."

"Which is why you'll never, not ever, pour yourself one in my presence, Simone. You deserve to be served a drink now and again."

"He always like this?" Sonia asked.

"Like what?" I frowned, not getting where she was going with her question.

"A gentleman?"

I grinned and watched while he made my sister and himself a drink. "Yeah." I said it with the awe I felt every minute in his presence.

"You're gone for him. I've never seen you like this with a man before. All swoony, shy, and blushing. Oh my God. You *are* blushing right now. My sister who could walk right into a sex shop and ask for the toy that gives the absolute best orgasms is bashful with her hunky boyfriend."

I nudged her shoulders and then winced when my wound smarted. "We haven't actually said those words. So, shut up."

"What words? Boyfriend?"

I gave her big eyes as he chuckled and handed her a glass. He wrapped his arm around me and kissed my temple. "You saying I'm not your boyfriend?"

"Just last night we told your parents that we were *seeing each* other. That's a big jump…from seeing one another to having an official title such as boyfriend and girlfriend."

"That was last night. Today is a new day," he stated simply.

"Well I don't think you should be deciding anything so life affirming when you're dealing with Helen's loss."

That had him closing his eyes as if he'd had a good fifteen minutes without thinking directly of what happened to his ex and the manner in which she died, and then I ruined it.

"I'm sorry. That was insensitive."

He shook his head. "No, it was the truth. And I'm beginning to find that the truth is all I ever want to hear from you. Don't try and hide behind things or tell me half-truths. I like you and your honesty exactly the way you are."

"He's a keeper, Simone. Lock him down and throw away the key. Marry the man and have his babies." Sonia tossed back the rest of her drink in one go.

Quinn entered the front door where the screaming media kept going even after he'd given my sister's statement. I could see two armed bodyguards standing by the front door on the outside before he closed it, so I knew we were safe. Not to mention as long as Jonah was around, I didn't feel fear. Even though I knew I needed to be paying attention to my surroundings at all times. Jonah just made me feel safe.

"Those guys are vultures, praying on the wounded and hoping to get fed. Sweet baby Jesus. You'd think they'd learn by now." Quinn scowled.

Sonia clapped her hands and rubbed them together. "I'm assuming we need to discuss how we're going to keep my sister safe. Sonia sat down on the couch and focused her attention on Jonah.

The three of us followed suit. Me sitting right next to Jonah, our thighs touching. Quinn perched himself on the arm of the couch Sonia was sitting on, his focus on the electronic device in his hands, though I knew he was paying attention. Very few things happened around Sonia that Quinn didn't know about. He took his job and my sister very seriously. She was not only his best friend but the sister he never had. Like us, he'd been a foster child and went to our same high school when they met. Though his experience in the system was nothing like ours. One horrible foster home after another. Mistreated, beaten, bullied for being openly gay. You name it, the guy suffered it. His and Sonia's bond was deep. The two didn't do much without the other. Which had been nice for me growing up because it gave me a break from my overbearing sister half the time.

"Actually, SoSo, Jonah believes that none of us are safe. He went after Helen, making things personal. If he doesn't get what he wants, which I'm guessing is me dead so he can move on, he'll go after our families. That means you and the girls are not safe. Neither is Mom nor any member of Jonah's family."

"Is that true?" She squinted at Jonah.

"Yeah. He's escalated and gone off his normal routine by killing Katrina. He killed Helen to prove he could and to get my attention. Well, he has it all right. Except my boss took me off the case indefinitely. Way too much conflict of interest with my connection to Helen and he isn't even aware of my growing relationship with Simone, since Ryan and I have kept that under wraps the past few days."

"You guys could move in with Sonia and of course Niko and I will gladly welcome any of the Kerrighan sisters. We could host four of them in our home if they shared a bed. We have two spare rooms. Our building is completely safe and protected. Under tight security at all times," Quinn offered. And yes, they lived in the same building, with apartments that were across the hall from one another like that TV show, *Will and Grace*. Completely codependent.

"We'll be okay here. Security system and two FBI agents. I still need to call my parents and discuss what happened see about having them take an unplanned vacation or visit to some family out of state. Check in on Helen's folks. It's a good idea for the two of you to have the sisters hole up in your building if possible."

"There's actually a fully furnished apartment in the building as well. One of my major campaign donors owns it. I haven't met the benefactor or owner but I'm sure if we contacted them, we could either secure it free of charge or for a small fee."

"I'll look into it now." Quinn tapped on his device.

Jonah nodded. "Good. Having your family safe during all of this will help a great deal."

"Done," Sonia said. "What else?"

As he was about to answer, we were disturbed by a pounding on the front door. Quinn pressed on his ear where he had a listening device connected to the guards outside. He looked at Jonah. "Someone claiming to be your brother, Luca Fontaine, is demanding access to you."

"Fuck." Jonah growled low under his breath. "Let him in. And that's only because I don't want a bigger media shit storm if they find out his connection to Helen, outside of being her brother-in-law for seven years."

Sonia's eyebrow rose in question, but I shook my head and whispered, "Don't ask."

A tall, well-built man in a pair of dark wash jeans that fitted his thick thighs perfectly and a polo that said "A+ Construction" embroidered over the heart entered. He had black hair like Loretta's, and light blue eyes like Marco. His facial features were a mix of his parents, just like Jonah. He was absolutely gorgeous but at least one notch down from Jonah in my opinion. I notched him lower on the hotness scale for his personality sucking rocks due to betraying his brother's trust.

"Jonah, I can't believe it…" He swiftly crossed the entryway and headed for my guy. Jonah stood up and held his hand out in a stop gesture. Luca stopped in his tracks, tears filling his eyes. "Brother, we need to be together through this."

"No, we don't."

"It was over a year ago, man. Hell, it was over before it began. A drunken, foolish mistake. How long are you going to punish me…punish Mom and Dad, forcing them to see their sons separately? We're family. *Brothers*," he rasped.

"Brothers don't fuck each other's wives," Jonah barked with such malice his body quaked. I stood up and gripped his biceps from behind and pressed my body close to his.

"Breathe, baby," I reminded him, concerned at his level of anger. His body and mind were taking on far too much and soon he was going to crash, hard.

He inhaled, his nostrils flaring, and clenched his jaw.

Luca looked at me then at Sonia and Quinn. "Uh, why is the Senator in your house?"

I nodded my head toward Sonia. "My sister."

"And you are?" Luca asked.

"None of your fucking business. You've come, you saw I was alive, now go."

"Jonah, I came for you. To be here for you. Family is everything to me."

He huffed. "You should have thought of that over a year ago when you fucked my wife and ended my marriage."

"Your marriage was toast long before I ever made the worst mistake of my life lying with her. She seduced me. I went there to see you. To confide in my brother over my breakup with Tiffany. You were gone. *Again.* Like always. We drank too much. Way too much. That's my cross to bear. My disease. I'm an alcoholic. That was my rock fucking bottom. I'd never have done that if I was in my right mind, Jonah, you have to know that. I'm in a program now. I haven't even had a sip of liquor since. Over a year now. I take full responsibility for my part in losing my mind in feeding my disease." He pointed to his chest as his face turned red. "I want my brother back. I want my family back."

Tears hit my eyes at the level of sincerity poured in every single word and the disgust he so obviously had in himself over what he did.

Jonah didn't speak but Luca kept on sharing. He looked at me, then at Sonia and Quinn. "I'm an alcoholic. I screwed up my life. Almost lost my business with my father, I did lose the woman I loved for three years and planned to marry over it, and I fucked my brother's wife, losing him too." He laid it all out in the open for all of us to hear.

I tried to move around Jonah and go to Luca. It was in my nature to help someone in need and he clearly was destroyed over what he did, even a year later.

Jonah locked me to his side.

"What is it going to take, Jonah? I've apologized over and over. I've sought help. I lost the only woman I ever loved. I haven't had my birthday or holidays with my family in a year. And now Helen's dead. I need to make amends, brother. I need you in my life. I love you. I want to be here for you, during this. What more do you need?" His shoulders sagged and I was surprised he didn't fall to his knees and beg for his brother's forgiveness.

"Time. I need more time," Jonah answered flatly. "Especially now."

Luca licked his lips, sniffed, and nodded. "You shouldn't be dealing with this alone."

"I'm not. I've got Simone. And Ryan."

"Ryan. Your brother by choice." He let out a harsh breath. "Got it. He's perfect, and I'm the piece of shit alcoholic. I get it. I bought that. Deserve it even."

"Yeah, you do," Jonah added.

Luca continued. "It doesn't change how much it hurts, brother." He put his hand in his back pocket, opened his wallet, and pulled out a business card. He looked at me and held it up between two fingers. "Please call me if either of you needs anything. And I mean anything." He set the card down on the table in front of us. "Simone, I wish we were meeting under better circumstances. I can see by the way he's holding onto you and shielding you from me, how much you mean to him. One day I hope to get to know you too."

Jonah's arms tightened on me. I stayed right where I was, not moving an inch or reaching out my hand to shake his. Especially since there was a very real possibility of a job with Luca and his father in the near future. Jonah was my priority, even though anyone could see how very much this man missed his brother and wanted to make amends. It was also obvious that Jonah was not ready to accept his apology or offer forgiveness.

Time would have to heal these wounds.

Luca offered a brief nod to Quinn and then to my sister before spinning around and leaving the same way he came.

Jonah turned to me and I lifted my hands to his shoulders. "You okay?"

He shook his head. "No, but I will be."

I nodded.

"Okay. Well, we're going to get moving on Operation Relocate My Family. Simone, please for the love of God, check in with us daily. It's more important now than ever before."

"Sorry, SoSo. I will, I promise."

She gave me a hug and then looked at Jonah for a moment and made a decision. She hugged him too. That was huge. My sister only hugged people she genuinely cared for. I was the touchy feely one in our duo.

"Take care of my sister. She's the most important person in the world to me." She pointed to him. "I'm counting on you."

He gave a soft smile just to her. "She's important to me too. I'll protect her with my life."

Swoon.

I went over to Quinn and he hugged me for a long time. "I'm glad you're alive and I don't have to kill you for making me deal with a frightened and angry SoSo."

I laughed. "Will you put me back on the chocolate almond butter clusters gift list for Christmas?" I puffed out my bottom lip and batted my eyelashes.

He grinned and smacked my cheek affectionately. "We'll see how you do with checking in over the next week."

"Come on! That's not fair. You know I'm crappy at touching base. It's like you're setting me up for failure." I crossed my arms and tapped my foot dramatically.

He shrugged. "If you want the clusters, you'll check

in. Simple as that. I want a happy and focused Senator, not a freaking out, often grouchy, and sometimes bitchy SoSo who's worried about her only living blood relative. Life's about choices, Simone. Make good ones."

I lifted my head to the ceiling and groaned. "Now you're being mean. Fine! But I better get a double batch!"

He winked, hooked his arm with Sonia's, and led her toward the door. She was already head down, eyes on her phone typing away. Work-a-holic. Still, he was right. I knew that my safety and ability to breathe were Sonia's biggest weaknesses. Anyone trying to wound her would only have to bruise me. That's all it would take.

"Love you, SoSo, and love you, Quinn. Good luck with the fam!" I called out as they were leaving then turned to Jonah. "That was a pretty intense smack down with your brother, baby…"

Jonah clenched his teeth and shook his head. "We're not talking about him. Not right now. Maybe not ever."

And of course, when I was about to grill him, his phone rang, Ryan's name appearing on the screen.

"Saved by the bell."

He smirked. "Mind getting us some pizza?"

"Oooh! I forgot." My mouth started to water, and my belly took notice. "Though no more whiskey. You're switching to beer."

"Sounds good."

Jonah answered the phone while I set about getting me and my hot FBI guy some food.

"What now?"

Chapter
ELEVEN

ONAH AND I SPENT THE REST OF THE DAY VEGGING, EATING, and watching mindless TV. Every hour or so he'd get a call from Ryan with an update. So far, we had Helen's last known whereabouts. Turned out she'd met some friends at a bar. Her phone's GPS stopped there. The authorities found the broken device smashed and tossed in the field adjacent to the poolhall. Jonah gave Ryan a list of friends of theirs to find out whether she'd met up with any of them. When they narrowed down the names to a few she'd been with that night, they guessed she'd left around eleven in the evening. Based on the timing from when she left Jonah's parents to the time she met up with her friends, those friends were the last to see her alive. The FBI's best guess was that she was followed from Jonah's parents' house to the bar. The killer must have waited for her to exit the establishment alone before he struck. Her car was still parked in the back near a dumpster.

No one heard or saw anything. The pool hall had cameras, but the car was parked out of the line of sight of the cameras.

The FBI and most especially Jonah seemed to be most interested in the autopsy results. Jonah had called Helen's parents and spent a good hour talking to them. He offered to handle her remains and thankfully they declined. Though it would be a while before they could lay Helen to rest properly since she was part of an ongoing murder investigation.

Me, I was fretting about work, waiting for my boss at Tracks to call me back. I'd informed the on-site manager about what was going on. I asked for a week or two off in order to give the FBI time to find their man, and she said she would relay it to Owen and have him call me back. He owned the bar but wasn't known for being the nicest guy. He paid a fair wage and didn't hit on the women who worked for him, but he didn't have any emotional connection to his staff nor was he cool about sick days and time off. He had the *'work your ass off for what you want'* mentality. Which I totally understood. That's all I'd ever been doing since I secured a work permit at fifteen. I just knew he wasn't going to be cool about me needing the time away regardless of the severity of the situation.

I jumped when my phone rang on the table as though it were a King cobra ready to strike. Jonah chuckled, stood up from the couch, and grabbed our empty beer bottles.

"Another?"

"Sure," I said and answered the phone. "Hello?"

"Simone, it's Owen. I understand you've got some trouble preventing you from coming to work?"

I gave him a quick rundown of the situation.

"Darling, I understand that you feel you need to be home in order to be safe. However, you need to look at it from my perspective too. I'm a business owner. I've already let you off two days of work for this shit. I can't allow for any more or I'm setting a precedent for the other staff. We're already understaffed. I'm afraid if you don't make it in for shift tomorrow, I'll have to let you go."

"What? No. I need this job, Owen. You know I do."

"And I'm offering to let you continue working it. We have plenty of bouncers and security here in order to keep you safe. I can make accommodations so that you stay behind the bar, and in view of one of our guys at all times, but either way we know shit can happen. You have to make the decision for yourself. If you don't show, I won't deny or put up a fight regarding your unemployment, but I prefer you here. If I see you here tomorrow, I'll know you're still working. If I don't, I'll have your final check ready for you to pick up, darlin'. Take care of yourself."

"Yeah, uh, thanks, Owen."

He hung up and I pressed my hand to my head and slumped into the back of the couch. Worry and fear about how the heck I was going to pay my bills shredded through me like a hundred tiny biting piranhas.

"What now?" Jonah entered with two cold ones in hand. He gave me one and I sucked back a long drink trying to cool my frustration at my predicament.

"My boss at Tracks says if I don't go in tomorrow, they're going to fire me."

"The fuck you say?" He growled, his face turning to granite.

"He's been as cool as he can be with me missing work. I need to go in."

"You're gonna have to quit, babe. You can't go in. It's unsafe."

I shook my head and stood up to pace the room. "Tracks is my primary source of income. As it is, I'm going to need to find a new place to live. And since I'm not going to give any notice, I'll lose my entire deposit. I'm going to have to move back into Kerrighan house again which is already a huge embarrassment. But if I don't make money, I can't pay for my coursework. I'm already behind on the fees. I've tried financial aid before but at my age and my lack of income coming and going with any real consistency, I never get approved. I'm going to need to get a new car, again, which I don't have any money for, and I only had the required liability insurance on it, and it wasn't worth much to begin with. I don't have insurance to replace the car. The flower shop was my gas and food on the go money."

"Simone, relax. Sit down with me and we'll discuss."

I ignored him. "You don't understand. Not having my own safety net financially is the worst. I try and work my fingers to the bone, but something always comes up. Then my sister has to step in as my big knight in shining Prada and pay off my debts so I can crawl out from under water." I blew a harsh breath from my mouth trying to let go of the anger and frustration coating my every thought.

"Do you have any idea how pathetic and demeaning that is? I swear, I can't catch a fucking break. And I'm tired, Jonah. I'm so fucking *tired* of working my ass off for pennies and even then, I can't hold on to them. And if I didn't take help from Sonia or Mama Kerri I'd be sleeping under a bridge. I don't want to sleep under a bridge, so my pride gets to take repeated kicks and I'm the loser of the sisterhood."

Jonah stood up and hooked me around the waist mid-pace and slammed me against his chest. "You're not going to sleep under a bridge. And you're not a loser. No one who works as hard as you do could ever be mistaken for a loser."

I sulked and cupped my cheek.

"I'll help you get back on your feet…"

White-hot anger boiled under the surface of my skin. I shoved out of his arms. "No way! Have you even been listening to me?" I grumbled.

"Simone, come on. Be realistic about this…"

I barely stopped myself from stomping my foot. "No, you be realistic. We've known each other *days,* not years. I'm not going to be your kept woman, and I'm definitely not going to take any of your handouts."

He frowned and placed his hands on his hips. I moved in front of him to put mine on the wall of his mighty chest. His T-shirt was so soft. A beautiful contrast to the warm, hard muscle underneath. I lifted my chin and looked into his eyes. "I'll figure it out. Though part of that is me going to work tomorrow. I'm sorry. I know you don't like it and Sonia's head will likely explode, but I have to work. I just have to."

He scowled so intensely I got more nervous. "If you're working, then I'll be sitting at the bar while you do it."

"You don't need to do that…"

He wrapped his arms around my body. "We starting something here. Me and you?"

I smiled softly, hope coating my response. "I think so, yeah."

"Well, I know so. That means if my woman is working slinging drinks in a bar filled with people and is at risk, my ass will be on a stool in perfect view while she does it. I'm on leave. There's nothing more important I need to be doing than keeping you safe."

I slumped against him. "I'm sorry my life is so jacked up."

He rubbed his chin along the crown of my hair. "I'm sorry mine is too. How's about you and me put our jacked-up lives together and work together toward making something beautiful?"

I kissed him over his heart. "You keep being so nice and I'm never going to let you get away. You'll be stuck with me and my crazy sisters and wild ways for the rest of your days."

He hugged me tighter. "Maybe that's not so bad from where I'm standing. Especially if it means I get a warm, cuddly Simone in my arms regularly."

"You're so swoonworthy." I lifted up onto my toes, clasped my hands behind his head, and kissed him. He tasted of beer and the rich taste that could only be Jonah. A flavor I was becoming obsessed with.

As was our luck, Ryan took that moment to enter the house, his loud footsteps clomping on the wood floor. He entered and grinned.

"I'm starting to make bets with myself on the various states of libidinous behavior I'm going to see upon entry to my own home."

Jonah looked at me and then back at Ryan and we both cracked up laughing, me pressing my face against his chest and letting loose.

It felt good to let go and laugh.

Ryan held up two white bags of what smelled like Chinese food.

"At least this time I come bearing gifts and updates!" He grinned and set the lot on top of the kitchen counter.

"Food first. Updates after. Especially if they're going to be icky. You can tell Jonah all the freaky stuff while I'm showering if that's cool with you."

160

Ryan's lips twitched and he nodded. "Noted, gorgeous." He winked.

Jonah groaned but didn't say anything. It seemed as though Ryan loved to get Jonah's goat as much as he could. With things being so uncertain, this must have brought a bit of consistency to his life during this situation that felt totally out of control.

Ryan pulled box after box out of the bags and laid three plates down next to them. He let me dig in first. I piled my plate high with the feast and waited to start until both men had their plates loaded and we were all sitting down at the small table.

"I don't have long, just enough time for dinner and to grab a change of clothes. How's everything going here?"

Jonah updated him on my need to work. Ryan glared at his plate, his jaw hardening. Seemed he didn't like the idea of me going back to work either but frankly, I didn't have a choice. I had to live even if it meant risking my safety for a period of eight hours a night a few nights a week.

Using this as happy time, I told Ryan about the idea that Jonah's dad had about me checking out their workplace.

"Wow. Yeah, that would be cool but what about uh, you know...the other partner who works there?" Ryan asked trying to be sly about not saying Luca's name.

"He was here today. Luca. Came to see if I was okay," Jonah offered.

"Are you fucking kidding me? I'll kick his ass for you." Ryan scowled and poked at the chicken bites on his plate so hard the tines made a loud clanking sound.

"It's fine. He said his piece."

"Yeah, and what did you say?" Ryan asked. Clearly, they

talked about the serious shit in their lives. Something I genuinely appreciated, because I had that with my sisters by choice too.

"Told him I needed more time."

Ryan nodded. "Took some serious balls to come here though. Especially as it pertains to Helen. The fuckwad." Ryan angrily scooped up some rice, half of it falling off his fork with his jerky movements.

"Yeah." Jonah sighed and leaned back in his chair running his hand behind his neck.

"You okay?"

"It's hard, you know? I'm still so angry at him but not because I lost Helen. Mostly because it was him that was the catalyst. My own brother betrayed me. Drink or no drink, how does someone get over that?"

Ryan shrugged as I ran my hand up and down Jonah's back wanting to show my support as he worked through this with his best friend.

"I guess it's a matter of do you believe it was the booze that did it or do you think there was more to it than that?"

"He never had a thing for Helen before. She's not even his ideal woman. Tall and lean, athletic build. I mean, Simone is more his type."

Ryan grinned at me. "Simone is every heterosexual man's type," he teased and smirked at me.

Jonah punched him in the shoulder hard enough for him to wince and rub at it through his laughter.

"You set yourself up for that one, bro."

"Whatever," Jonah grumbled, and bit into an egg roll.

"Thinking back on it, I saw Luca around Helen a lot. He never so much as looked at her twice."

"He claims she seduced him. They were drunk, she came on to him. He's gotten help for his alcoholism, yada... It doesn't really matter because it's over. My marriage ended and she's now dead." He tossed his fork on his plate and pushed it away from him barely half-eaten.

Ryan reached out and grabbed Jonah's wrist. "It does matter. Luca is your brother. I've known you a long time and I know how tight you two were before it all went down. And he *was* sauced all the time, man. You even told me how worried you were the last time you and Helen went out with him and Tiffany. He got so shitfaced that he made a huge scene in a restaurant knocking over a table. Remember?"

Jonah sighed again and nodded.

"He drank all the time. More than I think the family realized. Tiffany was constantly complaining at the family dinners I went to that he drank too much."

"Yeah. So?" Jonah bit out and yanked his arm out of his friend's hold.

"I'm just sayin' if he's an alcoholic and got help this past year, then maybe you oughta give him a little bit of your time now and again. Allow the family dinners with both of you there. Start small. You love your brother and I know you miss him..."

"He fucked my wife."

"And she fucked him. That says a lot about where she was at in your marriage. And worse, she blamed it on you. Never took the fall for her actions. Never apologized. From what I'm hearing, that's all Luca's doing."

"What are you trying to say? That I'm being unreasonable?" Jonah sneered.

I watched while Ryan eased back against his chair, wiped his mouth, and crossed his arms. The man's blond hair was a bit ruffled but sexy as ever. His jawline had a good two days of scruff that absolutely added to his appeal and his light eyes were searing with intensity. I so needed to get him around my sisters again when they weren't worried about my safety. See if nature could take its course with one of them. Though Blessing was my first choice.

"No, I don't think you are. Though I do think it's time you took the first step toward healing your family. You love Luca. I know you better than I know anyone, Jonah. You've been a little lost this past year without him in your life."

"I was dealing with losing him and ending a seven-year marriage. I had a lot on my mind."

"And obviously during that time he was taking the very hard steps toward healing the divide. Getting help for alcoholism is not easy. I watched one of my parents go through it. It was brutal. Nothing but hills and valleys, highs and lows, but eventually he came out on top and it sounds as though your brother is trying to get there as well, by making amends. Admitting he has a problem. Staying sober the last year. I'm not saying that what you went through wasn't hell on earth because I know it was, I was there during it. What I'm saying is that people do change if they want to. If they put the work in. And if he's changed, I'd hope you were the kind of man I know you to be, and could find a way to forgive him, or at the very least allow him back into your heart and the family fold."

Jonah clamped his mouth shut and I could tell he was clenching his teeth by how hard his jaw was, the skin stretched tight over his chin.

"I'll think on it," Jonah finally stated, rather low and under his breath.

"That's all I can ask. And let me know if you need an ear to bend. You know I'm here." His gaze swept to mine. "Though it looks like you've got a new source to share with too."

Jonah looped an arm across my shoulders, leaned to the side, and kissed my temple. "Yeah, I do, but it never hurts to get hit with the honesty from my best friend." He held his other hand out and Ryan clapped it and held it for a moment before letting go and standing.

"Hate to eat and run, but I've gotta get back. The coroner is doing an all-nighter. The case is leaking to the media and it's a nightmare out there with the connection to Senator Wright. She already has a lot of play in the media for being a looker and the youngest female Senator in history not to mention her having a unique take on politics as an Independent. Now her sister is entangled with a serial murderer."

"Damn. I haven't been following the media or watching anything on the news. It usually bums me out to be honest. I had no idea Sonia was dealing with more because of me." I sat back in my chair and pressed my fists to my eyes. "I wish I could just wake up tomorrow and it all be over."

Ryan took his plate and as he walked by, he ruffled my hair. "Don't worry, we've got you covered, girl."

I pushed my food around the plate, melancholy and sadness drifting over me like a black cloud.

Jonah got up and took our plates to the kitchen. He whispered some things to Ryan, but I didn't care. I was lost in my own pity party for one. I got up and headed to Jonah's room. I ran a super-hot bath and got in to soak away my troubles.

Turns out I was exhausted and slipped into a deep sleep within minutes of entering the bath.

The next thing I knew the water was stone cold and I was being hauled naked and shivering out of the bath and wrapped in a soft towel. Drowsily I allowed Jonah to lead me to the bed where he grabbed a clean shirt for me. He tugged the scrunchy holding my hair in a loose bun on the top of my head, and my dry hair came tumbling down around my shoulders. I lifted my arms dutifully and he put the shirt on over the towel. Then he stood me up and snagged the towel, yanking it off from under me, but allowing me the moment of modesty. It was cute because I was one of the least modest people in my family.

Then he pulled the covers back and I slipped in, but he surprised me by entering right behind me. One of my legs cocked up and he pressed his pajama-clad one right up against it. He pressed his face to the back of my hair and locked an arm around my waist.

"Mmm… I thought we weren't going to sleep together."

"Simone, I'm tired. Beyond tired. You fell asleep in the bath. My mind won't stop unless I'm lying right here. So, shut it and go to sleep, yeah?"

"I knew I'd get you to sleep with me." I snuggled back and yanked his arm up between my breasts and rested my lips against our clasped hands. "Not exactly the way I'd hoped, but I'll take what I can get."

He chuckled against my hair and yawned. "Goodnight, baby." He kissed me on my neck right under my ear.

I shivered and sighed, content as a kitten. "Night, Jonah. Things will get better tomorrow."

"They will if my woman would close her eyes and get some shut eye."

I snickered but pressed my lips to his fingers and kissed each one. I did this until his breathing got more consistent and I could feel his body weight turn heavy. When I knew for sure he was asleep, I closed my eyes and prayed.

I prayed to God that he'd let Ryan and the team find the man hurting us.

I then prayed to my parents for strength and the ability to see this through.

After, I prayed to Helen. Telling her I was sorry about what happened to her and asking her to watch over Jonah. Maybe put in a word with the big guy on his behalf.

Then I went back to God and did round after round of the "Our Father" prayer until I fell into a deep sleep, letting it all go for another day.

Chapter
TWELVE

WHEN I WOKE THE NEXT DAY, HE WAS ALREADY OUT OF bed. Which sucked. Big time. I'd hoped to finagle a little bed play. The gentlemanly behavior was starting to grate on my nerves. Every ounce of my being screamed to connect with every ounce of his. And yet, I also understood where he was coming from and why he wanted to take things slow. He hadn't had relations with a woman since he and his ex-wife ended their marriage. Now the woman was dead, and I had a sneaky suspicion he was adding that blame onto his already weighed-down shoulders.

I glanced at the clock and saw it was only eight in the morning. Today was going to be a long-ass day since I didn't go in for another twelve hours, and I was scheduled from eight in the evening to three in the morning. And Friday nights were always packed. I'd make some serious cash tonight, God willing.

My phone rang on the side table and I reached over to grab it. I saw Sonia's name as the caller.

"Good morning, SoSo," I chirped. I pressed up and leaned against the headboard. Just as I got settled the bedroom door opened and an already dressed and showered Jonah entered with steaming mugs of coffee in both hands.

I smiled wide at my beautiful man. He was wearing a simple pair of dark wash jeans that had some faded areas at the thighs and a tight-fitting, black T-shirt. His hair was wet and slicked back a bit. He handed me one of the mugs and I sipped the heavenly brew and whispered my thanks.

"Operation relocate family was a success!" My sister's voice rose in happiness.

"Excellent. Where is everyone?"

"Quinn and Niko have Liliana and Charlie, but they'd only do it if they got their own rooms. I have Blessing and Addison, and Quinn was able to secure the use of the fully furnished apartment by my biggest donor so Mom, Genesis, and Rory can spread out a bit. We're all using that place as home base."

"And Tabby?"

"I'm not gonna lie, Simone, I'm really worried about her. No one has heard a peep. We've all gone by her place, even used Mom's key a few days ago and she wasn't there. It didn't look like she'd been there in a couple weeks. Her plants were dead, and her mail had stacked up. Quinn and Niko, knowing we couldn't go out, went after hours and knocked on some doors on her floor. Turns out she was seen yesterday dashing into her apartment, and then leaving in a change of clothes and wet hair. One of them said she looked sickly and gaunt. I don't know what that means, but we're all freaked out."

Dread licked up my spine and I shivered. Jonah placed his hand on my thigh and rubbed back and forth, his face a mask of concern.

"Maybe Jonah and I can try to catch her before I go to work tonight."

"Work? At the shop? I didn't think you worked there on Fridays."

"No, at Tracks. And before you say anything…"

"Are you fucking insane! Oh my God!" she yelled and then a door slammed.

"SoSo I'm going to be fine…"

"Yeah you are, because you're not going to work. There is a serial killer after you. He's already shot you once and has killed close to a dozen women. You narrowly escaped but you know who didn't?" The diatribe became a screech. "Your boyfriend's ex-wife! Jesus, Simone! This is beyond stupid."

"Frankly, Sonia, I don't care what you think. It's either go to work or I'm fired. I don't have a choice."

"We all have choices, Simone. The right choice is your life. You tell the owner to stick it where the sun don't shine, and you quit."

"I can't." Tears filled my eyes and Jonah squeezed my knee. "I need the money."

"I'll give you money. Whatever you need. You want ten grand, I'll write you a check today. That should be enough to get you settled in a new place with some furniture, and then I'll cosign and put money down on a new car for you. Whatever it takes. Do not go to work."

I shook my head. "I'm sorry, but I have to make my own way. I have some new prospects for the future but in the meantime, I have to go to work. You don't understand…"

"No, I don't understand. Putting yourself willingly at risk is entirely selfish. Especially when I'm offering you an alternate route. One that will keep you alive, safe, and on the right track."

My heart felt like a vice was squeezing it so hard I could barely catch my breath. "Jonah is going to be with me. He'll stay right at the bar all night."

"It's not enough. Don't you see, Simone? This man is after you. He wants you dead. This is not a risk you should take."

"Well, here's the deal, SoSo. I'm my own person. I make my own choices, and this is something I have to do. I'm sorry that it offends or upsets you, but it's what I'm doing. You're just going to have to live with it. Now I've got a hunky FBI man who just brought me coffee and looks incredibly sexy all showered and dressed ready to take on the day. I'm going to spend some time showing him my appreciation for supporting me in what I need to do for me. Okay? Great. Nice chatting with you. Bye!" I pressed the red button so fast my finger smarted.

"That was some call." He canted his head and focused those dark eyes on me. "You okay?"

"My sister can be such a bitch," I grumbled.

"Definitely can relate to that." He cupped my cheek, leaned forward, and gave me an amazing kiss. "Morning, gorgeous."

I sighed against his mouth. "Good morning, handsome. How did you sleep?"

He grinned. "Best I've had in so long I can't remember. I'm completely rested."

I smiled wide. "Stick with me, kid, and you'll be sleeping easy for the rest of your life," I teased and stole another kiss.

When I tried to pull back Jonah pressed forward, kissing me harder, slicking his tongue along my lips until I opened. The kiss went wild, so much so I crawled up and into his lap. His hands came down to my thighs and ran the length of them until they encountered my bare ass.

He ripped his mouth away and dug his fingers into the flesh of my ass. I moaned and thrust against him.

"Fuck, I forgot you weren't wearing anything under my shirt." He ran his hand down the center of my ass until he cupped my sex from behind, dipping his fingers against my arousal. "Fuck, wet," he roared again, only this time he did so twisting us both until my back was to the bed and his body was over me, his mouth on mine.

Jonah found the edge of the T-shirt and shoved it up my body and off, tossing it behind him. One of his hands lifted my breast and he circled the tip with his tongue as I drowned in the unexpected turn of events. It was beautiful torture, his mouth on my breast, sucking rhythmically. He switched sides and repeated the same experience to the neglected one. Then he got onto his knees and he plucked and pinched lightly at the erect peaks while he watched seemingly fascinated until I was crooning and mewling, my upper body arching into his greedy fingertips.

He pulled off his shirt and I was gifted with the olive expanse of hard muscle. I ran my fingers down his ripped abdominals and groaned when he moved farther down the bed so I couldn't reach. I was about to complain when he cupped my knees and spread my legs wide.

Jonah up on his knees, his muscles pumping, veins protruding, shirtless, his nostrils flaring, and his teeth pressing into his bottom lip while he stared at the heart of me was beyond anything I could ever describe. It was feral, intense, and the closest thing to uncontrolled lust I'd seen in a person.

He licked his lips, rounded my ass with his large hands, and lifted my lower half up at the same time his mouth came down over me.

I cried out when he went straight for it, sinking his tongue as deep as he could go. I tried to close my legs, fight against the insane onslaught of pleasure because it was so intense, I thought I might explode with that single touch alone. He backed off a tad, bringing his tongue to the hot bundle of nerves between my thighs and swirling the tight knot in dizzying circles.

"Jonah," I pled, not knowing what I was begging for, but knowing I needed more. Something. Anything.

He laved at my clit, sucking it hard, and then releasing the pressure until I had no shame, putting my hands into his hair and grinding against his face while my ecstasy soared. It had been so long since I'd had a man go down on me, I was in utter bliss.

Every time I gripped his hair he growled into my sex, taking more, pressing harder, his hips humping against the bed.

"Turn around, give me your cock," I requested. He lifted his head but didn't leave me hanging with nothing but cool air against my soaked flesh. No, he used his thumb to tease around and around and then pressed it deep inside me.

"You want to suck me off, baby?" His voice was raw and gritty. A deep gravely sound that I'd not heard before.

I thrust my hips against his thumb as he fucked me with it.

"Yeah…" I gasped as he removed his thumb and inserted not one but two fingers. They reached so much deeper and I got into riding them.

"After. This first time I want to watch you come for me, Simone."

"Jonah." I groaned, and he went back to putting his mouth on me. He bit the inside of each of my thighs, licking and sucking in ways I'd never felt before. He took me to the pinnacle, almost pushing me over the edge, and then brought me back down. He did this three times until I was ready to kick him in the junk if he didn't finish me off.

"Let me come…" I begged.

"What is it that you want?" He made a sucking sound against my clit and it throbbed hotly.

"Please, Jonah, make me come." I gripped his hair and twisted, lifting my hips, mindless with the need to get off.

"Anything you want, baby." He murmured, spread my lips with both thumbs, licked me deep a few times, then pressed two fingers inside, hooked them high and tight, and laid his mouth on my hot spot. He sucked the bundle hard and fucked me with his fingers.

I shot off like a rocket. Humping his face wildly. He kept going, taking me higher and higher again, until he wrung another impressive orgasm out of me.

I rode both those waves to the absolute finish, pressing his head to me as though I were afraid he was going to leave me mid-orgasm. I shouldn't have been afraid. He took care of me better than any man ever had.

"Best ever," I sighed, pressing my arm over my face.

Jonah chuckled, wiped his mouth with his forearm, and came up over me, taking my lips in a juicy kiss that tasted of me and him. It was beyond sexy.

Which is of course was when there was a knock on the bedroom door.

"Hey, sleepyheads, got some news and not a lot of time. I'm making breakfast for everyone," Ryan's voice called out.

Jonah groaned and pressed his face to my neck where he kissed me and started to chuckle. Me, I got mad. Hell, fire, and damnation mad, but before I could say anything to my half-naked hero, he rolled off me and started walk to the door.

Oh. No. He. Didn't.

Before he could open the door, I flew off the bed buck-ass naked, grabbed his bicep, and twisted him around. Once he was facing me, confusion coating his features, I pushed him against the door and pressed my body to his until we were face to face.

"Don't you dare move." I glared, kissed his mouth briefly, and bit down on his bottom lip and snapping it the way he did to me. He grunted in reply and I grinned evilly, pressing my hands to his mighty pecs and sliding my hands down as I went to my knees before him.

"Simone…" he warned.

I reached for the button of his jeans and undid it, and then the zipper. "Shut it," I clipped, tugging his jeans down around his thighs.

"Baby, I don't think…" He tried again, but I cut him off by peeling down his boxer briefs until they were stretched against his thighs where his jeans were stuck.

I smirked. "Be quiet, baby, or Ryan will hear me blowing you," I said with a saucy wink before I took his beautiful, thick, nice-sized dick into my mouth.

He groaned and I pulled back, stopping just at the tip where I swirled my tongue around it the same way he did to me. "Shhh…" I reminded him.

Jonah's pitch-dark eyes were zeroed in on me. "Christ, you're so damn beautiful." He cupped my cheek as I took him down my throat. His head fell back with a thud against the door. I could hear pans clanking in the background which ratcheted up the excitement factor by about ten thousand degrees.

Once he started to get lost in what I was doing, I cupped his balls and rubbed and teased his taint with a finger.

"Jesus, Simone. Fuck." He growled and fucked my mouth, his entire body misting with sweat. I watched as his gloriously defined abs tightened and relaxed with each plunge of his cock into my mouth. I rolled his balls as his body got more rigid, his dick seeming to thicken in my mouth.

"Baby, I'm gonna blow," he warned.

I sucked until I let it go, leaving just my lips on the weeping tip. I tickled the slit at the top with the tip of my tongue and watched as his mouth dropped open, his eyes rolled back inside his head, and he fisted the hand that was not in my hair.

Knowing he was about to go off, I ramped up my efforts, sucking hard and deep. When I had him on the cusp of ecstasy, I hummed around his length. That was all it took. Jet after hot jet of his essence flooded my mouth and I swallowed it down, staying with his movements, ensuring his pleasure to the very end.

I loved fellatio. The power it gave me was intense. And as I watched him put a fist to his mouth and groan long and hard, I knew I'd given him something amazing. Before I could crawl my way up his body, he bent over and lifted me up by my ribcage. Then his mouth crashed over mine in a searing hot kiss. One of his hands cupped the back of my head and maneuvered my face from side to side as he took my mouth the way he took my pussy. With intention and enthusiasm.

For a long time, we drank from one another, solidifying all that just occurred with a kiss of true fulfillment. When we couldn't breathe, he let me go and pressed his face into my neck. "My sweet girl is incredible with her mouth," he rumbled against the heated skin of my neck.

I giggled like the girly girl I was in that moment. Happy that I'd pleased my man. I looped my arms around him. "Repeat tonight but this time with your dick fucking me somewhere else?"

"Anal on the second go? Wow. I mean, I'm definitely up for the job. If it needs to be filled, you know, I'm your man." He laughed, and I pushed away from him and smacked his chest.

"You're such a brat!" I laughed. "And I've never done that, so I don't know if I'd like it or not. Though I'm not against it. I just haven't been with the right person to work up to it." I moved to the bed and grabbed the T-shirt of his I'd worn to bed and put it on while I continued conversationally. "Trey wanted my ass, tried all the time, but he didn't want to put the work in to make it good for me. And my sister Charlie says if you're going to allow a man or a woman, she's bisexual by the way. Not sure I told you that. Anyway, she says that if you're going to do it, you need to do it with a person you trust and work up to. Start with small butt plugs while having normal sex, then graduate up to bigger ones, and so on…"

"Simone, honey," Jonah interrupted but I kept going as I put on the shirt.

"She says you have to be super lubed up, both you and him, or in my sister's case it might be a *her* sometimes, and then you need to be super turned on and be able to relax. Otherwise it can hurt a lot and be painful and then the entire experience is ruined."

"Baby," he said while pulling up his pants.

"So, it's not like I'm unwilling, I just feel we need to be further in our relationship and I haven't been in a relationship that went the distance, ya know what I mean? Though the idea does have its merits and Charlie says it's an amazingly full feeling that you can't really describe unless you're experiencing it. She says she comes crazy hard when she's doing anal from behind and he or she uses their fingers to double penetrate or a dildo. I'd so be up for that." I bit down into my bottom lip and thought about Jonah fucking me from behind, a vibrator in the front. A full body tremble went through me and I shook it off by wiggling around and shaking out my hands as though drying them.

"Simone, honey, shut up." Jonah laughed. "It was a joke. Though I'm glad you've really considered the possibility, but I haven't ever done it either. Helen and the couple women I had sex with before her weren't into it. It's not a big deal."

His comment stopped me where I stood while holding up a pair of lacy panties I'd just pulled from my suitcase. "Wait, you've only slept with three people?"

He frowned and tugged his shirt on. "Yeah. I met my wife freshman year in college. Been with her ever since. Didn't have much action in high school. Why? How many have you slept with?"

"Uh, more than three." I frowned and tried to count it up. Did people keep track of things like this? I mean I didn't fancy myself a ho, but I definitely liked to get laid and it wasn't often that I was without company of the male persuasion. I mean, I worked in a bar. It was super easy to find a hook up when I was between relationships.

"How many more?" His lips twitched, and I couldn't tell if it was with humor or disapproval.

"Just more. Can we leave it at that?"

He grinned. "You don't know off the top of your head!" he accused.

"I most certainly do." I lied through my teeth. "I'm going to go take a shower. You should probably go check on what Ryan's got to say."

And on that note, I escaped into the bathroom, pressing my body up against the door, my heart pounding a wild beat.

Shit. How many people had I slept with? I was determined to figure it out before the conversation came up again. When I entered the steaming shower's spray, I figured I'd count them in order of appearance starting with my first, Ben Taley, a high school senior. I was a sophomore and sixteen. For the next thirty minutes I went through my mind trying to come up with the magic number.

It definitely was not three.

From there I decided I would not be sharing my number with my new hot FBI guy.

Tracks was a crush when we arrived fifteen minutes before my shift. I introduced the security guys to Jonah who later informed me that they were not trained security professionals as much as they were muscular bouncers. This did not amuse him in the least. Therefore, Jonah parked his fine ass on the stool right next to my register so every time I had to ring up a drink, I had smiling dark eyes to drown in.

Until Trey showed, filling in for one of our bartenders. When Trey and I worked, we killed it. He was tall, fit, and good looking. His smile alone melted panties off the girls in droves. Including mine for the better part of a year. He had sandy blond hair, big blue eyes, and rocked the surfer-artist type vibe.

First thing he did was come straight up to me and pull me into his arms, his face going against my neck. I held my arms out to the side and stared horrified at Jonah who was grinding his teeth so hard I worried he wouldn't have any molars left. I patted Trey's back lightly and tried to ease out of his hold. This caused him to cup my cheeks.

"Baby girl, I was freaked, man. Word on the street is there's a killer after my babe. Why didn't you come to me? I would have kept you safe."

I tried to push him back while glancing over my shoulder at Jonah who was positively furious if the scowl on his face and his hands in fists were anything to go by.

"Um, you know, I uh…"

"Simone, baby girl." He wrapped one hand around the back of my head, the other on my ass smashing our bodies together.

The crowd whooped and hollered at the display.

"That's it," I heard growled from where Jonah was sitting.

"Trey, back up. We broke up a week ago."

He pressed us closer and took a bigger, rather vulgar grope of my ass. Not the cute little side cheek grab like Jonah often did but a full on, down the center grope like Jonah did to me this morning only I'd been naked and panting for it then. With Trey in that moment, not so much.

I tried to shove Trey off. "Trey, let go of me." I wedged my hands against his chest but it didn't matter because Jonah had already ripped Trey's hold off my ass and twisted his wrist and arm so fast I spun out of the way as Trey went face down over the bar.

Jonah leaned over Trey and spoke through his teeth. The music pumped loudly around us and our audience had grown to twice the size.

"Keep your filthy fucking hands off my woman," Jonah bellowed. "Simone is no longer on your radar, got it?" He twisted Trey's arm up his back a little harder ferreting out another cry of pain from my ex.

I had to get the situation under control and fast or I'd end up jobless anyway.

I pressed my hand to Jonah's back. "Honey, it's fine. Trey didn't know I'd entered into a new relationship nor does he know that my new boyfriend is a testy FBI agent."

"FBI? What the fuck, Simone. Dude, I didn't know!" he cried out.

Jonah let Trey up and pushed him down the long skinny row where we worked behind the bar. "Stay at your fucking end and do your job."

"What are you? Like, her bodyguard?" Trey rubbed at his wrist and up his arm.

"Yeah, something like that. Back the fuck off."

"Dude, I was with her like a week ago."

I crossed my arms and stepped in front of Trey. "You were with Melinda a week ago from what I heard. And you were with Sarah the week before that. Trey, we haven't been in a romantic relationship in at least a month regardless of the actual date you ended things. And let's not forget, you ended it. In a text. What kind of douche canoe ends a relationship in a text?"

"Baby girl, come on. You know I'm hard to tie down, and I gave you a lot of my time…"

"He can give me some of his time," a buxom brunette who twirled a strand of her hair around her finger spouted off.

Trey, already distracted by a pretty face and a pair of pushed-up tits lifted his chin, winked, and said, "Be right with you, babe."

I rolled my eyes and turned to Jonah. "He literally means nothing to me."

"Hey, that's fucked. You loved me. All the ladies do." He waggled his brows and grinned that sexy smile making at least three of the girls at the bar swoon.

Though there was a line of other women on my side that were sizing up Jonah as well.

"Like I said, he one hundred percent means absolutely nothing to me."

Jonah hooked me around the waist, plastered me against his chest, and took my mouth in a heated, delicious kiss. I went straight into a Jonah kiss haze getting lost in the moment.

"Damn, if my man kissed me like that, I'd be on my knees every night."

"Hell, I'd happily go to my knees right now if he didn't seem so into the blonde," I heard another say from behind my back.

Jonah ran his hands down my side and back up to cup my cheek. He pecked me once and then a second time before he whispered, "Get to work, baby. I'll be here waiting."

"Swoon-tastic!" A woman smacked the bar.

"Lucky bitch!" Another said laughing.

I turned and poured the mouthy chicks and myself a shot of Patron Silver. Then I pushed the shots toward them. "Cheers to good fucking men."

"And men that can fuck good!" One of them blurted back and clinked my glass.

"I'll definitely drink to that." I grinned at Jonah and he shook his head as I shot the tequila back.

As I worked, he monitored the club and Trey, who kept giving me sidelong glances every so often. I ignored him, served drinks, flirted with my man, and made some serious cash in tips.

Right at last call I heard a familiar voice call out, "Yo' bitch, can I get some service around here?"

I spun around as Jonah sat up straighter in his seat.

My gaze clapped onto her totally black ones and I held my breath. Her hair was a deep blue-black, cheeks sunken in, and her normally pink pouty lips dry and cracked.

I couldn't help the tears that filled in my eyes as I ran around the bar, flung up the little door, and smashed into my sister.

"Tabby," I cried against her extremely thin frame. On average she was always thin, never kept much weight on but this was in the territory of unhealthy emaciated thin.

I pulled my face out her neck and kept hold of her shoulders in order to be sure she didn't go poof and disappear.

"Where have you been? My God, Tab, so much has happened."

She looked left and right and twitched a little. I frowned and watched as she rubbed under her pert, reddened nose.

Her face was pointed and pixie-like though right now it was as if her skin was hanging on her skeleton by sheer force of will.

"I heard about you getting in trouble. Wanted to see you alive for myself. But now that I have, Si, I gotta go." She blinked several times in quick succession.

"You've got to go, no! What do you mean?" I cried, fisting my hands.

"Shit to do, girl. Gotta keep moving."

"Tab, please. There's a really bad guy out there right now. He wants to hurt me and maybe all of you. That's why we were all trying to find you. You needed to be warned…"

She flinched, twitched, rubbed under her nose, and looked around. "Can't be held back. Got shit to do. Just needed to check on my sister, ya know? Make sure you were still breathin' and shit."

"Tabby." I cupped her cheeks. "Are you using again, honey?"

Her eyes narrowed and she flinched, pushing out of my hold. "So, what if I am? What do you care? It's my life. I'll do what I want. And I fucking want to be free." She rubbed at her arms and then looked around. "Gotta go, girl. Just checking in."

"Mom needs to see you." I tried the big guns. Mama Kerri was everything to us. Our mother. The woman who took care of us when the world had forgotten we'd existed. Our light at the end of every dark tunnel.

She shook her head. "No, no, nut-uh. She doesn't want me around. I'm not good for her. No good for any of you. Got shit to do."

"Tabby, please come with me and Jonah. He's with the

FBI…" I gestured to Jonah who was standing not two feet behind me monitoring our conversation.

"Hey, Tabitha, I'm Jonah…"

"You're with the FBI?"

He nodded.

"Fuck! What the fuck, Si. You setting me up?"

I jerked my head back. "Tabby, you came here to see me. Why would I set you up?"

She plunged her fingers into her hair and looked around. "Shit. Shit. Gotta go."

I grabbed her wrist. "No, you need to come with me to the back room so we can talk. Call Mom. Get her here to help you. Honey, you're high as a kite and you're not making any sense. You look like you haven't eaten in a month, sister. Come on." I tried to get her to come with me, but she ripped her arm away.

"Si, Mom and the girls don't need me in their lives. I fuck everything up. I gotta go! I'll keep an eye on you, sister, but I gotta go!"

Feeling completely hopeless, I reached for her and she shoved me hard enough that I fell backward into Jonah who broke my fall.

Then as quick as she came, she disappeared into the crowd.

"Go after her!" I cried out.

He shook his head. "Baby, she's smoke. Gone. Wiry woman like that can disappear in broad daylight especially if she doesn't want to be found. And she doesn't seem to want to be found or receive any help right now."

I spun around and put my face against his chest. "She's using again. Probably selling too. She looks bad."

"We'll figure it out. Talk to your sisters and mother. See what we can do about nailing her down and getting her into a program."

I nodded. "She's already been through two of them. We thought this last one worked. She's been clean for two years since she left the six-month program."

He shook his head. "I don't know what to tell you. I don't know your sister, honey, but for now, all you can do is pray and bring the other women into it."

"Yeah, I gotta finish my shift." My shoulders dropped as the weight of Tabby using again truly hit me.

Mom was going to be devastated. Though I doubted she'd be surprised.

Chapter
THIRTEEN

"OH, MY POOR LITTLE CHICK." MAMA KERRI PACED the open space in the center of the rented apartment in Sonia's building while ringing her hands.

My heart hurt at the sight. The constant worry, concern, and fear that a young girl she raised, loved like her very own, and accepted into her life as her daughter had once again gone down the wrong path.

Jonah had left us, went out in the hallway to get an update from Ryan on the case. I knew he was eager for the autopsy results on Helen in the hopes that it would enlighten the team on new leads. Even though he wasn't officially on the case, they kept him fully updated in the event that he could shed some light on anything new.

For the past six months Jonah and Ryan had been chasing the Backseat Strangler across Illinois. The recent deaths of Katrina, my apartment manager, and Helen were the first they believed the Strangler had personally chosen. The rest seemed to be based on convenience. Wrong place, wrong time. Just like me. Originally. Now it's as though the killer had escalated focusing on first Katrina by killing her in my apartment and then Helen. She specifically was a message screaming loud and clear that the killer was biding his time.

He apparently didn't like loose ends and I feared he'd kill more people Jonah or I knew before he was done.

"Fuckin' Tabby," Charlie ranted on a huff. "There any liquor in this place? I need a drink." She stomped off into the kitchen, her red ponytail swinging along with her.

"Charlie," Mama chastised, and Charlie gave a murmured, "Sorry," as she entered the swinging door to the kitchen.

The room was unusual and seemed to be focused on entertaining in the combined living and dining space with a clear opening in the center and near the patio. There were three matching white leather sofas forming a U-shape in front of the fireplace, which had a flat screen TV hung above it. I imagined it could hold a good thirty people comfortably. More if you opened the sliding doors to the wide patio where people could mingle inside and out.

"I'm not sure what we can do at this point," Sonia stated on a sigh, her eyes glued to her phone. Her hair was a stunning shade of spun gold. One side was pressed behind her ear, the other side skimming her cheek in a pretty natural wave. She wore a sexy as hell red suit with black piping. I loved her in red. It upped her powerful politician vibe times a thousand.

"Kick some skinny girl ass, is what's going to happen if I get my hands on her." Blessing crossed her legs and pursed her lips, all sass and spitfire, ready to bring the smack down on Tabitha.

Mama Kerri glared at Blessing and she clamped her mouth shut and looked to me.

"I'm with Blessing. That girl needs a kick in the pants. Big time. You guys should have seen her. It was awful.

Repeating herself. Looking thin and sickly. It was almost as bad as when she was eighteen and had gotten in with that rave crowd." I frowned remembering that time as being awful.

Mama Kerri shook as though she were cold, then pressed her hand to her forehead. "Please Lord, take care of my girl or bring her home to me and I'll do it. Just keep her safe."

"*Si.* I agree. We need to find her, show her how much we love and need her in our lives. Help her to choose us over the drugs." Liliana wiped a tear from her eye.

Jonah entered the room from behind us, his face a mask of severity, jaw locked, dark gaze zeroed in on mine.

Last night after my shift I was barely functioning when Jonah took me home. I had gone straight to his bathroom and brushed my teeth. From there I yanked off my top, my bra, and my jeans, and hit the bed face first in nothing but my panties. Jonah had promptly covered me up and did whatever it is guys do to close up a house at night before sleeping. I didn't even feel him enter the bed, nor did I feel him leave it this morning when I woke. He'd been broody and serious all morning, even when driving us across town to Sonia's building where everyone was staying.

Genesis had taken a few days off work at the Department of Health and Human Services where she was a social worker who placed displaced and orphaned children into foster homes. Rory was sitting on her knees coloring in a Disney *Frozen* coloring book quietly at the glass square coffee table. For three years old, she did a damn fine job too.

"There are a couple new programs for drug addictions that I've researched. They have impressive success rates.

Though these ones are not only expensive, they are out of state, request no visitation from outside sources including family, and are deeply immersive. Tabitha would have to agree to it and sign herself into it. For serious cases like hers, they recommend a full year at their facility but no less than six months. We have to keep in mind, she's already been through two before. She may not be willing. And that's if we can find her first." Genesis frowned. Her hair was pulled back in a long French braid that fell almost to her bum. I had some serious hair envy because hers was the deepest espresso color, silky, shiny, and perfectly flat.

"Well, I don't know what to say other than I'll pay for the program this time. Mama Kerri paid for the first and Sonia paid for the second. I've got wads of cash in the bank and not a lot of time or desire to spend it. Besides, my agent just scored me a new bathing suit gig in the Mykonos that will pay off my condo downtown."

"Girl, you are rolling in it, as you should be with that fine full-figured sexy body." Charlie snapped her fingers and gave Addison a high-five.

"You are such an inspiration to women everywhere, *hermana*," Liliana added.

"Thanks, sprite." Addison winked at Liliana.

Liliana rolled her eyes and grinned. Sprite was a running nickname for Liliana because she was only five foot three. The smallest of us all. The woman was like a gorgeous Spanish doll. Perfect Latina features with her short curly dark hair, pointed chin, plump lips, rounded cheekbones, and skin the color of a pristine sandy beach made of crushed light brown coral.

"Speaking of work..." Addison stood, and her upper

body sagged. "I have a photoshoot scheduled for the next few days in New York. I have to go pack. I'm leaving tonight."

Her having to go to work had all of our attention, even Jonah's, who had sidled up next to me with his ass to the arm of the chair, his hand warmly resting on my shoulder. As he listened to her statement, he gripped me tighter.

She held her hands out. "No worries, the client secured a bodyguard to pick me up, drive me to and from the job and the airport, and to make sure I'm safely back in my hotel each night. Plus side, I'll be out of state."

Jonah crossed his arms. "It's not perfect, but we understand that you all need to live your lives. Please provide Simone with the information for the bodyguard and a detailed report of your schedule."

Addy nodded, grabbed her purse from the table, and laid a kiss to Rory's head. Each one of us stood and accepted hugs. By the time she got to me I held her tight. "Be insanely careful. I'm talking, looking over your shoulder, never going out unattended, and don't drink much. I know you need to put on a show for all the glamorous people you work with, but more than anything, you need to be on the lookout at all times. Okay?"

She held me tight, then kissed my cheek. "Scout's honor," she giggled.

"You weren't in the Girl Scouts!" I whined.

"I'll check in. Don't worry." Addison flipped her long brown hair. "Love you guys!"

After a round of love you's from all of us, Addy took her leave, Jonah entering as she exited.

"We have some more information that I'd like to share,

but it's not for little ears." He smiled at Rory who had her tongue sticking out while she was coloring Elsa's skin brown.

Genesis looked over her daughter's head at the picture. "Sweet Pea, you know that Elsa is white, right?"

Blessing stretched her body over to look at the page and grinned smugly.

Rory frowned and looked over her shoulder at her mama. "Auntie Bless says princesses are black too."

Blessing snickered. "And it looks to me you have one fine African American princess there. Just. Like. You." She tapped her nose and Rory giggled.

Genesis shook her head and smiled. "And she is perfect. Great job, Sweet Pea."

Rory beamed and then yawned and rubbed at her eyes with her small fists.

"I think it's past time for someone's nap. How about Grammy sets up a movie and watches a little with you?" Mama Kerri suggested.

Rory nodded enthusiastically.

"Wave to your aunties and your mama, baby," she instructed.

"Love you!" She waved and took her grandmother's hand, entering the back hall that led to the three separate bedrooms.

"That child owns my soul." Blessing tsked.

"Right?" Charlie agreed.

"One hundred percent," Liliana added.

"Absolutely. You've done such a good job with her, Gen. She's so smart and bright, even though her daddy is overseas on deployment and you two aren't together, she seems super well-adjusted and happy. It's gotta be hard doing it all on your own, though."

Genesis nodded. "Some days are harder than others. I have Mama Kerri so at the very least she gets family time every other day, but it is hard. And of course, I have all of you."

"We need to do better about allowing you some personal time. Once this is all over with, we should trade off. One of us taking her for a night every couple weeks. Give you an evening every so often so you can go out, let your hair down…"

"Meet a man." Charlie's tone was thick with innuendo. "When was the last time you went on a date?"

Genesis sighed and shifted her pretty amber gaze to my guy. "Don't you have an update for us, Jonah?"

Jonah stayed where he was and cleared his throat. "The preliminary autopsy results have come back. Helen was strangled as we suspected. Only the coroner found, uh, something really strange." He rubbed the back of his neck and a long breath shuddered through him. Talking about Helen had to be difficult on a good day. Talking about her body being autopsied, far worse.

"It's okay, baby, take your time." I ran my hand down his thigh.

He covered my hand with his and held it. He inhaled a long, slow breath while staring into my face. I smiled softly and held his hand pouring all the strength I had into it.

He swallowed and licked his lips. "Turns out there was a folded-up piece of paper lodged in her throat."

"Excuse me?" Sonia said, her tone wary.

"Yeah, it, uh, looks as though it was placed postmortem." He winced.

Blessing and Charlie both made a stink face while Liliana put both of her hands in prayer position at her chest.

Genesis just stared at Jonah with a compassionate expression.

"There was a series of numbers and a letter on the paper."

"Can you share it with us? Or is that confidential?" I asked.

"No, Ryan and the Director think it's some type of clue to where he is or perhaps it connects to a past or future victim. We wanted to see if the numbers made any sense to you. Keep in mind this is all extremely confidential. The FBI doesn't make a habit of sharing case details with civilians but in all honesty, we're at a dead end. This is pretty much all we have until we get her toxicology report and I doubt they'll find anything but alcohol since we know she was at the pool hall."

I shrugged. "Lay it on us."

Jonah pulled out his phone and read the number. "A121094."

"That's it?" Blessing asked. "No dashes or spaces? The numbers ran all together like that?"

"Yeah. We're thinking maybe it's an address or an ID of some kind. We've already checked drivers' licenses and license plates and have a list of addresses that have variations of the numbers. Boots are on the ground knocking on doors now, but I don't think he'd be so obvious as to give us an address or a license number. My gut says this is a clue to the next victim or someone he already has."

Liliana closed her eyes and started praying under her breath in Spanish.

"That's whack, leaving numbers on a sheet of paper in a dead woman's mouth." Blessing gagged and covered her mouth breathing deeply through her nose.

"Since this guy is obsessed with you and Simone, that number has to relate somehow," Charlie said. She reached for a crayon and a blank coloring page on Rory's book. "What's the number again?"

"A121094," Jonah repeated, and she wrote it down.

She wrote it down a few more times and ripped the scraps of the page and gave a piece to each one of us. "My theory is, keep looking at it. Let your mind wander, then do it again. Maybe it will make sense at some point. It has to be obvious. I mean this guy doesn't know that much about Simone. Maybe he knows more about you?" Charlie continued. "My guess is it's super simple and the odds are you're thinking too far outside the box." She shrugged and tapped the ripped piece she'd kept.

"It would be great if you all could think on it. Go over it with your mother and Addison too. I'll share it with my folks and her parents to see if the connection is on mine or Helen's side instead of yours."

"Sounds like a plan." Sonia stood up. "I have to go, Quinn is waiting for me. I have a press conference to attend about all of this. Would it be possible to talk to Agent Russell, maybe have him speak on the FBI's behalf?"

Jonah scrubbed his hand across his clean-shaven chin. Another thing he'd tended to before I got up, instead of waking me and having morning nookie. Dammit.

"I don't know. It's all hands on deck..."

"We have to address the public. The media is in an absolute tizzy over Simone's involvement and her being my sister. And according to Quinn, a few of the rag mags have put two and two together about your relationship. There're photos of you coming and going outside of your home in the same car. They've figured out that she is staying at your house and calling the whole thing a tawdry love triangle. Not only does that look bad on you, it looks bad on the FBI."

"There's no rule against me falling for a survivor," Jonah mentioned flatly.

"Aw, honey. A survivor instead of a victim. I like that." I stood up from my position on the couch and wrapped my arm around his back. "She's right, though. If something involves Sonia, the press goes nuts. And since I'm the wild child to her prim and proper, it's some juicy gossip."

"I'll talk to my Director and get back to you."

That appeased Sonia as she nodded, buttoned her blazer, and ran her hand down the sides of her hair. "Excellent. I look forward to hearing from you."

"The rest of you, please stay inside and with someone as much as possible. Any time you can take off work right now is a day more your safety is ensured. And speaking on behalf of myself and Ryan and the FBI, I want to thank you for keeping things quiet and uprooting your lives. I'm sure it hasn't been easy and I'm grateful to you all."

Charlie popped up off the couch and pulled Jonah into a hug. "No worries, dude. We're family. We do what needs to be done for one another."

Blessing got up and held her hand out. She was a hugger, but not by nature. Jonah would have to earn that by treating me well and staying around for a while. "We've got your back, brother." She shook his hand with both of hers. That was something.

Liliana dashed over to me and hugged me hard and kissed my cheek then got up on her tippy toes to hug Jonah who hunched his much larger frame over to hug her back. She also kissed his cheek. *"Ve con Dios."* Go with God, she said and smiled.

Genesis gave me a long hug. "You doing okay, sister?" My goodness, her amber eyes were mesmerizing against her soft brown skin. She was so beautiful it stunned me sometimes.

"Jonah's got me. I'm good, sis."

"Okay," she took a breath and let it out. "I'm gonna check on Mama and Rory. I'll bet Mama is asleep and Rory is awake singing along to the songs."

I chuckled and watched as she gave Jonah a hug. "Thank you for keeping my sister safe. If there's ever anything you need from me or anything I can do at my work, don't hesitate to reach out."

"Thank you, Genesis. That's very kind of you and I will. Sometimes I come across some wayward kids in my work that could use a little help."

"I'm there. Phone call away."

"Appreciate it."

Jonah turned to me now that the sisters were moving along to whatever it was they were going to be doing today.

"What next, FBI man?" I wrapped my arms around his neck and pressed my body to his.

"After the shit that went down at Tracks last night, I've come to really enjoy the idea of you working at A+ Construction. Figure we could visit my father, you could take a tour, meet some of the guys, chit chat with Lisa who has the job now, and maybe we can speed up that job change."

My eyes bulged because I felt like I'd been squeezed to the limits at the level of my excitement. I couldn't help but bounce up and down. "Really? Do you think he might consider hiring me before I finish my last class?"

He hooked his arm around my shoulders and kissed my temple. "Yeah, babe, I think he gets a load of how excited you are, driven, smart, and how much you mean to me, and he'll be jumping at the chance to bring you on board. I was thinking we could discuss a part-time situation with him. That way the other hours of the day you could devote to your studies and the flower shop until you're ready to go full time. This would also allow for you to have a full month of training."

I grinned. "And I could quit Tracks."

"And you could quit Tracks," he smirked.

"And be far away from Trey and his grabby hands," I added.

"Definite fuckin' plus."

I nudged his shoulder. "Don't pretend that isn't the real reason…"

He led me out the door and into the hallway. "You being safe with people I trust working around you is the goal. And it helps my father. My father deserves good help."

"And what about Luca?" I hedged because I didn't want to tiptoe around anything with Jonah. That's not who I was, and he made it clear he wanted me to be honest in all things.

He sucked in a breath and let it out on a sigh. "I'll have to deal."

I stopped at the front of the elevator. "Honey, I don't want you to have to deal with anything extra. If you don't want me working with Luca, I won't. Sure, it sounds like the most amazing opportunity but I'm not going to risk the opportunity I have with our relationship for a prospective job. It's just not worth it to me."

Jonah tipped his head to the side. "Simone, what's your end goal? Perfect world type scenario?"

I pursed my lips together and thought about it for a moment and then shrugged. "I want to have a good job where the work I do contributes and is important to the company. I want to feel needed. I want to be part of a team."

"All doable. And what about your personal life?"

I smile and placed my hands to his biceps. "I want to have a husband and kids one day. Have Mama Kerri watch my babies while I work, raise them in a similar manner as she raised me, with love and a kind hand toward discipline. And then I want to come home and be a mom and a wife. I don't want to change the world or invent the next best thing. I just want to make a solid day's pay for an honest day's work and enjoy my family time. Oh, and maybe a dog. I'd really like a dog. Dogs are awesome. How about you?"

Before he responded his lips crashed down over mine. He licked deep and kept the kiss going for so long we heard the elevator doors open and then close and the lift go back down with us not in it. I locked my arms around his neck and went right into my Jonah kiss haze where all things happy and good lived.

He pulled away but kept his forehead pressed to mine. "I keep wondering when you're going to turn."

"Turn?" I panted, still out of breath from his kiss.

"Yeah, turn into a bitch, or become needy, or crazy, or any of the above. Simone, you're too damn perfect to be true and I'm having trouble believing all I've ever wanted ended up in my lap during one of my cases. I went through hell with Helen, baby. Ever since I was promoted to a profiler five years ago, it all turned to shit. She became someone I didn't recognize. And maybe that had to do with me. We'd been together for so long we got used to one another. Then when I wasn't there all the time, she changed. Or maybe that's who she always was but I didn't see it. Whatever the case, I never felt this connected or on the same path with a woman. Are you sure you can handle a man whose career means you're going to be having a lot of those dinners alone with your children?"

I shrugged. "If my husband was out protecting other people from being killed and trying to put away extremely bad people for crimes I wouldn't want committed on my worst enemy, yeah I'm pretty sure I'd be fine. I'd miss you heaps, but that would just make it more exciting when you got home. Something to look forward to." I cupped his cheek. "Relationships are hard. Lord knows I've had my fair share. More than my fair share to be accurate. Though I never once saw myself in a white dress with kids underfoot like I have when I'm in your arms. You make me see a future. A real one that's all mine. One of my own making, and that's something to hold on to. I'm sure any marriage is hard, but if you keep the lines of communication open, anything can work. You just have to be willing to try."

He kissed me again and bit down on my bottom lip. Arousal slid through my form on gossamer wings. "Can we maybe go back to your place first?"

"Why?" He pressed the button on the elevator to bring it back to our floor.

I squirmed where I stood and bit into my own lip sizing him up.

He shook his head. "Oh no. No way. We stop back home we're not leaving, and I've made up my mind about Tracks. You don't love it. It's not your dream. It's not even a stepping stone to your dream so we need to get you checking into other options. And since I need to talk to my father anyway about the numbers, we should go there first."

I pouted. "Fine. Ruin all my fun."

"We'll have fun, baby. A lot of it. Tonight. When we're safely locked into a hotel."

"A hotel?" The surprise in my tone was obvious.

"Not making love to you for the first time and having Ryan busting in. I fear I may pull my gun on him."

I chuckled and the elevator doors opened. He led me inside.

"This is an excellent plan." I batted my eyelashes and stared into his handsome face.

He pecked me on the lips. "I know. You. Me. No interruptions. Candlelight dinner in. Chocolates. Champagne. The whole nine."

I covered my pitter-pattering heart. "You do have a plan. Still, I want to stop at your house on the way. Pick up something special to wear tonight and a change of clothes."

His eyes blazed white-hot fire with the amount of lust searing me. "Done."

"Any special requests?" I taunted.

"Black. Lace."

"Naughty." I grinned, knowing exactly what I was going to wear.

Jonah tugged at his collar and adjusted his crotch before the elevator opened.

Tonight, was going to be epic. I just knew it.

Chapter
FOURTEEN

A+ Construction headquarters were set up in an older part of town about twenty minutes from Oak Park. The front was made of horizontal windows with painted green slats surrounded by brick and beige-colored concrete. I had expected some type of rugged, rusted out warehouse, but was pleasantly surprised at how the front of the building was a bit contemporary with a touch of downhome Midwestern charm.

Jonah opened the door for me and placed a hand to my lower back as I entered.

The front had a crescent-shaped wall that separated the large reception desk from the waiting area. A set of six seats and a coffee table were on one side of the room. In the other corner was a pretty table with a pristine white orchid sitting on top, a gilded brass rectangular mirror hanging on the wall above it. Behind the reception desk I could see glass partitioned offices.

Luca was standing over the desk holding a file folder and discussing something with a heavily pregnant Asian woman. I lifted my hand and gave a jaunty wave. Luca smiled, finished his conversation, and left the woman's office. He walked the short hallway to the door that separated reception from where the bulk of their offices were.

"Hey, I uh, didn't expect to see the two of you so soon. Everything okay?"

Jonah tightened his hold on my hand. "Here to see Dad. He mentioned to Simone he'd show her around the company. If everyone feels she's a good fit, I'd like to see about him hiring her earlier, prior to her finishing her last class. Maybe in a part-time capacity. This would allow her the time to study and secure her degree, while giving Lisa time to train her on the position in advance."

Luca blinked slowly and didn't say anything for what seemed to me like a long time. My nerves were ramped up to the max and I had to keep myself from spewing all my thoughts a hundred miles an hour into the weighted silence.

"To be honest, Dad did tell me about the idea of Simone working here and I wasn't sure you'd be okay with that. Considering our history."

"Maybe this was a bad idea." Jonah grumbled and made to turn to the entrance, but I locked my other arm around his and held on.

"I'm very interested in working with you and Marco. I've had a ton of experience in customer service, and I filled in at Tracks any time the business manager was sick or on vacation. I'm a super-fast learner, intelligent, and you will not find a harder worker. And I'm looking for a position that I can stay with long term. Something that will support the future I want."

Jonah looped his arm over my shoulders. "Hope some of what you want in the future has me in it, baby."

I grinned and elbowed him in the ribs.

Jonah chuckled. "Ouch. Sorry. Okay, okay."

"Well, you've come to the right place. Dad was taken with you. You have been all he's talked about for the last couple days. Why don't you come on back and I'll introduce you to Lisa and the rest of the office team? Most of the men are out on jobs."

"Do they clock in here?"

He shook his head. "No. The office isn't open until eight. Our team starts when they step foot on the job usually around six-thirty or seven in the morning depending on the weather and what the job site entails. We trust them to do their job and follow their foreman's lead. We have five foremen. Each person has a team of four to five under him or her. We have one female foreman and two female construction workers."

"That's cool."

"Women can do most anything a man can, but we focus on our team's strengths. The female foreman we have is more talented in the design intricacies of a job. We send her in to work her magic. Then her team will either do the job or we'll pass it off to one of the other teams. It all depends on what's needed. The job determines the workers, if that makes sense."

I followed behind Luca as he spoke, and Jonah trailed us without interrupting.

"Actually, it makes perfect sense. You want to employ the right people in the right roles. That way, you'll get the best outcome."

"Spoken like a true business manager in training," Luca teased, and my heart started to pound. When Luca faced forward, I turned around and gave a thumbs up to Jonah who shook his head and rolled his eyes.

Chapter
FIFTEEN

"CAN YOU BELIEVE YOUR DAD HIRED ME ON THE SPOT!"
I spun around in a circle once Jonah led me through the hotel room door, tossing my bag into the chair in the corner. After I twirled, I went over to the bed and plopped backward, letting myself fall to the king-sized bed. The room was beautiful but not ostentatious. Hugging each side of the bed were black lacquered end tables with shiny silver handles. A squat, silver-based lamp sat on each side of the bed.

I watched as Jonah went to one lamp and turned it on, then repeated the process on the next.

Across from the bed were two huge windows. In between them was a matching black dresser with a flat screen TV hanging on the wall above it. To the left of the bed was a door that was already open, which I could tell led to a rather large bathroom, complete with an awesome tub that I figured two people could easily fit in. Imagining me and Jonah in the tub had me shivering with excitement to get on with tonight's activities.

I popped up and went over to the chair where my bag was, shimmying as I did so.

Jonah sat on the edge of the bed and chuckled. "You're really happy, baby."

I grinned and spun around. "So happy! You don't know what this means. He told me what the base salary is and it's more than all my jobs put together! Do you know what this means? I'll be able to finish my coursework, find a place of my own, buy some furniture, and live without fear about where my next dollar is going to come from." I clutched the pretty kimono-style satin robe I pulled from my bag and held it up to my chest. "And I'm going to have medical benefits! I haven't had any medical coverage since I lived at Kerrighan House and was under the government care plans. This. Is. Huge!"

Jonah patted the bed next to him. "Come here."

I dropped the kimono on my bag and practically skip-walked to his side. Instead of sitting next to him, I put my hands to his shoulders and sat across his lap, my knees beside each of his hips.

"It seems like since the day you crashed into my life, everything is changing for the better." I dipped my head and rubbed my nose against his. "Thank you, Jonah."

He moved his hands from where they'd been curled around the fleshy parts of my hips and slid them up my ribcage and around my back. "This smile on your face right now, it makes all the shit I've had to go through worth it. You light up my life, Simone. Make me see things differently. I'm now looking forward to the future."

I ran my fingers through his hair, and he tilted his head back. "Are you sure you're okay with me working for your dad and your brother?"

He inhaled so deeply I could feel his chest move with his intake of air where we were pressed together. "Wasn't it you who told me I couldn't let my past color my future?"

I grinned. "Not in those words exactly, but yeah. We can't take any of the past back and do it over again. We just have to move forward and make the best choices we can toward finding our happy."

"Which also means I can't convict you for the sins of my ex-wife," he murmured.

I scratched at the back of his head, allowing my nails to grate across the tension I felt there. "It wasn't all bad was it? With Helen."

He closed his eyes and I rested my forehead to his.

"You don't have to talk about it. Especially since this is supposed to be our night, but honey, you just lost her all over again in a way that's very permanent. I don't want you putting on a strong face for me, or not sharing your grief. You had a life before me, and I'm okay with you sharing all of it. I just want to know you're okay and I'm supporting you the best way I can."

Jonah smiled softly and opened his eyes. "I'm okay and dealing with a lot of it internally. I'm not going to lie and say it doesn't hurt that she left this world the way she did, but that's not on me, you, or anyone other than the bastard who took her life." He tightened his hold on me. "Would it be wrong to ask you to go to the funeral with me?"

I shook my head. "Not at all. She was an important part of your life. And you know, it's okay to let go of all the nastiness that was between you two in the end and just grieve for the woman you loved and married all those years ago."

He sighed and I felt his warm breath caress my cheek. "You're an amazing woman, Simone. I hope you know that."

I grinned, cupped his cheeks, and tilted his head to look

at me. "As long as my man believes it, that's all that matters," I said and took his mouth in a slow, deep kiss. Before long he fell back, palmed my ass with both his large hands, and let me take charge.

When I ran my hands down his chest in search of the button on his jeans, he encircled my wrists and sat back up abruptly. "Nope. No going further. We're having a dinner date here in the room and I am eager to see what you plan on putting under that pretty satin robe you just had in your hands."

I laughed and bit into my bottom lip. He cupped my cheek. "I'm going to have to start praying again," he said randomly.

His statement had me frowning. "Uh, okay. Why?"

He grinned. "Because you're such an anomaly. I'd never met a woman like you. One who seems so perfectly matched with me. Comfortable in her own skin. Takes life as it comes."

"Mmm hmm, butter me up some more, baby. I like it!" I teased. "But you know I'm a sure thing, right? I'm pretty confident that I want to jump your bones more than you want to jump mine." I ran my thumb across his plump bottom lip.

Jonah laughed out loud and for a very long time after I made my claim. "Not even close, Simone. You forget, it's been over a year since I've been with a woman. I'm certain my desire to fuck your brains out far surpasses anything you've cooked up in that wild imagination of yours." He kissed me hard and fast, tugging on my bottom lip and letting it go with a snap.

I licked the heated flesh and my eyes went half-lidded,

lust coiling at the base of my spine and lower. "Care to skip dinner?"

He chuckled, stood up, and let me drag down his muscular form. I whimpered like a wanton hussy but worse, I felt like one. I was one hundred percent ready to throw any plans he had out the window and just mount him right then and there.

"Cool it, baby. I'm going to order room service."

I sighed and took a deep breath, my arms still looped around his waist. "Okay, one more melt-my-panties kiss and then I'll go take a shower and leave you to order our food. Deal?"

He grinned, cupped the back of my head, and whispered "Deal," against my lips. Then he kissed me. It lasted a very long time. So long my panties were damp, my heartbeat was banging against my chest, and I was in a serious Jonah kiss haze, which consisted of my mind being mush, my body on fire with want, and my vision a little blurry.

Jonah chuckled as he walked me over to the bathroom. Then he left me inside as he stepped out, got my entire bag, and brought it to the counter and set it on top.

"You got what you need?" He cupped my cheek and I cupped his hard cock.

"Not even close, but things are looking up." I ran the palm of my hand over the length hidden behind his jeans. He groaned and thrust his hips against my hand once before backing up.

"Woman, you'd test the patience of a priest. Jesus," he grumbled. "Take your time. I think I'm going to need a bit of my own in order to be calm enough to sit and eat next to you." He shook his head and exited with a smile.

I moved to the door and curled my fingers around the jamb. "Sorry, not sorry," I called out playfully and grinned when I heard him chuckling as he picked up the phone to order our dinner.

When I exited the bathroom a full forty minutes later, I was rocking a black lace teddy and matching thong with my black satin kimono that had a badass colorful dragon design covering the entire back. Brilliant flowers covered the three-quarter sleeves and the waist tied with a huge red sash that double-wrapped around the body and then tied with a bow in back. It was cool and hot as hades. I thought about putting on heels but felt that would be a little too cliché. Instead, I dried my hair and left my face clean and moisturized. I'd shaved every inch of my body and lotioned up to the gills to ensure my skin was soft and smelling fantastic.

Jonah was sitting at a table that had been placed at the opposite end of the room with two chairs on each side. There were a pair of candlesticks on top and two silver domed heat covers over what I assumed was our dinner.

He stood and I was pleased to find he wore a pair of loose causal burgundy pajama pants and a white V-neck T-shirt. The shirt clung to the broad expanse of his chest and outlined the rigid abdominal muscles below.

I licked my lips, crossed my ankles, and leaned against the door jamb casually.

His gaze took in my body from top to toe before he grinned. "I see you got the casual dinner dress memo," he said and then winked.

I chuckled, pushed off the door, and moseyed over to the table. He pulled out my seat and I sat, allowing him to help me get settled.

With a flourish, he removed the food covers. "For your dining pleasure this evening," he said with a gentlemanly flair. "We have for the lady, filet mignon with a wild mushroom topping in a delicious wine sauce. Potatoes au gratin and seasonal veggies that are to die for, madam." His lips twitched as he bowed, clicked his bare heels together, and failed in his attempt to hold onto his composure.

Me, however, I was eating it up. I loved this fun and silly side to Jonah. The man was often the most serious person in any room. To know he had this carefree side hiding under all that brawn, responsibility, and stoicism was awesome and definitely welcome.

"Why thank you, kind sir. This looks magnificent." I used a knock off bad interpretation of someone who was rich, prim, and proper while lifting my empty wine glass. "If you'd be so kind as to fill my glass."

"Absolutely, madam, it would be my pleasure." Jonah grinned and filled up my glass and then his own before taking his seat. His tone changed the second he picked up his fork. "Damn, this looks good. I didn't realize how hungry I was until I caught a whiff."

I lifted my wine. "Let's toast."

He lifted his. "What should we toast to?"

"Finding the bad guy and living our best lives." I grinned wide.

"Now that I can drink to." He tapped my glass with his and we both drank.

For a few minutes we both got down to eating quietly.

I was as ravenous as he was. "Okay, so since this is technically only date number two, the first being Navy Pier, I suggest we quiz one another in order to fast track the getting to know you part." Mostly because we were absolutely going to have sex tonight. There was no way I was letting this man leave without an orgasm or two.

Jonah burst out laughing and sat back against the chair. "I'm game. What do you want to know?" he prodded.

I chewed on a bite of perfectly cooked beef and tilted my head. "Tell me something you don't like about yourself," I asked and scooped up a flat cheesy potato before plopping it in my mouth.

"Going straight for the kill, eh?" The side of his mouth lifted in a small smirk.

I shrugged. "I mean, you can tell me your favorite book, song, and movie but that doesn't really tell me much. Finding out something you don't like about yourself, that says a lot about what you find important or not."

He held up his fork and sucked in his bottom lip as though he were thinking about how to answer my question. I mostly just stared at the way his scruffy jaw moved as he chewed. The man was damn sexy, and I couldn't wait to finish dinner and take things to the next step. If that made me promiscuous to some, I didn't care. I'd been on fire for the man since the second I hugged him in the hospital after he'd saved my life. Besides, I'd never been one to care what others thought about me. Life was too short, and I was committed to truly living it to the fullest.

"Hmm, I guess I'd have to say my serious demeanor."

I frowned. "Why do you think that's a flaw?"

"Not a flaw exactly, more like it can put people off. I

don't mean to be standoffish or seem stiff and rude, but I know I come off that way a lot of the time."

"Fair enough. People are always thinking I'm too carefree and wild, which often happens to be the same thing they say they love about me. You can't really win." I shrugged.

He shook his head. "No, you can't."

"My theory is you just have to accept what you can't change, or don't want to change about yourself, and surround yourselves with people who care about you for what and who you are."

"Good advice. Okay, my turn. What is something you absolutely love about yourself?" He used my same line of questioning but went for the positive route.

I sucked back some more delicious wine. "I mean, besides the taking things in stride, I'd have to say I genuinely like all people."

"How so?"

"Well, I dig that you're serious, possessive, a little alpha because your heart is in the right place. Kinda like Sonia. You too have a lot in common actually." I laughed.

"Awesome, I have a lot in common with your sister. That bodes well for my manhood," he moaned.

I exploded in laugher as he made a sour face.

"No, you misunderstood me. What I mean is, I'm the type of chick who just appreciates people for who they are. I'm sure it has a lot to do with growing up in a home with eight other women, but I like the differences in people. If we were all the same, life would be extremely boring. I don't like to be bored. Always gotta keep moving, find something to do, see, experience."

"I hope together we can have a few of our own special experiences." His voice dipped low and had a sultry growl that made my blood heat with anticipation.

I grinned. "Oh, you have no choice, mister. When you're not on a case or out of town, you better believe we will be enjoying ourselves." I tapped my plate with the tines of my fork. "I mean, I'm not a maniac. I can settle down and just chill and relax with my hot FBI guy, but I'm looking forward to sharing new experiences with you."

He reached across and took my hand. "Me too, Simone."

"Okay, now tell me something no one knows about you." I bit down on my bottom lip and waggled my brows.

He shook his head and chuckled. "Ah, let me see. Something no one knows about me. Do you mean something that happened in the past that I'm embarrassed of, or something weird about me that I keep hidden like my sixth toe?"

"No fuckin' way! Let me see your feet," I blurted, shoved the white tablecloth back, and ducked my head under the table in order to stare at his perfect, five-toes-a-piece feet.

I maneuvered back up and glared at his smug face as he sat back and laughed so hard, he ended up clutching at his stomach. "Baby, you are too easy to tease. Man, I haven't laughed this much in ages."

I pursed my lips and picked up my wine. "Well, at least there's that. I'm a pretty good sport when things are funny, and I'll admit. You had me…for a second. Now spill it! Tell me something—anything—that someone doesn't know about you."

He leaned an elbow to the table and rested his chin on it. "Hmm, I'm thinking. Okay I've got it, but you cannot, under any circumstances, tell Ryan, my brother Luca, or my father. Got it?"

I rubbed my hands together as if he were going to lay something super juicy on me. "No telling your bestie, your bro, or your dad. Got it." I used a finger to make a cross shape over my heart. That did not mean I couldn't share with my sisters but all women did that. Men had to expect their women talked about them with their girlfriends.

He licked his lips and for a moment I got distracted and my heart started pumping thinking about what other things he could lick with that tongue.

"My favorite artist, singer, whatever you want to call it…"

I grinned. "Yeah?"

"Is Taylor Swift," he blurted out.

My mouth dropped open and I blinked slowly. Manly man, hot FBI guy, filled with muscles, carried a badge, a gun, and chased seriously bad dudes for a living loved Tay-Tay Swift. So much so he claimed she was his favorite artist and singer.

My silence must have freaked him out because suddenly he clipped, "Shit, I shouldn't have told you."

I shook my head and lifted my hands. "No, no. I'm glad you did. I just needed a minute to take that in. Not only is it endearing…" I pressed my lips flat together because I could barely hold back the laughter. "It's also hilarious!" I cracked up and he groaned.

"I'm going to regret this one day. I just know it." He sighed and rubbed at his temples with a thumb and a forefinger.

I waved my hand and breathed through the laughter

that continued to bubble up and come out in loud bursts. "No, no. I'm just surprised. A big, badass, FBI guy like you loves him some T-Swift. I'm a fan too. Swear!" I clamped down on my laughter and breathed through my nose in order to keep my mouth shut. "Have you purchased the new album everyone's talking about?"

"Downloaded it, yeah. It's actually pretty brilliant."

I chuckled but kept it under control. "After that, you can ask me anything you want, and I promise to bare all." I gushed, wanting him to feel better about sharing such a funny secret.

His lips twitched. "You done eating?"

I nodded, picked up my glass, and held it out toward him. He refilled both of ours, adding the last splash to my glass.

For a full minute he stared at me, a dark eyebrow cocked up on one side of his forehead. I loved when a man could do that. There was something insanely sexy about it.

"What is your absolute favorite part about your body?" His question came out in a lower timber, one that spoke to the seductress all women had hidden inside themselves.

"My tits." I answered honestly and instantly. I knew most women would say their eyes, or their smile, maybe even their hair. Those were all good features, but I had stellar boobs and was rather proud of what I'd been gifted in that arena.

He smirked and his eyes heated. "Show me," he taunted, as though I wouldn't.

Boy, was Jonah in for a surprise. I was not the type of woman who would back down from a dare. Especially one I wanted to do.

I took my glass, lifted it to my lips, and swallowed a healthy amount, then stood up and set it on the table. Jonah turned his chair and pushed the table to the side and out of the way. He crossed his arms over his broad chest, pushed his legs out in front of him, and eased back as though he were preparing to watch a show.

If he wanted a show, he was about to get one.

"My tits, huh? You want to see them?"

"Fuck yeah, I do." He lifted his chin which I took as encouragement.

I reached behind me and untied the bow and unwrapped the sash from around my waist then let it hang down at my sides, the robe parting down the center.

A good few inches of my bare stomach and bra and panty combo could be seen.

Jonah's nostrils flared. "Keep going, sweet girl." His voice was thick and had that growly possessive note that made my knees feel week.

I shrugged one shoulder and the robe fell to my elbow on that side. I repeated the process but kept my hands together, delaying the full view until he was panting for it.

He inhaled swiftly and sat up. He put his hands to his thighs and rubbed the material up and down as he took in my half-dressed appearance. I liked seeing him slowly become unhinged. It blossomed like power running through my veins, little electric bolts of lightning teasing my nerve endings.

I watched him swallow, his Adam's apple bobbing enticingly.

Heat pooled between my thighs and I trembled.

"Take it off, Simone," he demanded. He didn't request it. No, he *demanded* it.

I gave him my most sultry smile and let my arms fall to my sides as the satin slithered down my body in a silky caress before it pooled around my feet.

There I stood, not even a hint of modesty in a lacy bra that showcased my tits, lifting them up and making them look round and plump, held together by a wide satin bow tied in the center. On bottom I wore a slinky little thong that had two satin matching bows sitting at the curve of my hips. All one had to do was pull the satin bows and the lingerie would have fallen to the floor.

"Jesus, baby." He growled.

I grinned and walked slowly forward until I was right in front of his parted legs.

Surprisingly, he grabbed for my hips first and slowly spun me around until I faced the bed.

"Damn, woman." He growled and then shocked me momentarily when I felt the scruff of his chin at the soft cheek of my ass before his lips pressed down. Before I could respond, he dragged his teeth over the fleshy globe and bit down until I cried out.

"Fuck." He gripped my hips hard and then did the same thing to the other side. "Your ass is magnificent."

My heart rate was through the roof and every molecule inside of me was focused on the span of skin he was currently worshipping. He nudged his face lower and nipped, biting at the curve of my ass cheek where it met my thigh. I jumped at the sharp sensation but he held me still before turning me around.

His gaze slid all over my form as though he were touching me.

I shook in his hold. "Touch me," I whispered.

He traced his fingertips from my collar bone, down between my breasts, and over my stomach for an all too brief tickle against the lace of my panties.

I groaned. "Jonah," I pled.

Jonah moved his hands to the satin bow that held the cups of my bra together. He tugged sharply and I gasped as the lace fell away. He eased the fabric off my shoulders and the bra fell to the floor.

His focus was centered on my breasts when he slid his hands up and over my stomach and finally cupped my tits in his warm hands.

"You're right." He swiped the pale pink tips with his thumbs, and I sucked in a sharp breath. "These are some beautiful breasts, baby. You should be proud of them."

I swallowed my smile as he teased my breasts, plucking the tips until the pale pink turned into a bright rosy hue that burned along with each tug of his talented fingers.

He gave them one last delicious pinch before moving to my hips. He fingered the bows on each side and his crystal blue gaze lifted to meet mine as he waited to remove the final bit of clothing.

I was breathing raggedly through my mouth, but I nodded once to his silent request. He didn't even wait a second more before pulling both bows and letting the scrap of fabric fall to the floor.

His fingers dug into the flesh at my hips as he tugged me forcefully forward and latched his mouth over my sex.

On autopilot, my brain told my hands to keep his head locked to where I was experiencing this exceptional pleasure. I moaned and thrust my hips with the silky movements of his tongue and lips. He growled against my flesh, reached for my thigh, and forced my foot onto the arm of the chair, opening me wide in front of his face. I was at the perfect height for devouring.

He licked his lips, using his thumbs to spread me intimately, and went to town. It was carnal, loud, graphic, and wild in a way that let me know I was only scratching the surface of my serious, alpha FBI man.

One of his arms locked around my hips and used my ass as leverage to push his tongue deeper, taking more, taking it all.

Within minutes I was coming against his mouth, screaming out while humping his face as he kept at me until every last wave of pleasure crested and crashed to the shore.

I shook in his hold, maybe even blacked out because, somehow, he lifted me up and my legs were wrapped around his waist as he carried me to the bed.

Once there, he laid me down gently and nodded to the end table at my right. I turned my head and saw a strip of condoms had been laid out. Something he must have taken care of when I was showering. I turned over and grabbed the strip, ripped one off, and opened it. When I turned back around, Jonah's T-shirt was off and he was pushing down his pajama bottoms.

His cock was long, hard, and wet at the tip. I licked my lips and laid back down. "Come over me, let me suck you," I begged, and he shook his head.

"Need to fuck you, babe." He growled, his normally brown eyes looking pitch black when filled with nothing but desire and passion. I could have drowned in that inky darkness and felt complete.

I handed him the condom package. I watched in avid fascination as he rolled it down his hard length.

I whimpered.

"Spread your legs, baby. Let me inside." That deep growl would be the end of me.

When I heard it, I physically panted and complied, opening my legs wide without even a hint of restraint. I wanted that hard cock inside of me, maybe even more than he did.

He fell on me like a man who hadn't eaten in a week would fall on a juicy steak. His mouth crashed over mine, his tongue licking deep as he reached between us, centered the tip of his cock, and eased inside in one slow, torturously intense thrust.

"Baby," I gasped when he pressed to the absolute end and came over me, chest to chest, hips to hips, heart to heart.

Connected.

I felt greedy and wanton, impaled on his cock, my legs spread wide, his weight pressing me into the bed until I could hardly breathe.

I wouldn't have changed a second of it.

As Jonah eased up and out of me, balancing his weight on a forearm on the bed, his gaze met mine. In his eyes I saw what I was giving him.

Life.

Hope.

Salvation.

Absolution.

A future together. Nothing would ever compare to the feeling of having Jonah inside me. Of the two of us connected in this way. Not ever again. He was it for me and I knew beyond a shadow of a doubt that I was it for him. It was all there, painted across his face, open and honest for me to accept.

I locked one leg around his thigh, the other I held higher. He shifted one of his arms and pressed a hand to the back of that thigh, holding it high and out to the side, thrusting as deep as he could, splitting me in half in a way that was so liberally mixed with pleasure and pain I didn't know which I preferred more. What I did know was that I never wanted him to stop.

"Want everything, Simone. Want it all, every inch of you," he said nonsensically but I knew what he was talking about. Knew what plagued this man who'd had his wife cheat on him. Who traveled the world dealing with the scum of the earth regularly, not having a safe place to land that was all for him. Just for him.

He wanted *me*.

He wanted a safe place.

And in that moment, I vowed to be exactly what he needed.

"Take it all. Everything I have. I want to give it all to you." I confided blindly, knowing that giving myself to a man such as him, there would be no going back. And I didn't care. I wanted to be everything he could ever want and need.

His nostrils flared and his lips took on a snarl as he started pounding into me. Proving to himself, or to me, just how much this moment meant to him.

"Fuck, Simone," he panted, powering in and out, grinding against my throbbing, swollen bundle of nerves with each thrust. I arched into the pressure, took as much as I gave back, digging my nails into his shoulders as he fucked me into a mindless, blissful place I never wanted to leave.

I lifted my body, sucked on his neck, his chin, his lips, whatever I could reach as he took us both higher and higher into nothing but ecstasy.

I wrapped my legs around his waist, and he hauled me upright so I was in his lap. His hips lifted with each thrust, his calves against the bed as he powered up. I rode his cock, my head tipped forward, our mouths fused.

He sank deep on a mighty thrust and I shot into the heavens. My body locking around him so tight I was surprised he could still lift me up and down, forcing my body to take his rigid length until he too found his release on a mighty roar.

Jonah locked his arms around my back and waist, plastering me to his front while he took my mouth in the most passionate kiss of my life. Our tongues tangled and made love in the same powerful way our bodies had just moments before, wildly and relentless. Thoroughly and with wanton need.

I don't know how long we stayed together, him softening inside of me, my legs locked in a powerful vice around his trim waist, our mouths fused, but eventually he fell to the side taking me with him. Once there, he disconnected and turned me to face him. He tugged the sheets and blanket over our cooling bodies and locked me against his chest. I snuggled against his warmth, kissed him above his pounding heart, and closed my eyes.

"Sleep now, sweet Simone. I'll wake you soon for round two."

I grinned against his skin and then passed out.

Chapter
SIXTEEN

WE SPENT THE NEXT DAY AND NIGHT IN THE HOTEL room. Both of us unwilling to leave the safety and security of not only one another, but the little bubble of happiness we'd carved out for ourselves. Jonah was insatiable. Which I imagine had a lot to do with the fact that I was more than willing to reciprocate all the good he bestowed on me, but also the fact that he hadn't been intimate with a woman in over a year. We ordered room service for every meal, and ate it scarcely dressed. When done, we attacked one another as though we were starving. It felt as if we had been walking in the wilderness for a year with no hope of being saved or finding an ounce of human connection. This thing between Jonah and me was a living, breathing connection.

He made love to me as though it were his honor. A gift.

Connecting us in a way I'd never known with a man. And somehow through that link, we both felt saved.

Honestly, I didn't realize I was living half a life, going from job to job, attached to a man who *did not* love me and cheated on me repeatedly. Scrounging for every dollar I could in an attempt to make something of myself. I'd spent the last six years trying to complete a two-year degree, class by class, pinching pennies in order to do so.

Struggling was putting it mildly.

Sacrifice was all I knew.

Then along came Jonah.

Not only did he save my life physically that night, he saved my soul.

Now I had a man who genuinely cared for me and showed it. Protective. Generous. Kind. And a master in the bedroom. I had a new job that started Monday morning, making a larger salary than I'd hoped for, and I had one more class to complete to get my degree. Something Jonah's father was going to let me work on two hours a day while getting paid. He said you had to invest in your people, and he believed I was an investment. Actually, it was me who convinced him beyond a shadow of a doubt that I was worthy of such an investment. And I'd prove it. I intended to work my ass off for A+ Construction showing him, Luca, Jonah, Sonia, and all my sisters that I could be successful. I could turn my half a life into something truly worth living.

And all that started with Jonah.

The same man who was right then pouring the water from a sponge over my naked chest. He sat behind me in the gargantuan hotel tub, me between his spread thighs, my back against his front. His cock sated but not for long. My lady bits pleasantly sore.

I rested against him and sighed. Our bubble was soon to burst. We'd requested a late check out, which was only an hour away. We had to get back to the real world. Serial killers. A troubled sister. Helen's death. The FBI breathing down our necks and of course my family who was not only worried about me, they weren't safe.

"What are you thinking about?" Jonah traced the drops of water over one pebbled nipple with the tip of his finger.

"All that we have to go back to when we leave our hotel haven." I hummed and swirled my fingers around his kneecap and watched the water droplets fall down an enticing expanse of male, muscular flesh.

He chuckled and I felt it rumble through my back and out through my limbs in pleasurable waves of contentment.

Jonah wrapped his arms around me from behind in a sensual hug, pressing his chin to the crook of my neck and resting it there.

"We'll find our peace again, baby. Once this is all over. In the meantime, you stay with me at Ryan's and lay low. I'll take you to work tomorrow for your first day and my father and brother will ensure nothing happens to you. They're already upset about Helen and filled with grief over her loss. They'll be extra careful keeping an eye on you."

"And what about you? What will you be doing?"

He snuggled against my wet skin and kissed my neck. "I'll be trying to chase down whatever information Ryan needs. I may not be out in the field officially on the case, but I can still help the team back at our Chicago headquarters. I can chase down paper trails, make calls, connect dots. Try and figure out his next move."

I nodded and sighed.

"It's Sunday. What is your family doing today?" he asked.

"Normally I'd be having dinner at Kerrighan House. Mama always puts out a spread and if any of us are able to make it, we try to go and spend time together. Would you be interested in dinner with my mother and sisters?"

He nuzzled my ear and nipped at the cartilage there. "I could be persuaded," he said in that thick tone I was beginning to learn was his 'I'm-ready-to-ravish-you' timbre.

I twisted my body around in order to face him. There was just enough room in the tub for me to straddle his lap. Already his cock was full, hard, and resting against his abdomen.

"Do you have any idea how much it turns me on that you're always ready to fuck me?" I dug my nails into his shoulders.

He smirked, lifted his hands, and cupped my breasts. He tweaked both peaks simultaneously until I moaned, tipping my head back.

"Hop on, Simone," he encouraged before he cupped my left breast and fed it to his mouth.

For a full minute I enjoyed how ravenous he was for my breasts. Flicking the tips with his tongue, sucking them into bright red little berries until I couldn't take it anymore. My sex clenched and throbbed, needing him to complete the connection between us.

I lifted onto my knees as his teeth scraped along one heated tip. The other he pinched hard enough to make me gasp. Once I was centered over his length, I plunged down, water splashing over the edges of the bathtub as I did so.

Neither one of us cared.

I set up a beautiful rhythm of taking him inside of my body, lifting up, and slamming down. Jonah cupped the back of my nape and tugged my head down so he could kiss me.

I rode my man, his mouth sealed to mine, our tongues tangling, fingers gripping whatever skin we could find, completely lost to one another. By the time one heck of an orgasm coiled through my sex and out my body, Jonah was right on my heels, his face pressed between my breasts, powerful convulsions wracking his frame. I held on through it all, glorying in the ecstasy clearly written across his face.

By the time we both collapsed against the porcelain tub, there were barely a few inches of water left in it.

Once we'd cleaned up our huge mess, we checked out of the hotel. We were now heading up the elevator to the borrowed condo where Mama Kerri and Genesis were staying.

Gen let us in with a smile across her stunning face, and I was immediately bum-rushed by a three-year-old cyclone crashing into my legs. "Auntie Si, we are having pizza!" she cried out, holding her arms up for me to hold her.

I lifted her up and put her on my hip. "Yummy. Did you order it?"

She shook her head, espresso-colored curls bouncing all over the place. "Nana and me made it!"

"Homemade pizza is the best. Did you add lots of cheese? You know how I like a ton of cheese!" I tickled her stomach.

Rory nodded her head several times in quick succession and laughed before kicking her feet in the universal silent request to be put down. I set her down and she dashed off at a full run over to Blessing who was sipping a glass of wine, long, shiny dark bare legs crossed at the knee, a pair of bad-ass high-heeled leather sandals on her feet.

"Killer shoes," I noted.

She pointed to one of her legs and assessed her own foot. "They are pretty damn fabulous if I do say so myself." Then she looked me up and down from head to toe. "Looks like Simone already got her some Italian today. Mmm hmm."

My mouth dropped open in shock and Jonah had to cover his laugh with a fake cough.

Mama Kerri came bustling around the kitchen counter and narrowed her gaze at Blessing.

"Don't be mad at me for telling the truth. I call 'em like I see 'em." She sipped her wine and fluffed her hair as though she were queen of the castle. Then again, Blessing couldn't have looked more regal with the black corkscrew 'fro she dialed in perfectly, her impeccably tailored clothes, and always stunning accessories. It definitely paid to be a sought-after fashion designer.

From the hallway, Charlie bustled in cutting off Mama.

"Hey, sister," she said, then stopped and looked me up and down the same way that Blessing had. She walked over to me with a huge smile on her face, and lifted her hand for a high-five. I had no other choice but to play along. Everyone knew you didn't leave a high-five hanging. I bet it was bad luck or something. Either way, I wasn't going to risk any form of potential bad juju. I'd had enough for a lifetime already.

"Right on, Si. You're absolutely glowing." She lifted her hand to Jonah who chuckled but dutifully high-fived her. "Good man. Sealing the deal. I like it," Charlie added for Jonah's benefit.

"Mama," I groaned.

She smiled and waved me into her arms. I went straight in and nestled my face against her strawberry blonde hair. The floral scent I associated with her filled my lungs and I instantly felt a sense of peace flow over me.

Mama Kerri eased back and cupped my cheeks. "How's my chicklet doing?"

"Oh, you know, besides a serial killer coming after me and my family, I'm hanging in there."

She grinned and kissed my forehead. "Good." She let me go and then went over to Jonah and pulled him into a hug too. My heart swelled and I tried not to show how much it meant that she was accepting my new boyfriend into the fold.

"And how's our favorite FBI hero? Feeling better, I see. Your skin certainly has more color too." She kept her hands on her shoulders to assess him. "Any residual pain?"

He shook his head. "No, ma'am. I'm doing well. Your daughter has been taking good care of me. Except I did hear something about homemade pizzas from a little princess running around here…" He let the words trail off.

"Pizza!" Rory screeched from the other side of the room where she was sitting by Liliana playing Barbies.

I waved at Liliana and she smiled and made the Barbie wave on her behalf. This made Rory giggle which I assumed was the point.

"We have plenty of pizza. I've got a large cooling and two more larges ready to go. Would you like a beer or wine?"

"Wine for me, Mama, but I can get it. Jonah?"

"Beer me, sweetheart," he rumbled and followed me into the kitchen.

"Where're Sonia and Addy?" I didn't even ask about Tabitha. We all knew she was avoiding us due to her relapse.

Jonah took a load off on one of the high-backed white barstool seats at the large curved counter. I pulled a Miller Lite from the fridge, popped the top, and handed it to my man.

"Thanks, baby." He winked. I swooned. My heart pounded a happy rhythm in my chest as I smiled and danced over to where the glasses and wine had already been set out.

"I see someone is in a good mood." Mama grinned and handed me her glass to refill.

"Sonia and Addy?" I asked my question again.

"Sonia is right here and in desperate need of wine... stat!" My sister entered the room wearing a form-fitting black suit with a gray silk blouse. She shoved off her blazer and hung it over the chair next to Jonah. "Hello, Jonah. You're looking chipper today."

He grinned then his gaze cut to mine as a sexy as sin smile slipped across his face. "I'm doing good. Thank you. You seem rather frazzled?"

"Ugh. The media is going bonkers over the Backseat Strangler and my family connection. Ryan did the press release with me today and updated the public the best we could. They're still ravenous." She sighed long and deep. "Simone, that wine got a funnel? You could just put it in my mouth and pour."

I chuckled and used a heavy hand pouring her glass. Instead of the standard four ounces, I went with a solid seven. I carefully brought it over to her and set it down. It barely touched the counter before she murmured, "Bless you," and picked it up, sucking back a wallop of wine. She winced but did it again.

"We could probably break out the tequila if your day was that bad," I teased.

She shook her head and took another large drink. "Nope. I'm good. Just needed to get a head start on numbing the many voices swirling in my head."

I nodded, poured Mama's wine and my own, then handed Mama hers.

Mama had just cut the pizza and was serving slices to Jonah and Sonia. She set aside a slice of cheese she'd cut into three really skinny pieces then took the plate over to the glass table where Rory's booster seat already was buckled into one of the chic dining chairs. "Come on, baby, pizza's done."

"You spoil her, Mama." Genesis entered the space, her long dark hair hanging beautifully down her back in a perfectly flat sheet, the white romper she wore with a gold belt tied around her waist giving her a golden goddess appeal. She kissed Mama on the cheek and then came to me and wrapped me in her arms.

I held on to her while Mama fussed over Rory.

"Why do you think I had eight daughters? Multiply that by one or two and you've got eight to sixteen grandchildren. I have the rest of my life to spoil my grandbabies and there is nothing any of you can do about it." She patted Rory's cheek and gazed at her granddaughter as though she made the sun set each day and the moon rise each night.

There was no "adopted" in Mama Kerri's world. We were just her girls. Her baby chicks. And any children we had would be her grandchildren. And not a word would sway her differently.

"How you really doin', Si?" Genesis asked.

I hugged her tight. "Good. Really good."

"Simone, you haven't told them your news?" Jonah reminded me as he took a monster bite of pizza and closed his eyes as though he had just tasted a little bit of Heaven.

My temperature rose and excited butterflies took flight in my stomach. "Oh my God! Guess what?"

Blessing entered the kitchen, snagged a plate and a cheesy piece of pizza, and shoved an unladylike amount into her mouth. "What?" she asked around a mouthful.

"I got a new job! One with a real salary and medical benefits. And they are going to let me finish up my last course to get my Associates degree...get this. While on the job! Can you believe it?"

Sonia set her wine glass down. "Does this mean you're quitting the bar and the waitressing job?"

I nodded excitedly. "Yep! Well technically I already quit the greasy spoon but I'll be calling Tracks tomorrow. Probably during my lunch break as the office manager in training at A+ Construction." I let my voice rise with my joy.

Blessing held out a fist and I bumped it with my own. We both allowed them to explode. Genesis held me tight. "That's amazing, Simone. I'm so proud of you. I know you've been having a rough go of it, even before all this stuff," she waved her hand in the air for emphasis, "was happening. This is awesome."

"Thanks, Gen."

Sonia got up from her chair and came to me with her arms out. "I'm so happy for you." She tugged me into her arms and held on tight.

I patted her back, but she kept holding me. "I hated you working in that bar downtown. You're finally going to be appreciated for your skills and talents. And best of all, you'll be safe." She let out a breath as she looked into my eyes. "I'm happy for you, honey."

I grinned. "Thanks. I'm excited. But I have to admit, I didn't just get it on my own. A+ Construction is owned and operated by Jonah's dad and brother. However, he didn't even know about the conversation when I spoke with his dad about finishing my schooling and wanting to go into office management. It just happened to be at the same time that their office manager was leaving to have a baby and not planning to come back."

Charlie entered the kitchen, her red ponytail flapping with her bouncy steps looking cute as a button in her skinny jeans, vintage Pink Floyd tight tee, and bare feet. "Who cares how you got the job? All that matters is you got it and you're going to slay at managing that office." She came over to me and hip- bumped me. "Now where's Addy? I thought her plane landed at noon. It's six." A frown marred her peachy lips and pearlescent complexion.

Sonia picked up her phone. "Let me check her flight."

Blessing snorted. "Of course, you're keeping track of her flight."

Sonia glared at Blessing. "Right now, we can't be too careful." She kept punching buttons as the rest of us got pizza and munched.

Jonah got a call and squinted at his phone. "Hey, Ryan. How goes it? Still no leads on that number?" He shook his head and sighed.

"Speaking of…that number sequence has been driving me insane." Charlie pulled out a crumpled piece of paper from her pocket. I recognized it as one of the pieces she'd made each of us that she'd written in crayon on Friday. "A-1-2-1-0-9-4." She read each number out loud.

I chomped down on some veggie pizza, capturing a huge chunk of artichoke and plopping it in my mouth. So good.

Charlie continued. "A-121-094," she said.

"Her flight landed on time," Sonia stated still typing away at her cell. "I've texted her to come to the condo Mama and Gen are in. I also texted Quinn to call me if she was there sleeping off her travel."

I nodded and sipped my wine.

Charlie spoke out loud again, determined to figure out the code. "A-12-10-94?"

"That's Addison's birthday." Mama Kerri smiled and pushed through our huddle and looked at the piece of paper. "Yep. She was born December 10th, 1994. A for Addison, right? I love puzzles," she hummed, not realizing what she'd said as she went over to the oven and pulled out the second bubbling hot pizza.

"Ryan, hold up, man. What did you say?" Jonah held the phone away from his ear. "Mrs. Kerrighan. Did you just say that number was Addison's birthday?"

Chills raced across my skin and the hairs on the back of my neck rose to attention. I started to tremble.

"And she's not here." Genesis gasped then put her arms back around me. "She's late. Why is she late?"

"No…" I choked out and stared into Jonah's eyes, telling him every fear I had with that single look.

Blessing tossed her plate down on the counter and pulled her phone out of her back pocket. She furiously pressed a series of buttons then put the phone to her ear. "Addy, you better call me the very second you get this message. We are freaked way the fuck out, sister! We're at Mama Kerri's condo in Sonia's building. Call me." She growled and then hung up. Her chest moved up and down, her dark gaze focused and fearful.

Tears filled my own eyes as the possibility of what that number could mean raced across my mind.

"Yes. I know every one of my daughters' birthdays by heart. Every mother does. Why?" Mama turned around and noticed how the vibe in the room became thick with emotion and coated in fear. "What in the world is going on?"

Charlie swallowed. "None of us showed you this number before now." Charlie closed her eyes and a tear slipped down her cheek. "It's okay. No. It's okay. We're probably wrong. We received this note on Friday. It's Sunday now and Addison was in New York. Safe and in New York. With a bodyguard."

Sonia had her phone to her and was talking. "Yes, hello, this is Senator Wright. My assistant hired your service to protect my sister. She's a well-known model. Addison Michaels Kerrighan? Yes, that's the one. Yes, I know, she's very beautiful. Can you look up her detail and tell me where they are right now or patch me through to him? We're afraid she may have been intercepted by a criminal which is the exact reason we hired your agency. Yes, of course I can wait while you look it up." Sonia's bright blue eyes stared holes through mine.

Jonah spoke softly to Ryan, but his gaze was on Sonia. All eyes were.

"He hasn't checked in? The airport? The Town Car is still at the airport. Well can you get through?" Sonia's voice lost any sense of patience or calm, her fear bleeding through her tone.

"Give me the phone, Sonia," Jonah demanded.

She let it fall into his hand her face pale and her eyes matching mine, filling with tears.

"Yes, this is Agent Fontaine with the Federal Bureau of Investigation. I'm going to need to speak to your manager. We're going to need an exact location of the car and driver. Now."

Jonah took Sonia's phone and exited the kitchen heading for the hallway toward the bedrooms.

Quinn raced into the kitchen from the front living room. "Addison hasn't arrived back from her trip. I left Niko at home in case she shows. What's the status? I got your text that she's missing."

Sonia licked her lips and spoke with a clear, concise tone. It was her Senator-in-charge voice. "Addison was supposed to arrive at noon. Her plane landed. None of us have heard from her. Mama Kerri figured out that the code the Backseat Strangler crumbled up and put in Helen's mouth after he killed her was Addison's birthday."

Quinn gasped, his hand fluttering to rest over his heart. Mama Kerri braced her body at the edge of the counter. I let go of Genesis and went over to her and wrapped my arms around her beloved form from behind and rested my chin to her neck.

"Jonah and Ryan are going to find out what's going on. Maybe we're all wrong and she stayed in New York. Maybe she got caught in traffic. Maybe…"

Mama Kerri shook her head her body shaking uncontrollably as her fingers turned white with the effort to hold herself up. "He has my daughter. A madman has my Addy."

Chapter
SEVENTEEN

"TABBY, HONEY, IF YOU GET THIS MESSAGE, PLEASE CALL one of us. The man who tried to hurt me might have Addy, Tab. I'm scared. Mama's freaking out. We're all frightened out of our minds. If you could find a way to call or text us, let us know you're okay…" I shivered and pressed the phone tight to my ear. "I just need to know you're safe. I love you, Tab. We all do, sister."

Jonah's arm wrapped around my waist from behind. I was hiding out on the patio looking out over the city of Chicago. I hadn't even heard him come up behind me. The city was beautiful from way up there. Buildings jutted up toward the sky like Lego bricks stacked in every color, shape, and size. Lights twinkled from rectangular-shaped windows in varying shades of white, yellow, and gold. Car lights and bright yellow taxi cabs trailed like caterpillars along the busy streets.

Life moved on while ours stood still.

The waiting was the hardest and something inside me knew it was only going to get worse with whatever Jonah had come out here to tell me.

"Baby…" He held me close.

"You have news." I whispered to the wind and the breeze stole off with it.

"I have bad news, honey. We need to gather everyone." He squeezed me tighter to his form.

"Is she dead?" I asked, as unbelievable pain ripped through my heart, reminding me of the day I lost my parents in that horrible fire. Like the physical pain of sliding down the roof of my first childhood home in my nightgown. The flames had engulfed every inch of the hallway outside of our room. Sonia lifted me up and shoved me out the window into the cool night air. I was so scared, barely six years old. Screaming for my parents, my thighs and legs abrading along every shingle as we slid down the side of the first story roofline. Flames crackled and groaned in our ears as ember and ash sizzled into the soft skin of my arms as we narrowly escaped the fire that took my parents' lives.

"Simone." He breathed against my neck bringing me back while I trembled in his arms.

"Is. My. Sister. Dead?" I choked out, staring at the skyline and watching the blackness get darker, my vision focused on a single square inch of light in the distance as I waited to hear if my sister was still breathing.

"We don't know. She wasn't in the car. Come on. What I have to say, honey, I don't want to say it twice. At this point…" His voice cracked, the only hint that the information he had to share was breaking him in half. He took a breath. "At this point, it doesn't look good," he finished.

I closed my eyes and let the pain fill me up. It was the only thing that would keep me standing. If I succumbed to the grief, it would take me away. Right now, for Addison, for my sisters, for Mama Kerri, I had to be as strong as possible. I held on to my pain and dug my fingernails into my hands, piercing indentations in my palms until the pain turned into anger and not sadness.

"Let's go." I turned around and started to enter the condo. Jonah took my hand, interlaced our fingers, and pressed my sore palm against his warm one.

I gasped as our connection zapped through our palms reminding me of his presence. Of his loyalty. His commitment to me. To us.

"You're not alone in this." His dark gaze was lasered on mine, so much compassion filling them. Too much. I had to hold on to the anger, the pain.

"I know. I have my family." The statement came out flat, emotionless. This was not the time for emotions. This was the time for action.

"And you have me, Simone. Me. I'm here. Right here. Standing in front of you. Alive. Fighting alongside you." His expression was ravaged with unease and desperation. He too was probably holding on by a thread. The thin rope that we'd built between us since this all started pulling tight, reminding me of my anchor.

Jonah.

I squeezed his hand and held back the tears. Instead, I nodded curtly and opened the patio door.

We entered the living room hand in hand.

Mama Kerri's head lifted off of Blessing's shoulder. Liliana sat on the other side, both of her hands holding one of our Mama's.

"Did you find her at the airport? Does he have her?" she asked, rapid fire.

"The FBI found the Town Car and no sign of Addison." Jonah's words were gentle yet direct.

"What does that mean?" Genesis spoke softly.

Jonah cleared his throat and rubbed at the back of his neck with his free hand but kept hold of one of mine.

"Unfortunately, we found her bodyguard in the trunk of the Town Car. He had been strangled with the same tool the Backseat Strangler used on almost all of his other victims. The car was then moved and abandoned in long term parking. The FBI were able to work with airport security to review the security cameras. The cameras show a white man with a dark mustache and beard and a hat pull up to baggage claim at the same time that Addison came out of the airport. He got out, showed her a sign with her name on it. He took her luggage and put it in the trunk of his car. The license plate was covered with a piece of paper with a fake number on it. Addison got in the backseat and the man drove off. We don't have more than that at this time, but I can promise you the FBI has every man in the vicinity and the boys in blue on the lookout."

I let go of Jonah's hand and went straight into the kitchen and opened every cabinet until I found what I was looking for. The booze. I pulled down the tequila and sucked it back straight from the bottle. From the other room I could hear my sisters crying and whispering soft words to one another.

Anger sizzled through my blood as I got a tumbler and poured four fingers of straight tequila and then took a full mouthful and let it burn my throat and stomach as it went down. I gloried in the heat. The bite of pain.

What was Addy experiencing right now? Did he knock her out? Strangle her already? Or was he holding her as bait?

What was his plan?

I could hear Jonah murmuring softly to my sisters and mother.

Jonah.

My God, the man's ex-wife had been killed only a short few days ago and now he was dealing with his girlfriend's sister being kidnapped.

I closed my eyes and lifted the drink, sucking back some more.

"You better have enough for me, sister." Blessing entered the kitchen and leaned her back to the counter I was standing in front of.

I handed her my glass with two fingers' worth still inside. She curled her long fingers around it and shot the entire lot back in one go.

"Fuck." She hissed. "I'm gonna call my dad. Get him and his gang brothers looking out for a black Town Car with a white dude in it carrying a comatose pretty brunette woman around."

I reached out my hand and gripped her wrist. "I'm not sure if that will help. And you know it's a risk every time you connect with your dad, especially if you're asking for gang assistance. Not only do we want you far away from Tyrell Jones and his goons, *he* wants you away from that life. Otherwise, he would have stopped at nothing to take you away from Kerrighan House all those years ago. He wouldn't have made that deal with Mama Kerri. Getting you away from that gang is the one thing he did right for his daughter in his entire life. Don't ruin that now."

She set the glass down, grabbed the bottle of tequila, and filled that sucker back up. She took another drink, then passed it back to me.

"Gotta do something, boo." Her lips pressed together but her eyes filled with tears. She was feeling this as deep as we all were.

Blessing Jones-Kerrighan was a hard ass, beautiful, take-no-shit, Black businesswoman. She did not let anyone mess with her or any of us. She'd watched her mother get murdered right in front of her eyes at a young age. Her father had been and still was big in the gang scene in Chicago. After her mother's murder, the Child Protective Services got involved. They needed to ensure Blessing's safety. Which is when Mama Kerri took her on. It wasn't easy at first. She was a street kid who had lived a hard life by the time she was ten. She got in all kinds of trouble until Mama Kerri showed her another way to live. Mama's way was love, kindness, and sisterhood. Eventually Blessing grew into the successful fashionista she was today. But seeing that hollow look in her eye, I knew she was not going to let this sit.

I took her hand. "Promise me you'll give the FBI a full day before you do anything."

She frowned, stole the tequila back, and sipped it. Her coal-black gaze came to me and she pointed an accusing finger around the tumbler. "They have twenty-four hours."

I closed my eyes. "Thank you, Blessing."

She tilted her head. "Don't thank me yet. Twenty-four hours goes by and no Addison, I call Tyrell. Ain't nothing any of you can do to stop me." She handed me the glass and went back into the living room.

I looked down at my bare feet and painted toes and prayed. "God, I'll do anything it takes. Anything to get Addison back. I just need a sign. Please send me a sign." I closed my eyes. "At the very least, please keep Addison safe until help can arrive."

Mama Kerri, Genesis, Liliana, and Charlie were all in the king-sized bed huddled around a sleeping Rory. I'm not sure any of them were sleeping, but it had been a full night with no news.

I glanced at the clock. Five sharp.

Sonia was curled up in one corner of the couch, typing on her phone. I imagined doing Senator-type things. Or maybe she was playing a game on her phone. Blessing was stretched out, her head in Sonia's lap, her eyes glued to the news.

Sixteen hours.

A madman had had Addison for sixteen hours.

Jonah was out on the balcony, phone glued to his ear, which was how he'd been much of the night.

Me, I was numb.

My anger, gone.

Pain, gone.

Sadness, gone.

I was empty.

Moving my body into the kitchen was the most amount of effort I could commit to. I found the cupboard that held the coffee and filters and set them out before grabbing the pot. I filled the pot and was just about finished pouring it into the coffee container when I felt my phone buzz my ass with a text.

I pulled it out as fast as I could. Everyone I loved besides Tabby and Addison were here.

It was from Tabby. I covered my mouth with my hand and read what it said.

I'm fine. Don't worry. Got eyes on the lookout. More later. Love you all.

I shook my head and read her words at least five more times. She had eyes on the lookout? What in the world did that mean? My shoulders sank and I sighed, trying to focus on the one thing I did understand. She was fine and she loved us. I wished she'd be here with us, but beggars couldn't be choosers. Simply knowing she was not in the hands of the Backseat Strangler was a small win and I'd take whatever win I could get.

Quickly, I fired off a text in return.

Thank you, Tab. Be safe. I love you. We all do. Always. Come home soon.

I started the coffee and checked the fridge. There was cut-up fruit, eggs, bacon, and all the standard fixings. Even if I wasn't hungry, I thought maybe I could pull something together for everyone else.

As I was rummaging through the cabinets to see if there was pancake mix, because Mama Kerri always had pancake mix, my phone buzzed again.

I hoped it was Tabby saying she had changed her mind and was heading over now when I noticed it was from Addison.

I clicked the message icon so fast and had to bite my tongue not to scream at what I saw. It wasn't a message, it was a video.

Addison was tied up in a chair in a dark space. Her luxurious brown and gold locks where stringy and wet. There was a dirty bandana-type thing tied around her mouth. Her teeth were stark white biting around it. Her face was speckled with dirt and grime and sweat. Her arms were tied to the wooden rails of the chair she was in, forearms facing up. Both her hands were held in tight fists, the knuckles bright white at how tight she was clenching them.

I squinted to see better, and noticed up and down her inner forearms were bloody and blackened circular-shaped pock marks or wounds. Then out of nowhere, a gloved hand entered the video holding a lit cigarette. Addy started to wiggle around desperately trying to move her body back and away from the glowing red-tipped ember.

As I watched in horror, the hand turned the cigarette around and pressed the hot tip into Addison's arm. The sound on my phone wasn't on but I swear I could hear her screaming in my soul. It reverberated within my chest until I was practically hyperventilating. Still, my eyes were glued to the image before me. Addison looked right into the camera and her normally stunning green eyes were hollow, the light that always shined completely blacked out, devoid of anything but extreme pain.

Tears streaked down my face as the cigarette that had been snuffed out in my sister's flesh was dropped to the ground outside of the camera's view. Then a white piece of paper was held aloft.

The note said three words.

You For Her

The video ended and my phone buzzed with a text.

Go to your apartment.

Alone.

Now.

That was all it said. My entire body shook so hard I fell to the tile floor. He wanted me in exchange for her.

"Simone!" Jonah cried, falling to his knees, one hand cupping my cheek, the other my shoulder. "Baby, what's wrong?"

I opened and closed my mouth as my vision waved in and out. Eventually, it all just went black.

When I woke, I was lying on the couch, a cool cloth to my forehead, Sonia petting my hair with tears in her pretty blue eyes. Jonah paced behind the couch. My sisters and my mother were all huddled around me with various expressions of worry plastered across their pretty faces.

Then it dawned on me. I had to get to my old apartment. Now.

"I've gotta go!" I called out and attempted to sit up.

My body still shook, and my teeth chattered.

"You need to lay your ass down, boo." Blessing demanded on a growl pacing the other side of the couch, rubbing her hands up and down the sides of her hips.

I shook my head. "No, you don't understand. I've got somewhere to be."

"There is no way in hell you are trading yourself for Addison. Not now. Not ever. Get that out of your head right fucking now, Simone." Jonah's words brooked absolutely no argument.

Tears filled my eyes. "He's going to kill her. But he *wants* me. I'll let him have me for her. I don't care."

Sonia let out a sob and Mama Kerri pulled her into her

arms and petted her hair, her sad eyes on me when she spoke. "Simone, we'd never let that happen. Addy wouldn't want that, and you know it. There has to be another way, baby girl. There just has to be." A tear fell down her cheek, but she swiped it away quickly.

Jonah approached and Charlie and Lilian made room for him. "I've seen the video. It's already being reviewed by the FBI. We've got our best hacks working the GPS to see if we can get a read on his location. We have a team in place at your apartment. If he shows, we'll get him. If he texts or sends another video, we'll have a lock. And we'll get him. You have to have faith, sweetheart." He took my hand, brought my fingers up to his lips, and kissed each one.

I closed my eyes and let the tears take me.

Jonah pulled me up and into his arms where I sobbed into his chest. I let all my fear and grief go against him and he took it all without complaint. Then he held me tighter. Closer. Whispered softly into my ear. Promises I wasn't sure he could keep but I prayed he could.

When I was all cried out, Charlie handed me a steaming cup of coffee. "Here, Si, let this warm you up."

I nodded numbly, wrapped my hands around the cup, and let the heat soak into my chilled hands.

You For Her.

Addison silently screaming behind her gag as he burned her flesh.

I twitched and convulsed as I too felt the pain she must have felt, a phantom-like wound searing into the tender skin of my forearm.

Nausea built up in my throat. I set the cup down and dashed to the bathroom where I hurled until I couldn't physically anymore. Vomit had splashed on my shirt and clung to my chest and neck.

Gross.

I washed my hands and skin as best as I could and then rinsed out my mouth. I needed a shower, a toothbrush, and a clean shirt. I opened the door and Sonia stood leaning against the opposite wall.

"Come on, I'll take you down to my place. You can shower and change into something of mine."

I nodded but didn't speak. There were no words left inside me.

Sonia put her arm around my shoulder and led me into the living room.

"Oh, baby girl." Mama Kerri clucked sweetly but I didn't have it in me to respond.

The numbness had taken over.

"I'm going to take Simone down to my place, get her a shower and a change of clothes. Tell Jonah where we went when he gets off his call." She gestured to where Jonah was pacing on the balcony.

"Okay, my darling chicklets. Be back quick. I need you all in the same place right now."

Sonia nodded and led me out of the apartment, onto the elevator, and to her condo. I followed her into her room where she took me straight to the shower. She yanked off my stinky, vomit-coated shirt and tossed it into her hamper. I kicked off my shoes and toed off my socks, unbuttoned my jeans, and removed my underwear while she started the shower. The second it was steaming she left the bathroom to me but kept the door open.

Probably because she was worried I'd pass out again.

I stepped into the steamy space and ducked my head under the water, allowing it to heat my body from the outside in. For a long time, I stood there just letting the water pound against me. My mind playing the image of Addison being tortured on that video over and over.

Eventually my skin got so hot it broke me out of the horror cyclone of imagery spinning in my brain and I quickly washed my hair and body. Once completed, I got out and found a new toothbrush, a soft towel, clean underwear, and a sports bra, along with a pair of black yoga pants, a tank top, and a purple zip-up hoodie.

I brushed my teeth so hard my gums bled. Again, I didn't care. There wasn't much I cared about except how bad I'd screwed up my opportunity to save my sister from uncertain torture and likely death.

I'd never forgive myself if Addison died. Not ever. It was my fault she was in that chair and not me. I'd gotten away. She might not. And I'd have to live with that reality.

You For Her.

Those three little words would destroy me.

It should have been me and not her.

Not sweet, kind, beautiful, filled with life Addison. The girl had a hard enough upbringing before she came to stay at Kerrighan House. Left at the fire station as a brand new baby. Shuffled from foster home to foster home. Some okay, most not. Addison had her own demons, but she'd been saved. By Mama Kerri and her love. Just like we all had.

We'd been given a second chance at life.

I should have died on that dark road at the hands of the Backseat Strangler. If I had, Addison wouldn't be where she is right now. Helen wouldn't be dead. Katrina from my apartment wouldn't be dead. That bodyguard who'd been sent to keep Addy safe wouldn't be dead. That was three lives, not including Addy's, that were hanging over my head.

You For Her.

I closed my eyes and finished getting dressed. Sonia was waiting for me in a similar outfit when I came out.

"Feel better?"

I nodded but I wasn't sure I'd ever feel better. Not if Addison didn't walk away from this alive.

Sonia hugged me and I gave her that. She needed it. I'd give my sisters anything I had to give. Even trade me for them.

She let out a long breath and put her arm around my shoulders again. Which was probably a good thing because I might have actually crumbled to the floor in a ball of misery if she hadn't.

"Let's go. Mama will worry."

We left her condo and walked to the elevator. She pressed the button and then stood next to me. I stared at my feet; visions of Addy tied up flashed across my mind in a twisted horror reel I couldn't shake.

When the doors opened, Sonia cried out as an electrical sound pierced the air. Her body jolted forward and tumbled through the open elevator doors, and she fell to the floor in a lifeless heap.

My survival instincts must have kicked in because I'd barely realized my sister had been tased as I spun around to face my attacker. I saw nothing but a man in black with two cut out eyeholes and a third for his mouth when a black gun came barreling at my face. It was too fast to block. Too fast to fight. Light exploded behind my eyes as I was clocked with the butt of the gun. And for the second time that day I blacked out.

Chapter
EIGHTEEN

RIP. DRIP. DRIP.

The sound of water hitting metal sounded through my head. Something icy cold and flat was pressed up against the side of my face. I'd attempted to blink open my eyes, but a rush of pain exploded throughout my head.

"Psssst. Simone, wake up. Wake up, honey. Hurry." I heard a voice I recognized, not far away, but still the sound was waving in and out.

Drip. Drip. Drip.

What the hell was that noise?

"Simone, come on. Get up!" I heard it louder, the words spinning in my brain on a useless empty hamster wheel until the dots started to connect.

I'd been hit in the face with a gun.

Sonia had been tased.

Addison had been kidnapped.

"Si, please, sister, wake up. Now before he gets back." A sob tore from that familiar voice and I rubbed my face against the cold, flat surface and opened my good eye. It was dark. Dank. Cold. My face was smushed flat to the gritty cold concrete under me.

Drip. Drip. Drip.

I rolled over onto my side. My hands were tied behind my back and I was in the corner of a big open space. Maybe a basement.

"Simone…please wake up."

I heard the plea rasp low and throaty from the female figure twenty feet away. Her head was down in front of her as if she couldn't hold it up any longer. There was rope tying her chest, legs, and arms to an old wooden chair.

"Addy?" I croaked, my voice sounding as though I'd swallowed glass shards.

Her head came up and those green eyes I adored met my gaze. "Simone!" She gave a shaky small smile. "Can you move? Can you get up?"

I swallowed against the nausea filling my stomach, ebbing up my throat. I breathed in and out slowly for a minute getting a hold on my physical issues.

"Um, I don't know. Where is he?" I grated through a throat that was so dry it felt like sand coated my esophagus.

She shook her head. "I don't know. He came in an hour ago and dumped you there. Then he left."

I used my core strength and swiveled up to sit on my hip with my legs tucked to the side. They were zip-tied together, but if I could get on my back and stretch my arms, dislocating my shoulder, maybe I could get them under me.

"I'm gonna get my arms in front of me." I announced my plan.

"How the hell are you going to do that?"

I gritted my teeth and rolled back to my side. I shimmied all over the place trying to get my arms under my ass, but it was no use. Pain shot through my arms, shoulders, and head as I tried and failed.

"Maybe if I dislocate my shoulder, I can get my arms out."

"Are you insane! You'll pass out again from the pain. Just try to ease up and bounce to me. Then I might be able to untie your arms," Addy pleaded.

Now that idea was a good one.

I maneuvered back onto my hip then shifted my body until I was up on my knees. The world swayed as nausea stole up my throat again. I breathed through it and waited until it passed. Then I jumped as best I could, landing in an awkward crouch. With as much power as I could muster, I slowly stood up.

"Okay, good. Now jump over to me but try to be quiet. We don't know where he is or when he'll come back."

I nodded and started to hop. It felt like it took a hundred years to get over to Addy and what I saw when I got there made a sour taste fill my mouth, so much so I had to spit on the ground in order to avoid being sick.

Her beautiful, long, elegant forearms had been destroyed by cigarette burns, the skin and flesh molten and black. Some of the wounds were deep enough he must have used the same spot more than once because I could see straight to the meat of her. I spat again and turned around.

Her fingers tugged on my zip ties to no avail.

"It's not working." Her voice cracked, and tears slid down her cheeks.

"Just keep trying." I looked around the open space to see if there was anything sharp I could grate the plastic against but didn't see anything but pipes, concrete bricks, rat droppings, garbage, and water dripping randomly from pipes. "Where are we?"

"Not sure. I think an old basement, where the heating and pipes run. I just barely got the gag out of my mouth right before you woke up. But he's rarely gone for more than an hour or two. I passed the time by counting the minutes. He must live in this building. We have to get out of here, Si."

I nodded and my body started to shake when we heard a door creak open somewhere in the back of the space and a quick sliver of unnatural yellow light broke through the dark. The light came and went so fast I barely had a chance to notice there must have been a door in the back of the room, behind the big pipes and metal, square-shaped machinery.

I stood in front of Addison, ready to take on whatever this monster had in store as long as he spared my sister.

What I saw made tears fill my eyes and fall down my face.

Tabby.

Dressed in black from head to toe, like I'd seen her at the bar. Her dark cap of short hair spiked up all over her head. Her body was barely skin and bones and yet she was the most beautiful thing I'd ever seen in that moment.

A huge wave of relief poured over my form.

"Tabby!" I cried out, tears falling down my cheeks.

She ran over to us, reached into her back pocket, and pulled out a switchblade. "Fucking hell, what did he do to you, Addy?" She swore, her hands behind me cutting the plastic.

Pain and pleasure shot to my aching shoulders in ribbons of heat, ice, and sizzling pin pricks the moment they were released.

Before long she'd cut the ties around my ankles and set about releasing Addison.

I moved around to the back of the chair to work on unknotting the huge rope he'd used to keep her upper body in the chair.

We couldn't have noticed we weren't alone.

The door didn't make a single noise.

No light streaked across the room warning of his presence.

While I was bent behind Addison's chair, Tabby was crouched over working on the ropes around each of Addison's wounded arms.

"Stand up, skank," I heard called out from somewhere behind Tabby.

My body reacted before I did, jolting to attention. I stood up, as did Tabby. Addison choked out a sob. Her shoulders sinking in defeat.

Tabby held her knife in her hand, gripping the small blade as though she were holding a kitchen butcher knife ready to strike. Her nostrils flared and she stared into my eyes. Hers were the deepest, darkest midnight blue and filled with determination. Her skin was pale. Cheeks hollow. There were smudges under her eyes but it didn't take one speck away from her strength of character. The arrogant confidence exuding from every one of her pores.

"Remember, this was my choice. I love you all so much." Her words were whispered but direct.

"Now turn around, bitch," the man behind her demanded, his voice oily and gritty. I could see he was still wearing a mask. I shook, my body trembling in fear.

Tabby licked her lips and gripped the knife. "Mama

Kerri and my sisters were the best thing to ever happen in my life."

"Tabby…" I choked out. "Do what he says. Just follow along," I begged.

She sniffed, firmed her jaw. "My love will never die," she promised us. Then, she spun around on a booted heal and pushed her body to move at a dead run, knife held above her head. She looked like a modern gladiator, poised to strike with a mighty spear, not a small switchblade.

Two ear-splitting shots rang out.

Bang. Bang.

I watched in horror as Tabby's thin frame took those shots to her chest, her form jarring with each hit, but it didn't stop her trajectory as she came down on her target, arm in the perfect location.

She struck, the knife sinking right into the side of our attacker's neck. It caught and she yanked as they both started to fall. Red liquid spurted out of his neck like a vulgar water sprinkler, painting the space in blood.

"Tabby!" I screamed.

"No!" Addison cried.

Both bodies went down, Tabitha right on top of the masked man as the door creaked from behind them and men in SWAT suits and black FBI bulletproof vests stormed in, massive guns at the ready.

Only they were a minute too late.

I ran toward Tabitha, but Ryan came out of nowhere and cut me off, body-slamming me and wrapping me up in his hold.

"No! Tabby!" I screeched.

"She's getting help." He turned my form to the side. A

pair of paramedics rolled my sister off the man but even from here I knew what they'd find.

Her eyes were open and she stared lifelessly at nothing. One of the paramedics held his fingers to her neck.

I waited with my heart in my throat.

Time seemed to become sluggish as if everything was in slow motion around me. Blood pooled around her body, the mess growing larger with every second.

Then I watched as he shook his head and closed her eyes with his hand. Ryan tightened his hold. I bucked, my body losing control as the devastation tore through me like a two-hundred mile an hour bullet train moving between countries.

"Shhh, shhh, focus on my voice." Ryan held me tight to his form and whispered into my ear. "It's going to be okay. It's going to be okay. Eventually, honey, it will be okay."

I shook my head knowing it would never be okay.

Tabby gave her life to save ours.

Remember, this was my choice.

She planned this. She'd planned to fall on the sword to save me and Addy.

I crumbled in Ryan's arms.

My love will never die.

Her last words permeated my emotion-soaked mind on rapid repeat. I closed my eyes as I was passed into another pair of arms. Addison locked her body around mine and we held onto one another as time sped back up. FBI and other cops or medical personnel moved around us in a flurry of activity. Large sheets were put over both the attacker's and my sister's bodies.

We were led out of the basement by Ryan and another

member of the team, caging us both in. We went up several flights of dark concrete stairs until we came upon a wide-open metal door that led to a bright rectangle of daylight.

The two men maneuvered us over the blacktop and through a patch of parking lot that was littered with black SUVs, SWAT vans, and cop cars. They brought us to an ambulance with another set of paramedics.

One started to mess with my eye wound, but I waved them off. "Take care of my sister." I lifted my chin to Addison who was now barely standing. She was visibly dehydrated, her skin green and grimy. The wounds up and down her arms would need serious treatment. For now, the paramedic simply wrapped her from wrist to bicep.

"Miss, you're bleeding from your head. You have a rather large gash above your eye that will not only need stitches but could get infected if we don't treat you."

"I don't give a fuck about me!" I roared in her face. My body got hot and then icy cold as I started to shake.

Out of nowhere, a presence unlike any other came up behind me. A masculine arm looped around my waist and tugged me back against a very warm, familiar, and beloved body. I felt him surround me in a bubble of peace and serenity as his lips came to my ear.

"Baby, let her take care of you, yeah?"

Tears fell from my good eye and I slowly turned around at hearing his voice.

Jonah was there. His expression was ravaged with fear and concern but still was more handsome and welcoming than anything else could possibly be.

One of his hands came up and tunneled into the back of

my hair curling around my nape. The other hovered over my face tracing the damage. Tears filled his dark eyes but didn't fall as he winced then let his hand curl around my waist. His voice was broken and barely a whisper when he spoke. "I was so scared I'd lost you, and I'd only just found you."

That was it. All I could take.

It was all too damned much.

Tabby was dead.

Addison had been tortured.

Jonah had lost Helen.

I almost lost him. This perfect soul. The other half to my broken one.

And that was when I threw my arms around him, shoved my face into his neck, and soaked up his woodsy and fresh linen scent until there was nothing else but him surrounding me with protection and love.

Jonah Fontaine.

The man for me.

The man I loved.

And I wasn't going to wait even a moment before sharing this revelation with him. It wouldn't be right. Not after everything we'd gone through. Not after what Tabitha sacrificed in order for me to have this.

"I love you, Jonah."

"Baby, Jesus." He locked his arms around me. "Christ, Simone. I've loved you since you lost your mind on the ferris wheel, so wrapped up in kissing me you forgot where you were."

He has loved me since our first date. I convulsed against his frame, body-wracking sobs pouring from me in endless waves. But he didn't let me go. He held on tight. Gave me what I needed until I found enough strength to pull myself together. Once I had, he led me to the paramedics, but held my hand as they tended to me. Then Jonah got the paramedics to load me and Addy into the same ambulance, saying something about the FBI needing us together and he'd be our escort.

Whatever he had to do to keep us together, he did. Putting me and Addy as his priority, making sure we felt safe after the horror we'd just experienced.

I loved him even more because of it.

Turns out, getting whopped upside the head is the reason I'd been so nauseous. I had a full-blown concussion from taking the hit to the temple. I'd been seen, stitched up, bandaged, and given instructions on how to deal with this new ailment.

Not that I gave two shits. My focus was entirely on seeing Addison and finding out how Sonia was.

Dutifully, Jonah brought me to Addison's room where my entire family was stationed. They'd put Addison in a private room instead of handling her in the ER because she was related to a senator and we were informed the news vans were already parked outside. I'd seen Mama Kerri when I was being checked out in the ER but not the rest of my sisters.

I was bum-rushed by Sonia first. When she wrapped her arms around me, I returned her hold just as tight.

"I love you, SoSo," I croaked into her hair, emotion coating my throat.

She sniffed, nodded, and pulled back. "I love you more than anything." She smiled half-heartedly but I figured for a long time the Kerrighan clan would be half-alive after sustaining such a loss.

Mama Kerri was next. Heartbreak and grief felt thick in the very air around her form. It would take us all a long time to find any sort of peace after Tabby's loss.

Blessing, Liliana, Charlie, and Genesis each hugged me. I told every last one of them that I loved them, needing them to know it and hear it from my lips.

"Rory?" I scanned the space and didn't see my niece.

"Aunt Delores has her at Kerrighan House," Genesis confirmed.

After the round of hugs, I went over to Addy's bed. She was staring vacantly out the window even in a room filled with her family.

"Hey, sis. How you doin'?" I took her hand, careful not to touch the bulky bandages running up both arms from wrist to bicep.

She blinked slowly and turned her head toward me as if she'd just realized someone was there and holding her hand.

"I'm alive," was all she said. Though it sure as hell didn't sound like she was any happier for it.

"Yeah. Me too," I said flatly. There was no judgement. No score. No positives in any of it.

We'd made it out alive. Tabby did not. Now the two of us had to live with those circumstances.

"Do you remember her last words?" I asked softly.

She nodded. "My love will never die." The phrase left her chapped lips as though each word sliced straight through her heart.

"And it won't. We'll make sure of it," I promised.

A tear slipped down Addy's cheek. "No. Her love will never die, and ours for her won't either."

I swallowed down the cotton lodged in my throat. "She died so we could live."

Addy nodded.

"How do we live with that knowledge?" I whispered, not knowing how the hell to carry on without our sister there.

"I don't know. One day at a time, I guess." She sighed deeply.

I squeezed her hand. "One day at a time."

And that is when Addison and I formed our own connection. It went beyond the sisterhood, beyond our family by choice. We'd survived something together. Something life changing. Our lives had been threatened, we'd suffered tremendous loss, but we'd made it out alive.

We'd been saved.

Spared.

When Tabitha sacrificed it all for us, she'd connected us in a way others might never understand. She'd given us a gift—one we could neither take back nor return. We'd have to carry it with us forever.

I looked at Addy. For a long time, we stared into one another's eyes, both lost to thoughts of our fallen sister.

Mama Kerri walked to the side of Addison's bed and sat down and took her other hand. Jonah came up behind me.

"You ready to go home?" he asked.

I frowned and a fissure of fear skated up my spine.

"I need to be at Kerrighan House," I announced, matter of fact.

Home.

I needed to be *home*. The only home I'd ever known.

"Me too," Addison said, her eyes locked on mine.

"I think maybe it's a good idea if all my babies come home until they're ready to enter back into the world after all we've endured." Mama Kerri's voice was filled with heartbreak but her request would not be denied.

"When everyone's back at Kerrighan House, I can go over the details behind the rest of what happened," Jonah shared.

I nodded, as did Addy and Mama Kerri. Which was also when Quinn slipped into the room. He waved at Sonia. "They're not being put off. The press have surrounded the hospital. If you don't make a statement and let them see you, we're going to have problems."

Sonia clenched her teeth and made fists with her hands. She looked around the room and her face contorted into one of sadness and fury. "Fine. Let's go. Now. I'll see you all back at Kerrighan House."

"I'll wait until Addison is released. Why don't you all head on over and I'll bring our girl when she's out," Mama Kerri stated.

Jonah nodded and curled his hand around my shoulder. "Come on, baby. Let me take you to your ma's."

I clenched my fingers around the railing of the hospital bed, surprised at my sudden reluctance to let go or leave Addison's side.

"Um, I think I'd rather wait until Addy's released," I whispered.

"Si, I'm okay. I'll be there soon." She sighed tiredly.

I frowned at my white knuckles gripped around the rail. "But what if something happens between now and then?" I choked the question out, emotion clogging my throat.

She reached her arm out and covered one of my hands with hers. "Let go of the railing, Si. I'm fine. I'm alive. And I'm right here. No one's gonna get to me in the hospital. And besides, he's gone. Dead. Remember?"

I peeled my hand away but kept hold of hers then sat down on the side of her bed. "I'm gonna wait until you're released."

Jonah rubbed a hand up and down my back soothingly. "No problem. We'll wait for your sister."

I nodded, still not sure why I couldn't break away, just knowing I wasn't ready to do so.

Not long after the others left a nurse came in and went over the outpatient information and discharged Addison.

Together, the four of us piled into Mama Kerri's Subaru Outback. Jonah drove. Mama Kerri in the passenger seat, me and Addy huddled together in the back.

As each mile passed and we got closer to Mama Kerri's, the exhaustion took over. I leaned my head onto Addison's shoulder, and she leaned hers on to mine.

In the safety of my mother's vehicle, my mother present, my man ever watchful, Addison safely sitting next to me, I closed my eyes and allowed sleep to take me.

Chapter
NINETEEN

BACK AT KERRIGHAN HOUSE, WE ALL HUDDLED AROUND ONE another on the giant U-shaped sectional. Mama Kerri sat in the single chair, a plate with an uneaten grilled cheese sandwich on her lap. She'd made a bunch of sandwiches. I ate mine tasting absolutely nothing. I could have been eating a block of Play-Doh for all I cared. The rest of the sisters were in various stages of eating or not eating.

Jonah entered from the kitchen with his plate in hand. He set the plate on the coffee table and sat beside me. Addison was on my other side, which was exactly where I needed her to be.

Jonah took a deep breath and scanned each of our sorrow-filled faces.

"Wayne Gilbert Black was a thirty-five-year-old sociopath. The building you were found in was where he lived. He was the building owner but mostly a slumlord. After his mother was killed when he was a child, he was in and out of foster homes. This is the reason the FBI thinks he snapped when he didn't finish the job with you, Simone. He found out that you too had been a foster kid, living a happy life. We can't know for sure, but it's part of the theory."

I nodded and clenched my teeth, breathing through my nose. Jonah's warm hand surrounded mine and held it in both of his over his thigh.

"His mother was a well-known prostitute. According to the information we found in his apartment, he'd seen her killed and journaled about it incessantly. Apparently, she would regularly park her car down an alley out of sight in order to do business. She'd force Wayne to stand in a dark corner while she brought the clients to the backseat of her car. There she'd do the deed. None of this hidden from her child. Until one of her client's kinks got out of hand. He strangled her during the act by accident. Or so he claimed when he turned himself in. Apparently, Wayne saw it happen. This is likely when he had his first psychotic break."

Mami Kerri covered her mouth and closed her eyes.

"He was a deeply demented man, set on killing women in the same manner his mother died. We'll learn more when we get his foster care details and any psych evals he had in the past," Jonah continued.

"I don't care about Wayne Black. What I want to know is how he got into my building," Sonia groused.

Jonah winced and swallowed slowly.

That meant more bad information was forthcoming.

"He tased the security guard out back and then strangled him," Jonah stated gently.

I wanted to cry. I really did. Another life lost due to this monster and I had no tears left to give. I was dried up. Empty inside.

"How the hell did Tabby get involved?" Sonia asked directly, arms crossed over her shoulders as though she were angry. She probably was. Sonia had a temper that often exploded if she was hurting.

I cleared my throat and then spoke up. "I'd called Tabby and left a message when Addison went missing. Begged her to come home. Told her none of us were safe, including her. She said she was fine but that she had eyes on the lookout."

"Our team discovered from the video footage of Sonia's building that Tabby had been hanging out across the street at the small cafe, watching the front door. Our best guess is that she saw a stranger headed around the back of the building and followed him because not long after we saw the masked man, we saw Tabitha sliding along the outskirts. We got an anonymous lead that a strange man had entered the back of the building and a guard was knocked out. That was the last call I got when I was on the balcony. The timing was a perfect storm." He rubbed at the back of his neck.

"She must have seen Simone taken and followed them, because when the video shows Simone being carried unconscious, over the shoulder of the man we know now was Wayne Black, we could see a skinny woman all in black running down the long alley and disappearing. Two hours after Simone was taken, we got another call. I spoke to Tabitha," he said, his voice cracking.

My nose tingled and I shoved my body to his side, cuddling against his chest. He wrapped an arm around my back and took a breath.

"The operator was told if we got another anonymous call to direct it to me, but this time Tabitha asked for me by name. She was either following the case in the media and saw pictures of me and Simone or heard my name when she showed up at Tracks that night. Whatever the case may be, she called and gave me the location of where they took you."

"Jesus, that girl." Blessing shook her head as a wave of sadness flashed across her face.

Jonah took a deep breath and then let it out shakily. "She told me she'd been following the man that kidnapped you. Notified me where he'd taken you and told me to hurry. That's it. Then she hung up. Which must have been not long before she entered the building on her own mission to save you."

"My Tabby would never allow anyone to harm her sisters. She was more protective than Blessing and Sonia put together." Mama Kerri sniffed and wiped at her nose with an old-fashioned handkerchief. "She always said if she didn't have us, she'd have nothing. Which is why she would go to the ends of the earth to protect us."

"And she did," I whispered. "She gave her life for ours."

Addy grabbed my hand and I held it so tight I could feel her heartbeat against my palm.

"My girl had a lot of demons but the one thing that gave her pride was us. We were the only good she could see in the world. It had been that way since she arrived here at thirteen years old. I can easily see why she'd make such a sacrifice. Her love was bigger than any drug that riddled her brain and body. And in the end, she did exactly what she set out to do. She gave it all up for the family she loved. As twisted and gut-wrenching as losing Tabby is for each and every one of us, her death was very noble. I'm going to choose to see my baby as a hero and I would encourage each one of you to do so." Mama Kerri's words were filled with compassion and sorrow, but she meant every word.

She firmed her spine and sat up in her chair. "You lost a sister today and I lost a daughter. That is going to take us a long time to accept. But let us feel comforted in the fact that she died doing what she loved. Protecting her family." Her blue green eyes came to me, then Addison. "It would have been the same if it had been Blessing and Liliana or Sonia, Genesis or Charlie. I do not want the two of you taking this on as though it were your fault. It is the fault of a very sick man. Now, we have to set about healing. That alone will be hard enough without you two attempting to accept blame. You hear me?"

I licked my lips and nodded. "Yeah, Mama. I hear you."

"Yes, Mama," Addison reiterated.

"Okay, I'm going to go check on my grandbaby outside with Aunt Delores in the garden. You all have your beds here; I expect each of you to be in them tonight." Her gaze scanned every woman and waited until they nodded or gave their own murmured, "Yes, Mama."

"Now, I love all my girls with my whole heart. I loved Tabby, and together, we'll find a way through this pain. Part of that will be putting my girl to rest."

"I'll help you with all the details, Mama Kerri," Genesis offered.

Mama nodded. "We'll set about looking at her place next weekend. We need this week to heal. I expect all of you to lay your heads down on a pillow in this house until I'm confident everyone is emotionally and physically okay. And that includes me. Okay, my chicklets?"

Again, each of us either nodded numbly or said okay.

"Jonah, I suspect you will be staying here with Simone?" Mama Kerri asked.

He perked up by my side. "I didn't want to beg, but I would have."

She smiled sweetly and that small smile was all it took for the emptiness inside me to start to fill up again with love.

I didn't have Tabby and would grieve her the rest of my life. But I did have Mama Kerri, Sonia, Blessing, Addison, Liliana, Charlie, and the man I loved holding me up.

We all had a long road to go, but together I knew we could make it through anything.

Even the loss of a sister.

Drip. Drip. Drip.

I jolted awake, my entire body so hot, sweat misted around the edges of my hairline and down my spine.

I was back there. In that basement. Addison tied up, blood pouring down her arms and dripping against the cold concrete floor. Her lifeless eyes open staring unseeing at the ceiling as her life source continued to drip out of her.

Tabby lay dead at her feet.

But that wasn't how it happened.

Addy was alive.

I blinked against the darkness of the room while the familiar breath against the back of my hair took away a little of the panic. I focused on that breath from behind me as Jonah slept, his body curled around mine. Still, I couldn't shake the unease clawing at my stomach.

Addy.

I *needed* to see Addy. Make sure she was okay.

Make sure she was alive.

With extreme effort, I eased slowly out of the bed. On bare feet, I padded out of my old room, the one I'd shared with Sonia that I was now sharing with Jonah. Sonia and Charlie had bunked up in the spare room because neither of them wanted to sleep in the room that Charlie used to share with Tabby growing up. It was too soon. It might always be too soon.

I maneuvered past the squeaky board that I knew would wake Mama Kerri and kept on past Lilian and Genesis's room. Past Charlie and Tabby's old room to the one at the end. Addison and Blessing had always been thicker than thieves. Sharing a room with a woman half your life would definitely build that relationship. It was also why they were so good working together a lot of the time. Blessing as the designer, Addy as her model. Had a lot to do with why they were hired for special shoots too. They just worked well together.

As quietly as I could, I pushed open the door to their room. Blessing slept deep. Always had. She was also the last to rise. No matter what. The woman liked her sleep and never had a problem falling to sleep or staying that way. You could run the vacuum right by her bed and she'd sleep through it.

Addy sat up a little when I entered.

I dashed over to her bed as she pulled back the covers. I slid in and faced her. She grabbed both of my hands and we stared at one another in the mostly dark room.

"Can't sleep?" she asked.

I shook my head. "Nightmare. You?"

"Same."

I nodded, brought our hands toward my face, and kissed her fingers. She squeezed mine.

"Are we ever going to be able to close our eyes again and not see what happened?" she whispered.

My heart cracked open and more sorrow poured out.

"I don't know. I hope so. Probably when a little time has passed. Maybe not."

She hummed and closed her eyes.

I closed my eyes and listened to her humming. She did it for so long it lulled me sleep.

Sometime in the night or early morning, Jonah came into the room and I was lifted into the air and held in his arms as he carried me back to his bed.

This became a nightly routine. Me waking with a nightmare and crawling into bed with Addison until I could sleep again. Later, Jonah would come and get me, carrying me back to my place at his side.

He never complained. Not once.

Friday, we cremated Tabby's remains and set her soul free. Tabby's ashes were put into an etched, ornate metal urn that Mama Kerri put front and center on her mantle over the fireplace. None of us were ready to spread her ashes anywhere. We needed the reminder of her presence in our lives and we all agreed Tab would be cool with that.

Mama Kerri held a small gathering at her house, and we put an announcement in the paper. Few people showed. Mostly friends of ours or Mama Kerri's. Of course, the media mongrels were camped outside waiting to catch any sight of the grieving family. Not only was the media obsessed with the fact a serial killer had been caught and taken out, but the connection to the youngest Senator in history, one who was beautiful, strong, and firm in her political convictions? They simply couldn't harness their fascination.

Sonia had been followed incessantly and it didn't look like it would be slowing down any time soon.

Worse, we were coming up on a presidential election and for some reason the media were calling for Sonia to run. This news shocked Sonia more than any of us, but she politely demurred and reiterated that she was happy serving the great state of Illinois as a Senator.

It was now Saturday and the remaining eight of us descended on Tabby's rathole apartment downtown. We had boxes, newspaper, packing tape, and everything else we'd need to box up our sister's life. Jonah was out doing something with Ryan and Aunt Delores had Rory for the day.

I swore you could hear a pin drop with how quiet all of us were when Mama Kerri opened Tab's door and let us all in. We stood in the center of a very sparsely furnished place. The only thing of true value seemed to be the framed images on the walls.

When Tabby wasn't going from crummy job to her dealers, she would take photos. I remember all the years she had a camera hanging around her neck. It was the first present she'd gotten from Mama Kerri on her fourteenth birthday with us. Instantly she set about taking photos of everything. Us. The garden plants and flowers. Landscapes. Broken down things that she somehow made cool through her lens.

I walked around to each photo starting with the one over her ratty couch. It was a gorgeous one of Mama Kerri with her big sun hat on, her long strawberry hair falling down her back in curly waves looking a stunning pinky gold. She was pruning her wildflowers and the sun caught her smile perfectly as she'd turned just half her face toward the camera.

I kept going, walking around the room until I found the one that always devasted me. It was of a woman leaning against the side of a brick building. A cigarette lit and hanging out of her mouth. She had black hair and even darker eyes that were hollowed out and empty. Her body was thin and pale. A junkie. Next to her feet was a small child. A little girl with a filthy mop of black hair and light, haunting eyes. She had smudges of dirt on her cheeks and she was playing with a single feather. It was as though she'd been captured running her fingers up and down the feather, feeling the life that had been attached to it. A different life. One that was free. There was a small smile to that little girl's face as though she hadn't yet been broken down or was doing her best to survive the circumstances she'd been given. The little girl still had hope in those eyes.

I knew in my whole heart why Tabby took a picture of that junkie mother and her daughter. She saw herself in that little girl.

The hope for more.

I lifted the picture off the wall and announced, "I'd like to have this picture." I turned it around and showed the group.

None of them made any case for wanting it themselves. Either because they didn't see what Tabby saw, or they did and wanted me to have what I needed to remember Tabitha by. I carefully brought the picture to a side wall. Each of the sisters chose an image they liked that Tabby had taken herself and enjoyed it enough to put it on her wall, and then set their choice next to mine. I put sticky notes on each one with the corresponding sister's name.

After a couple hours we were making good progress.

Each of us focused on a different area of the small apartment. We'd selected pieces of her clothing that we wanted to keep and boxed up the rest for donation. Any sentimental items we remembered and wanted, we set aside for ourselves. Addy had found Tab's camera and told everyone that she wanted it. Whatever Addy needed to get through the horrendous experience she'd suffered, any one of us would give her.

We continued at a solid pace, boxing up her kitchen for immediate donation. Everything was mismatched, nothing of any real value.

"What's this?" Addison called out, after she lifted a multicolored scarf off of a chest that Tabby had been using as a coffee table. She still had bandages wrapped around her arms, but she hid them by wearing a loose long-sleeve shirt.

I went over to her side and sat on the ratty couch as she lifted the latch and opened it. Inside were nothing but what looked like matching photo albums and extra blankets. I ran my finger over the huge three-inch-wide spines that faced the opening of the chest. There was one with each of our names on them.

I pulled out the one that said *Simone* as Addy grabbed the one that said *Addison*.

The photo book was rather heavy and huge. At least fourteen inches by fourteen inches. A perfect fat square. They were all a shiny black with silver imprint.

Addy and I opened ours at the same time. The first page had an awesome image of me. My blonde hair was blowing all over the place. I was wearing this baby blue button-up sleeveless shirt and a burgundy wide-brimmed hat that I was trying to keep from blowing away. A teasing smirk was plastered across my lips. I remembered Tabby taking that picture when we were downtown at the Taste of Chicago, a huge festival that was held every summer. We were hanging out overlooking Lake Michigan when Tabby started taking pictures. Across my chest in a super cool font were the words WILD CHILD. The image reminded me of a wicked cool book cover.

"Wow, this is badass." Addison traced her image and the words WILD BEAUTY graphically designed over her picture.

I turned the page and there was picture after picture of me, or me with Tabby, or me with the rest of my sisters and Mama Kerri. I kept turning. It was years' worth of pictures. More than a decade's worth. I went to the very back. The first image was one she'd had to have taken when she first got the camera at fourteen. I would have been just barely twelve. It was a selfie of me and Tabby. Under it she wrote, *Soul Sisters Forever*.

Soul Sisters.

That's what we were.

That's what she died for.

That's why I had to accept her sacrifice as the gift it was intended to be.

I reached for Sonia's and Blessing's books. Addison took Liliana's and Charlie's except hers said *Charlotte* which was her real name. I didn't look inside to see what she'd named them, though I hoped one day they would share. For now, whatever was in their picture book was for them and Tabby alone.

Sonia frowned when I stood in front of her with the heavy book.

"We found these picture books in a chest. There's one for each of us." I handed her the one with her name on it.

The only way I could see how affected Sonia was in that moment was because her hands shook when she reached for the book that had *Sonia* in beautiful silver etching down the spine.

She ran the flat of her hand over it lovingly then looked up at me. Her eyes were filled with tears when she said, "Thank you."

I handed Blessing's to her. She reached for it, saw her beautiful name, and held it against her chest as she looked up at the ceiling. "God dammit, Tabby, why did you do this to us! I miss your face. I miss your awkward hugs. I miss your bony white ass dancing around Mama's house taking pictures. I miss my sister!" She sucked back a sob. Sonia got up and pulled Blessing into her arms.

"Me too, Bless, me too." She cooed over her shoulder.

"We didn't get enough time with her." Blessing sobbed which truly was a miracle. The woman was such a hard ass, she rarely shed tears. Her response to emotional conflict was usually to get mad and get even. There was no getting even when the person you're mad at was no longer living.

"Sister, it would never have been enough time." I ran my hand down her back as Sonia served as her rock, holding Blessing up while she gave in to the grief.

Addison gave the other girls their books and I went back, got Genesis's and Mama's, and brought them to where they were boxing up Tabitha's small bedroom items. I handed the respective books to Gen, then to Mama.

Mama put her hand over her heart and sighed, then took the book and immediately opened it. The first page was of course an image of Mama Kerri. It was a candid shot of her dancing in the yard. I remember exactly when it was taken too. Mama Kerri had just turned fifty. Tab would have been just hitting twenty. That had been a great party because we were all mostly old enough to enjoy it. I was around eighteen, and Addison, the youngest, was seventeen. Mama Kerri wore a bright yellow dress with flowers and vines running all over it. She was spinning around, her hair aloft, and the dress was flowing with the breeze.

I ran my finger over the image as Mama Kerri stared at it. "She was extremely talented. I wish she'd known that," I confided.

Mama nodded. "I tried to tell her. Get her to enter photo competitions but she said her images were for her and her alone. To capture the good she had in her life, because it was too easy to focus on the bad." She sighed, turned the page, and traced an image of Tabitha's pixie-like features. There was no smile there. Tabitha had never been known for her smiles, but there was awe and wonder in her eyes as Mama Kerri had hugged her from behind and smiled into the camera that Tab must have been holding up.

"You know, she once told me every beautiful picture she took she felt as though she'd covered up a negative moment in her life with something positive. I guess the only things she truly saw as positives were us."

I nodded.

Mama Kerri stood up and looked around the now empty room. The bed had a few small boxes on top but that was it.

"I'll check on the girls, but I think we're done here. I'll meet the charity on Monday to ensure they pick up everything and I'll leave the key with the manager."

With my mother and sister Gen in tow, we entered the living space. About twenty boxes were stacked up against the long kitchen wall. The rest of us had one box each with a few mementos and keepsakes.

I laid my photo book inside the box where I'd put a few pieces of clothing and jewelry that reminded me of Tab as well as the framed picture she'd taken of the woman and child.

In a little over two hours and we'd packed up our sister's entire life.

Two hours was all it had taken.

I couldn't say a weight was lifted off my chest or my grief suddenly disappeared, because it didn't. What I did know was that after spending time there, seeing the photo-books she'd made of each of us, was that Tabby loved deep. Far deeper than we could have imagined. She didn't always know how to share it or even how to say it most of the time, but she sure as hell *showed* it.

Through these priceless books.

Though her sacrifice.

One by one, each sister walked out of the door until Addison and I were the last ones standing. The others already making their way back down the stairs to their cars.

Addison took my hand and we looked around the empty space. It didn't feel like Tabitha had ever lived there in the first place.

Probably because she hadn't.

Tabitha's true home wasn't a place.

It was us.

Soul Sisters forever.

And that's how it would always be.

EPILOGUE

One month later…

ONAH PULLED UP IN FRONT OF A+ CONSTRUCTION, GOT OUT of his car, and sauntered to the front door. I watched all that sexiness in a black suit with a crisp white dress shirt open the door. He'd already removed his tie, which was something I found fascinating because he told me it was the first thing he did when he got in the car after work each day. Apparently, it was his way of mentally shutting off work. Me, I just really appreciated the generous expanse of supremely yummy olive skin that showed through the two buttons he'd undone.

He had his aviators on, and his dark hair was slicked back and to the side in a trendy but hunky hairstyle I loved on him. My man was the epitome of a hot FBI guy.

"Um, I think you've got a little bit of drool there at the corner of your mouth," Luca teased and chuckled. We'd been going over the company's outstanding invoices.

I nudged his shoulder hard and he side stepped playfully as Jonah approached. "Shut up! I can gawk at my man all day long. Look at him!" I gestured with the file I had in my hand toward Jonah.

He pulled off his aviators and grinned. "Gawk away, baby."

Luca groaned and lifted his hands. "I'm going to go back to my desk. Just remember, these walls are glass. No hanky panky out in the open."

My mouth dropped open and if he hadn't escaped, I would have smacked his chest with the file. "Can you believe that? Suggesting I'd get freaky at work. Pah-leese." I narrowed my gaze and watched Luca head back to his office until I was hauled into the arms of my favorite guy.

He tucked his head against my neck and kissed my neck. "I'd get freaky with you in a heartbeat. Glass windows be damned." He grabbed my bum and ground against me.

I let my head fall back and laughed at his shenanigans. "Cool it, buddy. We can hit Ryan's place and have a little fun of our own. But what are you doing here? I thought you were picking me up at Kerrighan House to have dinner."

He smiled and looped his arms around my waist. "I have a surprise I want to share with you. Are you done here?"

I glanced at the clock and noticed it was five-fifteen in the evening. "Heck, yeah. Let me grab my purse and tell the guys I'm out."

Jonah pecked me on the lips and then left me alone to go through my shutting down the office routine. Even if people stayed, I still made sure that the doors were locked, everything with personal information about clients was locked away, and any staff that were hourly left on time. Jonah busied himself shooting the breeze with his dad and brother.

Over the last month a lot had changed. Jonah and Luca had made amends and the Fontaine clan were back to having dinners every Thursday together. His parents were ecstatic and gave me all the credit.

After we'd cleared out Tabby's house, I started that very next week working at A+ Construction. I'd been there three weeks now and it felt as though I was in the perfect place for me. I had only a month more to work on my coursework and I'd be done. Marco and Luca were thrilled with my skills and the rest of the staff had been giving them a thumbs up about my performance so far. All in all, it was awesome. I'd never been happier at a job and I couldn't wait to learn more and work my magic wherever I could.

Since I was too freaked out to go in my old apartment, and I wanted absolutely none of my sisters or Mama Kerri in that place, Jonah, Luca, his dad, and his mom went and packed up everything that was salvageable. It wasn't a lot, but at least I didn't have to buy a new wardrobe, books, CDs, and replace some of the special items I'd saved over the years from my family. The furniture was all gone, and I couldn't have cared less. What they could save was currently all boxed up and in Jonah's storage unit where he kept the few things he'd taken from his time with Helen.

We still slept at Mama Kerri's most nights. The first two times we tried to sleep at Ryan's I ended up waking up Jonah and making him take me to Mama Kerri's so I could check on Addison. I didn't need to crawl into bed with her in order to sleep anymore, but the need to physically see her alive was still wearing on me. Jonah, Mama Kerri, and Sonia were openly worried about this coping mechanism so last week I started therapy. I'd only had one session so far, but I told the therapist what was happening and how it was a bit disrupting and she told me it was perfectly normal. She also gave me tips on how to slowly minimize the issue. The first was not getting into bed with her. Which was why I was now able to just peek in, see that she was breathing, and feel more comfortable. According to her, this would take time because my brain had created some connection to the trauma with Addison in a way that manifested itself in this need to see her alive.

Jonah left the back just as I put my purse over my shoulder.

"Ready?"

"Yep." I put my hand in his and let him lead me out to his car. I still hadn't gotten a vehicle yet. It was on the list of things to do but I had Jonah bringing me to and from work which he told me flat out he needed to do in order to cope with his fear for my safety.

Basically, we were all a little messed up but working through it and getting healthier every day.

After twenty minutes I realized he was heading to Mama Kerri's neighborhood. "I thought we were going to dinner?"

"I have a surprise, remember?'

"Oh yeah. Is your surprise at Mama Kerri's?" I laughed.

He shook his head. "Nope, but close." He reached over and put his hand on my thigh where he gave me a little squeeze.

I rolled my eyes and sighed overly dramatic. "FBI hot guy and man of mystery. You sure you don't have a big red S and a blue spandex suit hiding under those government threads, mister?" I prodded at his ribs and he laughed.

Randomly he put on a blinker and turned down a street two blocks from Mama Kerri's. Then he pulled to a stop alongside the front curb of a pretty two-story house. It had a single big oak tree to the right of it that would give the house awesome shade in the dead of a humid Illinois summer. It looked like a quaint doll house with wooden slats in a slate-grayish seafoam green color with pristine white trim around the windows, the door, and the fencing that surrounded the open porch that ran the length of the house. There were white stairs that led up to a dark forest green door with four cute little window cutouts at the top half.

The grass ran the entire front yard with a concrete path up to the stairs. The garage and driveway must have been in the back like many of the others in this neighborhood.

"Wow, this is beautiful. Who lives here?"

Jonah ignored the question or maybe didn't hear it as he got out of car and opened my door. I shifted my booty to the side and took his outstretched hand as it wasn't super easy to get in and out of a car in a tight-fitting pencil skirt, and I always dressed up for work. I had a serious job and I dressed as though I felt that way. Even though almost everyone there wore jeans and polo shirts with the company name embroidered on the chest.

I followed Jonah's quick movements up the stairs as a woman I'd never met before exited the front door. "It's all set," she said and handed him a set of keys. She looked at me and smiled huge. "You must be Simone."

I nodded. "And you are?"

"Deni. Nice to meet you, but I have to run!" The woman of about sixty or so moved quickly down the stairs and around the corner where I assumed she drove off in the sweet Cadillac I'd seen parked on the other side of the house.

Jonah opened the door and took my hand, tugging me inside.

"What in the world?" I breathed as I tripped on my tall heels.

"Surprise!" He said it with such joy, I smiled but had no clue why.

I glanced around at the empty open living room. Everything was painted bright white. You could still smell the hint of fresh paint in the air.

I shook my head as I walked around the empty living room. "I'm not sure I understand."

He grinned and then turned me around in the entryway to face the opposite wall. There in plain view was a series of four pictures. Two side by side and one on each of the other walls in the U-shaped space. Front and center was Tabitha's picture of the woman and her child. Next to it was the first image of Tabitha and me as kids. The one to the left was the picture of all of us sisters and Mama Kerri in front of Kerrighan House that he must have got from one of the girls. The other wall had a candid shot of Jonah and me his mother had taken a week or so ago at dinner. I was sitting in his lap and he was cuddling me and making me laugh.

I gasped and covered my mouth with my hand.

"Why are these pictures here?"

He wrapped his arms around me from behind and put his chin to my neck. Together we looked at the images. "Because I want this to be our home. I bought it for us to start our life in. It's twenty minutes from work for you, not far for me, and super close to your mother and my parents."

Tears filled my eyes. "You bought this for us?" I choked out and spun around, clamping my hands to his shoulders.

"Want to build a beautiful life with you here, Simone. Marry you and have babies and bring them home here."

I covered my mouth and trembled. "It's all too soon. Marriage? Babies? Oh my god!"

He chuckled. "We have time for all of that. For now though, I thought we could start out in our own place and take it one day at a time." His words reminded me of the promise that Addy and I had made in the hospital a month ago.

"Really?" I let the tears fall. "But what if…" I swallowed against the emotion clogging my throat. "What if I can't be away from Addy?"

He wrapped his hands around my waist and pressed his forehead to mine. "Sweetheart, you're working on that. And Addison has no desire to leave Mama Kerri's any time soon. Now if you feel the need to check on her, she'll be only two blocks away."

I smiled. Loving this man so much more for understanding my issue and not making me wrong for it. He wanted to help me through it but continue moving our lives forward.

"How did I get so lucky that you were the man that saved me that night? The man just for me?"

He kissed me softly. "The universe works in mysterious ways."

"I love you," I whispered against his lips.

"And I love you." He kissed me for a long time as we stood in our new home together. He kissed me for so long we both became breathless.

"Come on, let me show you the house." He interlaced our fingers. He led me through the incredible open kitchen, the three empty bedrooms and two baths, including the awesome master suite with a killer shower that had these amazing white subway tiles. Everything was bright, white, and ready to move in.

"This is the most amazing house." I started to worry he'd spent way too much. Three bedrooms and two bathrooms in Oak Park wasn't exactly cheap.

"Room to grow into." He waggled his brows. Jonah had been talking a lot about our future and having children. We both wanted a good-sized family. Him because he was Italian, and his mother wanted lots of grandbabies, which she talked about nonstop at every family dinner. Me because I had a ton of sisters and wanted to always be surrounded by the people I loved.

He brought me down to a huge basement that was entirely empty. Meaning it literally had no walls.

"Unfinished basement."

"Now I know why you could afford this place," I teased.

"My father, brother, and woman work at the best construction company in the state. They could whip this into something amazing so we have a big lounge area, another bathroom, maybe even a small kitchenette and another bedroom for guests." He curled his arm around my back as we faced the large space. "It's as big as the top half. It would double our square footage and my brother and father would do it at cost for materials. It'll take a while. Probably six months or more as they'll have to do it when they have time. Of course I'd help, plus Ryan will pitch in. We don't need it right away so it'll be no bother to have it in a state of disarray until it's done."

I nodded, seeing his vision. "True. And we'll have pride in it because we'll make it our own."

He kissed my cheek. "Exactly. Now, I have one more surprise."

"More? You bought us a house!"

He grinned wildly. "Something tells me this next surprise is going to be even better."

I scoffed. "Not possible. Did you see where I'm going to be living? It's a palace compared to my old tiny apartment, your one room at Ryan's, or even my old room at Kerrighan House." I started to hop up and down as the reality set in. My man not only asked me to move in with him, he bought us a freakin' house to build a life in. I squealed like a little girl.

Jonah smiled so wide I had to wrap my arms around him and kiss him silly.

After I'd shown my man my gratitude, he led me back up the basement stairs, through the house, and out into the yard.

Oddly, he whistled and from around the corner came a bouncing, auburn-colored golden retriever puppy.

Chills raced over the surface of my skin as I kicked off my heels, dashed down the stairs, and fell to my knees in the grass. The adorable puppy jumped all over me.

"Oh my goodness, you are the most beautiful thing in the entire world, yes you are." I put my face to the dog's and she licked me like crazy. I snuggled her close and pressed my nose against her soft fur. "Who do you belong to, sweet girl?" I asked the puppy who wiggled all around until I let her go. Then she scampered around my form, jumping at me then running in a circle, then pouncing back. She had the most stunning auburn coat and dark amber eyes.

"She's ours, sweetheart. Well, our first baby."

I picked her up and stood barefoot in the grass cuddling the precious angel. "You bought us a dog," I whispered through the tears. I'd always wanted a dog.

He casually walked down the stairs, put his hand to the fur baby, and pet her. "I knew you wanted one along with a family one day. I love dogs. And I thought it might be good to have something that's loving but can be protective when trained, which I plan to do as soon as she's a bit older. Then I'll feel more comfortable when I have to travel and leave you alone."

"I love her so much," I confided, kissing the soft brown of her nose.

"I can tell. So does this mean you're moving in today?" He grinned.

I nodded. "We don't have a bed."

"Which is why Ryan and his buddy should be arriving any time with mine."

I let my pretty girl down and walked right into Jonah's chest. He wrapped his arms around me as I hugged him tight, pressing my ear over his heart so I could hear it beating.

"You've made me so happy, Jonah. I'm not sure what to do with it all. I feel like it's going to explode out of me, and I'll be a pile of goo on the ground."

He chuckled and cupped the back of my head until I lifted my chin and our gazes met. Blue eyes to a dark espresso brown I planned to live my entire life looking into and loving for the rest of my days.

"After everything we've been through, Simone, after Tabby, and Helen, we deserve this. We deserve to carve out some happy for ourselves without feeling guilty."

My bottom lip trembled as the emotions soared through my form. "I want to believe that. I really do. It's just so hard after such loss."

He nodded and cupped my cheek. "That's why we need to live every single day to the fullest. Starting with making this house our home. Naming our fur baby."

I chuckled and looked at the gorgeous girl pawing at Jonah's pant leg. "What about Amber?"

He ducked down and scooped up the dog. He pointed her body so her muzzle was facing him. "How's about Amber? Do you like that name?"

The dog licked his face. Then again, she probably would have done that anyway.

"She likes it. Amber it is."

I smiled and petted our dog. "Welcome home, Amber. We're your parents and we're going to give you so much love and tons of treats!" I promised and snuggled her soft neck. She licked my cheek.

"Hey, yo! Can someone open up the door! We got a giant bed out here!" We heard Ryan calling from the side of the house.

I laughed and dashed up the steps, jetted through my gorgeous house, and opened the front door.

Shockingly, it wasn't just Ryan at the door. It was our entire family. His parents and brother. My mother and sisters all holding boxes. A small moving truck was parked behind Jonah's car.

"Wh-what are you guys all doing here?"

Blessing nudged her way through holding a box with my name on it. "Moving our sister into her new home, of course."

I clasped both of my cheeks and spun around. "Did you do this too?"

He held up our pretty girl. "Mama is happy, Amber."

"Aw, you named her Amber." Charlie cooed at my dog as she set down a box in the open space and reached for the dog. "Look, your auntie is a redhead too."

I went over to Jonah smiling with stupid girly happy tears in my eyes. I held up my hands in the air. "I'm so happy!"

He tugged me into his arms and laid a hot and heavy one on me.

Later that night, after all of the boxes were moved in, we ordered pizza and beer for everyone. We still had to unpack what we had and go out and buy furniture but we were in our own bed, Amber curled in a cute little dog bed on Jonah's side so he could take her out regularly to potty train.

Jonah and I had just made love for the first time in our house.

He twiddled my fingers over the bare thigh that I had slung across his naked form. My head was to his warm chest and I was listening to his heartbeat.

"You like our home, baby?" he asked.

I grinned against his chest then kissed him there. "Love is the word I'd use. I can see us being blissfully happy here."

He hummed happily but kept playing with my fingers. "And that marriage idea…how's that percolating in your mind?"

"Honestly, planning a wedding is not something I've ever had a desire to do. Though I'd marry you if it was something super small."

"I had the big shindig traditional thing with Helen. I wouldn't want that either. Plus, we now have a decent mortgage and a basement to renovate," he added thoughtfully.

"This is true. I think that will be fun though. We can take our time, do it how we want."

"What about a destination wedding?" he hinted.

"Like Vegas?" I scrunched my nose. I'd spent a lot of time working in bars and smoky spaces over the years. Plus, I was not the type to gamble away my hard-earned dollars.

He groaned. "Not my scene. I was thinking more along the lines of Hawaii."

"I've never been to Hawaii," I breathed, awe in my tone.

"You in a sundress, me in a linen shirt and khakis. The beach, flowers in your hair, the sun at our backs. Nothing but you and me and a man of the cloth."

I traced my fingers down his chest. "Sounds beautiful but I think my sisters, mother, and your parents would be pretty disappointed if they didn't get to participate. I have another idea?"

"Yeah?" he murmured, sounding tired.

"What about here? We have a small service and reception in the backyard. Then Hawaii for the honeymoon."

"Now you're talking." He cupped my head and kissed me slow and sweet. "So, when I ask you to marry me really soon, pretend to be surprised okay?" He yawned.

I grinned and put my head back over his chest. "Okay. Just give it some time. We need to set up our house first and I need a little more time at my job before I tell them I need a couple weeks off for a wedding and honeymoon."

Jonah wrapped his arms around me and tucked me close. "Deal."

I waited a few minutes, and as sleep started to take me, I pressed my hand over Jonah's heart and asked him the same question he'd asked me. "You happy, baby?"

He hugged me close and kissed the top of my head before he answered. "I've never been happier than I am lying in our bed, in our house, beside you, our dog safe in her bed, with a bright future ahead of us."

I sighed and snuggled into the man I knew in my heart I'd spend the rest of my life loving.

And for the first time in a month, I slept the entire night through, held in the safety of my man's arms, without a single nightmare marring the happiness in my life.

The End

If you want to read more in the world of the Kerrighan foster sisters, check out Addison's book in Wild Beauty. *Each book will be a complete but interconnected standalone novel. I may write three total books of select sisters or one for each. It all depends on the muse and the readership.*

Read a sneak peek of Addy's book on the next pages.

Wild
BEAUTY
(A SOUL SISTER NOVEL)
SNEAK PEEK

C*LICK.* THE CAMERA FLASHED AND I WAS BACK *THERE*.
In that chair.

That dark, freezing cold basement, with rats and other vermin scurrying around my feet.

My chest was tied with thick, uncompromising ropes. My arms zip tied, forearms up so he could continue with his torture.

I glanced down at the blistered, ravaged tissue of my forearms with a detached, vacant assessment. Seeing the torn, bleeding, black wounds on my arms in the only way I could—as if they weren't mine. The scent of burnt flesh seared my nostrils. I desperately held back my need to vomit as my mouth watered around the cloth gag. It was tied so tight it dug into the edges of my mouth, abrading the sensitive tissue every time I attempted to free myself.

Another camera flash.

"Addison…" A somewhat familiar voice reverberated in the cavernous space around me. My mind swirled as I tried to focus on that tone. It was kind. Compassionate. Connected to someone I loved.

Blessing.

Click.

I shuddered at the sound and shook where I stood, sky-rocketing back into that dreaded chair.

The masked attacker was coming back.

He would continue hurting me.

He was going to *kill me* just like all those other women.

My only hope was they'd find him before they got to my sister Simone. If she were spared, my soul would be free. I could die knowing she was safe.

I had no idea when I got off that plane and met the driver out front of the airport holding a sign with my name on it that I was willingly walking straight into my own personal Hell. He looked the part. Wore all black. Had a Town Car. Knew my name, when I was to arrive. Everything.

Smart girls knew better.

And I was a smart girl. Mama Kerri made sure all of her foster daughters got the appropriate education, graduating high school with good grades. I had a dream and worked toward making that dream a reality. She told us there was no mountain too high when it came to our life and career goals. I believed her. Took everything she said as gospel and worked my ass off...literally.

I was one of the most coveted plus-size models in the industry. I had millions in the bank. But there was no amount of money in the world that would save me from the Backseat Strangler.

"Addison, honey, you're scaring me!" Blessing's voice broke me out of a cold sweat and catapulted me back to the present. I shook like a leaf where I stood under the unnaturally hot lights of the backdrop for the photoshoot.

"Where am I?" I trembled in her arms.

Blessing put her hands to the sides of my neck. They were cool and steady. I shivered in her arms. She placed her face directly in front of mine, her dark eyes fixated on me.

I locked onto those familiar loving eyes like they were my talisman. The only connection I had to my safe place.

"Addy, you are in the middle of a photoshoot," she said calmly.

I shook my head. "He's here…" I choked out on a guttural whisper.

She shook her head, her black curls bouncing along with her. "Boo, he's not. He's dead. You're in the middle of a shoot in downtown Chicago. Behind me are your clients and the photographer."

I looked over her shoulder at the myriad of bodies standing around and staring at us. I clenched my jaw realizing I'd had another *moment*. That's what we were calling them. "Moments." Which was essentially a really kind way of describing my mini-freak-outs. I lost all time, space, or any sense of where I actually was and found myself stuck back in that basement with a serial killer. The place where both Simone and I watched our sister Tabitha sacrifice herself in order to save us.

Tears filled my eyes and started to fall.

"Okay, that's a wrap. Bring me her robe." Blessing snapped her fingers to the young fashion design student that she had mentoring under her.

The girl brought my robe and Blessing helped me put it on over the delicate pink bra and panty set I wore.

I wrapped my frozen form and allowed the soft chenille fabric to remind me there were soft and beautiful things I could count on to bring me back to the here and now. Something sizzled in the air, an electricity I felt tease the air forcing me to look up.

Click.

The photographer on the job, took a random, candid shot. He was positioned at the lens, his face hidden behind his equipment. I hadn't been concerned with who was behind the camera, only that this was my first job back after *the incident*. Now I needed to see the individual or I might go back to when "he" was taking pictures and filming me.

All I was able to see was the man's long sandy brownish blond hair falling around his shoulders. He moved his face and his brown-eyed gaze met mine.

It was as if in that second, he'd seen right through my eyes to the empty, broken, frightened woman beneath the perfect hair and makeup.

Click.

I twitched as gooseflesh rose on my skin, but as long as I was looking into those earthy, tranquil brown eyes, I felt grounded. No longer floating aimlessly across an endless expanse of deep, pitch black waters with no hope for shore. But in his eyes, I found my footing. I curled my toes against the cool floor, cementing where I was in that moment.

This man, the photographer with his soulful eyes, trimmed beard, and mustache held me centered to the here and now with a single look. No longer was I wading back into the dark memory of that night when my entire life changed.

I removed the robe, stared into his gaze, and handed the robe to Blessing. "I'm okay. I'm going to finish."

"You sure? You don't have to. The clients understand what you've gone through. They've agreed to photoshop the scars marring your arms, but I know them well. They'll understand if you're not ready," she assured me.

I shook my head, my gaze set on the photographer.

I lifted my chin toward him. "I've never seen you before."

One side of his lips twitched up into a small yet sexy smile. "I'm new to fashion photography. And if you're okay to continue, I'd love to finish." His gaze darted to the lens. "We've gotten some great shots. Most of them after you took a breather. You're a wild beauty. The camera loves you."

I smiled. "That's what they all say when a half-naked woman is standing in front of them."

He chuckled and the rich baritone sound warmed my body from the inside out.

"I'm Addison Michaels-Kerrighan. And you are?"

"Killian Fitzpatrick."

Interesting name for an intriguing man.

"You ready to continue or do you want a break?" he asked, no hint of judgement in his tone.

I pursed my lips. "As long as you don't hide behind the camera," I stated shakily then added a soft, "Please and thank you. Apparently, faceless men behind cameras are a new trigger for one of my *moments*." I shared that, but then balked at my own stupidity. I had no idea why I'd give up something so personal to someone I didn't know, besides the fact that he had honest, kind eyes, great hair, and a sexy smile.

"I'm here for you, whatever you need."

Surprisingly, I laughed. "Again, that's what they all say," I teased, taking a deep breath and letting out all the fear and ugliness that had crept up. I shook my arms and legs as though I were flinging off water, but mostly was just trying to fling off the negative tragedy that plagued my every waking minute. "Just get a good shot."

"With you, Addison, I'm not sure there are any bad shots. Though I think with a little time and focus, we could find magic together." His voice had a warm, comforting tone, laced with a hint of innuendo.

My cheeks heated and I quirked my head and smirked.

Click.

I hope you enjoyed this sneak peek of *Wild Beauty*, the next soul sister novel. Order your copy now.

AUDREY CARLAN
Titles

Soul Sister Novels
Wild Child
Wild Beauty

Wish Series
What the Heart Wants
To Catch a Dream

Love Under Quarantine

Biker Beauties
Biker Babe
Biker Beloved
Biker Brit
Biker Boss

International Guy Series

Paris
New York
Copenhagen
Milan
San Francisco
Montreal
London
Berlin
Washington, D.C.
Madrid
Rio
Los Angeles

Lotus House Series

Resisting Roots
Sacred Serenity
Divine Desire
Limitless Love
Silent Sins
Intimate Intuition
Enlightened End

Trinity Trilogy

Body

Mind

Soul

Life

Fate

Calendar Girl

January

February

March

April

May

June

July

August

September

October

November

December

Falling Series

Angel Falling

London Falling

Justice Falling

ACKNOWLEDGEMENTS

To my husband, **Eric,** for supporting me in everything I do. I love you more.

To the world's greatest PA, **Jeananna Goodall**, it's all your fault this book went crazy suspenseful! I blame your addiction on *Criminal Minds* and your love of cops and special agents. It turned out amazing and I loved every second of writing it. Our numerous plot phone conversations were hilarious. Phrases like, "I don't want to hurt her too much," and "I'm definitely killing off that chick," were warped and also hilarious. Thank you for always being willing to dive into the creative brain with me and toss around ideas. It truly makes the process so much fun and feel less lonely. Love you, woman!

To **Jeanne De Vita** my personal editor for not only blasting through this manuscript and making it better, but for always being so positive. You are a true gem in this literary world and this novel would NOT have been completed and released on time without your help. Thank you for being part of Team AC and taking that position seriously. I hope every new author out there, or person wanting to be a writer attends the *Romance Writing Academy*. They will not only gain expert knowledge but will feel supported and part of a team. You rock lady! Interested people should check it out! www.romancewritingacademy.com

To my alpha beta team **Tracey Wilson-Vuolo, Tammy Hamilton-Green**, **Gabby McEachern**, **Elaine Hennig**, and **Dorothy Bircher** for being the absolute best cheerleading beta team in the world. You ladies are my safe place. My touchstone. I can't imagine not having you at my back. Thank you from deep within my soul. I adore each and every one of you.

To my literary agent **Amy Tannenbaum**, with Jane Rotrosen Agency, for always knowing exactly how to make me feel special, and finding all my babies the right homes.

To my foreign literary agent **Sabrina Prestia,** with Jane Rotrosen Agency, I can't wait to see where Wild Child shows up in the world! It's always such a gift to see my words translated into other languages. Thank you for spreading the love.

To **Jenn Watson** and the entire **Social Butterfly** team, you guys blow my mind. Your professionalism, creativity, and business prowess is unprecedented. Thank you for adding me to your clientele. I look forward to teaming up on many more projects in the future.

To the **Readers**, I couldn't do what I love or pay my bills if it weren't for all of you. Thank you for every review, kind word, like and shares of my work on social media and everything in between. You are what make it possible for me to live my dream. #SisterhoodFTW

About
AUDREY CARLAN

Audrey Carlan is a No. 1 *New York Times*, *USA Today*, and *Wall Street Journal* best-selling author. She writes stories that help the reader find themselves while falling in love. Some of her works include the worldwide phenomenon Calendar Girl serial, Trinity series and the International Guy series. Her books have been translated into over thirty languages across the globe.

She lives in the California Valley, where she enjoys her two children and the love of her life. When she's not writing, you can find her teaching yoga, sipping wine with her "soul sisters," or with her nose stuck in a sexy romance novel.

NEWSLETTER

For new release updates and giveaway news, sign up for Audrey's newsletter: audreycarlan.com/sign-up

SOCIAL MEDIA

Audrey loves communicating with her readers. You can follow or contact her on any of the following:

Website: www.audreycarlan.com

Email: audrey.carlanpa@gmail.com

Facebook: www.facebook.com/AudreyCarlan

Twitter: twitter.com/AudreyCarlan

Pinterest: www.pinterest.com/audreycarlan1

Instagram: www.instagram.com/audreycarlan

Readers Group: www.facebook.com/groups/ AudreyCarlanWickedHotReaders

Book Bub: www.bookbub.com/authors/audrey-carlan

Goodreads: www.goodreads.com/author/show/7831156. Audrey_Carlan

Amazon: www.amazon.com/Audrey-Carlan/e/ B00JAVVG8U

Printed in Great Britain
by Amazon